I0680789

COMFORT ZONE

ALEXA MILNE

Comfort Zone
ISBN # 978-1-78430-993-0
©Copyright Alexa Milne 2016
Cover Art by Posh Gosh ©Copyright February 2016
Interior text design by Claire Siemaszkiewicz
Pride Publishing

Published in 2015 by Pride Publishing, Newland House, The Point, Weaver Road, Lincoln, LN6 3QN, United Kingdom.

Pride Publishing is a subsidiary of Totally Entwined Group Limited.

COMFORT ZONE

Dedication

For you.

Chapter One

"All right, all right, I'm coming." Aron Roberts opened his front door, relieved the ringing had stopped.

"Could you grab the top one for me, please?" the voice behind the boxes asked. "Sorry about the bell. No hands."

"Sure. You look as if you're fully loaded there." He picked off the top box then stood and stared. He'd seen those green eyes before, but once seen never forgotten. "Joe!" he said in surprise. "It is you, isn't it? Wow, I didn't realize when Margaret said she'd booked a caterer for tonight it would be you. So, is this your company, or do you work for them?"

Joe smiled. "Any chance of getting the food in the fridge before catching up? Wouldn't want it to spoil for your guests now, would we?"

Somewhat flustered, Aron let Joe move past him. "Sorry. Right. Yes. The kitchen is that way, on the left. We'll be eating in the conservatory." He followed Joe down the corridor, unable to resist casting his eyes appreciatively up and down his sturdy frame. He guessed Joe worked out if the biceps, currently straining the arms of his T-shirt, were anything to go by. "Yes, through there. There'll be enough room in the fridge."

Joe put the boxes on the table and started to open them. "I had no idea it would be you. I guess I spoke to your wife on the phone." He whipped out a sheet of paper. "Yeah, it says Margaret Pearce. Oh, and yes, *Croeso I Cymraeg Catering* is mine. It's a play on my name."

"Welcome to Welsh Catering?" Aron questioned.

"Yeah, that's me, Joe Welsh, and you must be Aron Pearce. We never did get around to swapping surnames at the side of the road, did we?" He held out his hand. "Good to meet you again in much better circumstances."

Aron shook his hand. His grip was firm, and Aron found it hard not to run his thumb across the back of Joe's hand. "Margaret is my personal assistant, not my wife. She thinks she's my mother most of the time, and she organized this evening for me as she organizes the rest of my life. I'm Aron Roberts, and I'm not married."

Aron couldn't help but notice the way Joe lowered his gaze, seemingly looking him over. Was Joe checking him out? He glanced away, as if aware he'd been caught.

"Well, that's cleared that up then. I'll get this lot put in the fridge and get started, shall I? If you can point me toward the crockery and cutlery you want to use, I'll make sure the table is laid. Most of the prep work is done, so I can cook and present. I'll be the waiter for tonight as well. Is there somewhere I can change?"

Aron pulled out a few drawers and opened the relevant cupboards to show Joe where to find everything he might need. "There are seven of us for dinner tonight," he explained. "It's the first anniversary of me setting up my company. When we met last year, I'd recently started Aztechnologies."

"Sounds clever," Joe said as he busied himself around the room. "And I'm obviously not the only one who can play with names. You said your name was Az."

"It's a nickname I'm trying to grow out of," Aron said.

"Oh, right. It'll be Mr. Roberts tonight in front of your guests." Joe continued to talk as he removed items from the boxes and placed them on the table.

Aron stared when he unwrapped a roll of cloth to reveal an impressive set of knives.

"Most chefs have their own. We have to make sure we have IDs on us because carrying knives is an offense. I had to explain to an overzealous cop once."

He stopped for a moment, as if feeling the weight of the knife he'd selected in his hand. "You know, it's such a weird coincidence us meeting again a year after I nearly crashed into you. Mrs. Pearce said someone recommended me."

"Yeah, you did a party for Dan Morgan and his partner for their civil partnership ceremony. I couldn't go because I was abroad, but he went on and on about the wonderful food. I didn't know the company was yours when I asked Margaret to book you." He wasn't exactly lying about Dan, but being abroad had been a convenient excuse to avoid seeing the man he'd once loved committing himself to another.

Joe interrupted his thoughts. "I see. That night went well, and I got quite a few bookings afterward. I had to keep pinching myself, you know, being there with all those Welsh rugby players and me being a Giants fan all my life." He chuckled ruefully. "Strangely, I had no trouble getting my family to volunteer to help me serve on that occasion."

Maybe it was the wrong thing to say, but Aron opened his mouth, and the words flowed out. "You know I came to see you at the pub in Llandaff a while after we met."

Joe stopped and glanced up before continuing. "Oh, yeah?"

"You weren't working there, though, and they were a bit cagey about where you were."

"No, I left. I decided being on my own gave me more independence and flexibility."

"It must be good having your family working with you." Yes, he was digging. When Aron had met Joe at the side of the road the year before, he'd been about to become a father for the first time. They'd stood together in the rain, waiting for the rescue services to sort out their broken-down cars. Aron had warmed to the man in front of him. Joe had been shaken up after his brakes had failed. Aron considered him again. His black hair was shorter and neater than it had been. He stood an inch or two taller than Aron, but still under six feet. Aron speculated about the body under his chef's jacket. But above everything else, it was his green eyes that had caught Aron's attention, and the smattering of freckles across his nose and cheeks, totally unexpected for a man with his coloring.

"Yes, it can be when they can be bothered," Joe replied, bringing him back into the room. "How do you know Dan Morgan?"

The subject had been changed. Aron didn't want to admit he and Dan had been an item for many years. He didn't want Joe to know he was gay, not yet anyway. Although everyone among his friends, family and colleagues knew. It was always awkward with someone new.

"Dan? I went to school with him. We've known each other since we were eleven. Right, I'd better get out of your way and leave you to get on with things — unless there's anything else you need."

"No, everything's in order. I'll get the vegetables sorted then the main course. The scallops don't need much cooking, and the dessert is mostly done. You said you wanted to be ready to serve at eight?"

"That's right." Suddenly, the room had become smaller, and he wanted to get out of there. "I'd better go and get ready. Margaret is a great believer in the idea that clothes make the man, and I need to get the oil out from underneath my fingernails. My production manager likes me to be hands on. To be honest, so do I. We're trying to get a new piece of tech sorted at the moment. I won't bother you with the details."

Joe chopped carrots without stopping.

Aron shifted uneasily from foot to foot. "I'll leave you to it, then."

Joe murmured something and continued chopping.

* * * *

Upstairs, Aron sat on his bed and stared at his reflection in the mirror. His suit hung over the door behind him. It was beautiful, he had to admit, but he hated dressing up and was happiest in his jeans and lab coat. However, Margaret nagged him often and reminded him that he did, as managing director, have a professional image to project to buyers.

His thoughts turned to the man downstairs cooking in his kitchen. He'd been out to dinner with Dan, his partner Iestyn and some other school friends, and they'd enthused over the food from their party. He'd liked the name of the company and the menu, especially the emphasis on healthy meals and local produce, but the man... When they'd met the first time, they'd talked at the side of the motorway until the police had arrived. Joe and his wife had been together since they were fifteen. His eyes had shone and his hands hadn't stopped moving. Most of the time, Aron had listened, knowing letting Joe talk would help him to calm down. He'd talked about being a chef, and his family, and how excited he was about becoming a dad for the first time. Strange, he hadn't mentioned whether he'd had a son or a daughter. In Aron's experience, parents did little else but expound the virtues of their children. He eyeballed himself in the mirror.

"Stop it, you fool. He's a married man, who loves his wife, and you aren't going to get into his pants." He peered down. "And you aren't, either." Maybe he should have a cold shower.

* * * *

Twenty minutes later, he'd relieved some of his tension under the water and washed his hair. Stroking himself, he'd tried desperately to imagine anyone other than Joe, finally settling on the actor cast as *Poldark*, with his dark hair and good looks. Standing in front of the mirror, he turned back and forth, gazing at himself in the suit. Margaret would say he needed to eat a pie. True, he was on the skinny side of thin, but he loved to run, and tried to make sure he managed about twenty miles a week. Once he got into the zone, he felt freer than he did at any other time — except for flying — but he couldn't do that every day. He'd lost weight since last year, and the suit hung loose around his shoulders. His brown hair skimmed the collar. He got some gel and ran it through, finding an arrangement he could live with.

There would be six others at the table tonight. Margaret and her husband Harry, a semiretired accountant who did the company's books. Their son lived in Australia, so Margaret mothered Aron instead. Without her undoubted efficiency, he wasn't sure his fledgling company would have survived its early days. Also coming were his production manager, Dai Morris, and his wife Pauline. Dai liked the hands-on stuff as well, and they'd taken to working together like ducks to water. Dai was as straight as a die, honest and down to earth. He and Pauline had two children, Mel now at university and Rhodri, who'd recently declared his bisexuality. Dai saw Aron as his gay guru as he struggled to understand his teenage son's choices. Aron thought Rhodri's only aim was to get laid, and the gender of the person didn't matter to him. The final two guests were two of his school friends, Evan Williams, the company solicitor, and his wife Beth. He glanced at the alarm clock—seven-thirty. He knew Margaret would be early to make sure everything was ready, so he hurried downstairs.

The smell coming from the kitchen stopped him in his tracks and made his mouth water. He threaded his way through the lounge to the conservatory. The table had been laid out beautifully. Joe had obviously been busy.

Aron listened to Joe hum while he worked. He coughed. "The food smells wonderful," he said. "Do you do all the cooking at home, or just at work? If I was your wife, I'd leave you to it." He hesitated, but he had to ask. "Your baby must be getting on a year old now. What did you have?" He'd said it casually, but Joe stiffened at his words and put his knife aside.

"Ellie's nearly twelve months old and as cute as a button." Aron couldn't help noticing Joe didn't appear happy when he spoke. "She's crawling everywhere."

"I bet she keeps you and your wife on your toes."

Joe gazed at Aron. "There were complications. Ellie came early, and Angie had a traumatic time giving birth. She hemorrhaged and died twenty-four hours later. It was the best and worst day of my life."

Chapter Two

Aron stared at Joe while trying to get his head around what the man in front of him had said. Joe had returned to his task, having dropped his bombshell, but the tautness in his upper body betrayed his struggle to maintain control. Aron had no idea what to say. Conflicting emotions assailed his senses, but this wasn't about him. He wanted to pull Joe into his arms to comfort him, make him feel better, or something, but that would have been truly self-indulgent. How the hell did anyone live with what had happened? How did you lose your wife, then deal with having a baby, and do all of that in your early twenties? Aron realized how little he knew about Joe. No wonder he'd left his job at the pub. No wonder they'd been cagey about telling Aron why.

Joe stopped chopping and raised his head. As if he'd read Aron's mind, he put the utensil down and came over to where he stood.

"I'm sorry, sometimes my anger still gets the better of me. I shouldn't have announced it like that."

Aron shook himself. "Please, it's me who should be sorry."

"You weren't to know." Joe placed a hand on Aron's arm. The connection was instant. They gazed at each other, eyes wide open with shock. He wanted to reach out to grab something, but that would mean losing the connection. It was like he was falling, and although his body didn't move, only Joe's hand kept him from flailing about. They must have stood there for seconds, but it might have been a lifetime. Time had no meaning.

The sound of the doorbell pulled them both out of the moment.

"I'd better answer that," Aron said, his voice barely more than a whisper.

"Shit! The sauce." Joe scooted back to the food, while Aron went to the front door, unsure whether his feet were touching the floor. He opened it to find Margaret on the doorstep, early as he'd expected.

"Something smells good," she said as she came through the door.

Her husband smiled and handed over a bottle of wine.

"Good to see you, Harry." Aron shook his hand.

Margaret had disappeared to check on the kitchen. Aron considered going to rescue Joe.

"Leave her to it, lad. You know what she's like. Whatever he's cooking, it smells delicious. I don't know what she thinks she's going to do. Maggie has many talents, but cooking isn't one of them, that's for sure." Harry was the only person who used the name Maggie. Aron called her Margaret, but although Aron's employees might call him by his first name, they called her Mrs. Pearce.

"Really?" Aron said, surprised there was something his capable PA couldn't do.

"Oh, don't get me wrong," Harry whispered. "She can do the basics, but she's not interested enough. She always has something else to do that matters more. Still…" Harry patted his more than ample stomach. "Nothing wrong with a good takeaway curry and a beer!"

Aron laughed. "No, there isn't. Take a seat, Harry. I'll get you a beer now."

The other guests arrived soon after. Dai, obviously uncomfortable in his suit, had undone his top button and loosened his tie. Like Aron, he was much happier in his overalls. Pauline handed over a large bouquet of flowers.

"Thank you, these are lovely. I'll take them into Margaret in a minute. She'll make a much better effort at arranging them than me. You're looking lovely this evening, Pauline."

"Thank you, kind sir. Staff discount helps."

"Those shoes aren't from your store," Aron said.

"No, but I found them in the sales, and they are gorgeous, aren't they?" She turned one foot around to show off each side.

"I'm in awe you can even stand in them," Aron replied.

She smiled indulgently at him and pushed his shoulder. "Oh, Aron, you're such a disappointing gay, not a 'fabulous darling' in sight, or any mention of the rhinestones. Rhodri helped me to pick them out."

"How fortunate that your son has such good taste," Aron said in what he hoped were more bitchy tones.

"That's better," Pauline replied, laughing.

Dai harrumphed and went into the living room to talk to Harry. When Evan and Beth arrived, and Aron had finally dragged Margaret out of the kitchen, they were ready to eat.

* * * *

It had taken all Joe's concentration not to chop his fingers off after Aron left to answer the door. Something had happened between them, but he wasn't sure what. Aron's soft brown eyes had stared into his. Joe recognized all the signs of someone desperate to comfort him. Usually he hated all that. He'd become accustomed to the pity-filled looks, or the predatory ones, he received. Why was a bereaved man with a baby like catnip for some women? Still, they weren't to know he was dead inside. Oh, he hid it well. He took care of Ellie, he did his job, and he smiled in all the right places when his and Angie's family offered help, but he knew he was going through the motions, being who everybody else needed him to be. But when he'd touched Aron's arm and stared into his eyes, something inside him had woken up—a tiny flame had flickered in the darkness. For the first time since Angie's death, a shaft of light had illuminated the great big black hole she'd left. He'd experienced a spark of joy, of not wishing that he, like his wife, had been taken from this world. Her voice, telling him not to be alone filled his mind.

"Find someone, Joe. Don't set up a shrine for me. Find someone to love, who'll love you and Ellie and make your lives better again." Her eyes had closed for the last time minutes later. They'd had no secrets. She'd known of his interest in men as well as women and used to joke that he only fancied her because she was built like a boy and kept her hair short. She'd been the most perfect person in the world for him, but every day he lost another memory of her, no matter how desperately he tried to hold on to every smile, every curve of her face, the way she walked, and the sounds she made when he touched her.

"Is everything okay?" a voice said, pulling him away from his musings. He glanced up to see a gray-haired, comfortably built woman dressed immaculately in a navy blue dress.

"Yes, Mrs. Pearce." He held out his hand. Her firm grasp suggested a no-nonsense sort of person used to other people doing what she asked them to do. "I'll be ready to serve at eight as instructed. The table is laid. The white wine is cooling and the red breathing. I'll serve when you're ready, then afterward, I'll box up any leftovers and leave the place clean before I go."

"Excellent. You came highly recommended, and I want this dinner to go well."

"Aron mentioned it was a celebration."

A look of surprise crossed her face when he called Aron by name. "Yes, and fingers crossed, we're about to land a major contract."

Joe smiled, unable to miss the obvious pride in her voice. Aron interrupted them, bringing in the flowers. Before he could say anything, Margaret quickly pushed him out then set about finding a vase and arranging them.

Once finished, she announced, "I'll leave you to it then."

Joe prepared food for seven. He hoped Aron might be the odd one out, that he would be the single one in the party. But why? He knew almost nothing about the man. After the accident, they'd talked and Aron had sprung to his defense when the grumpy policeman had accused him of dangerous driving. Okay, so maybe he'd appreciated his smirk and the slim body underneath it, but he'd never expected to meet him again. He'd had a wife, whom he'd adored, and they'd been expecting a child. His life had been all mapped out, but now that he'd found Aron had come searching for him, he couldn't help wondering why. He allowed himself to imagine the possibility of finding someone else who filled his senses in the same way Angie had, then he shut it down. There was no future in such thoughts. He got his work jacket out of the suit cover and changed. He fried the scallops and arranged them on plates with bacon, salad leaves and his own special dressing.

Aron was sitting at the head of the table with the three couples on either side of him when Joe brought the starters.

"This looks wonderful," Mrs. Pearce said as he picked up his cutlery and tucked in.

For a few moments, Aron held his fork in midair unable to stop thinking about the way Joe's body filled his suit. The dark color made his green eyes stand out even more. Pauline tapped his arm.

"Are you all right?" she asked.

"Yes, sorry. Don't mind me. I was thinking about the presentation next week."

She patted his arm and glanced toward the kitchen. "Yes, of course you were."

"These are so good," Evan said. "They're practically melting in my mouth, and the bacon is gorgeous."

Evan and Beth were two of Aron's oldest friends from school. After he and Dan had split, their mutual friends had been unsure of what to do at first, wary of taking sides, but when the dust had settled, he'd been able to maintain contact with most of them. They talked about the company and the new deal they were hoping to seal, but also of babies and children. Aron smiled and made what he hoped were appropriate comments.

"I can't believe you've never held a baby," Pauline said at last.

"I'll bring Scottie over," Beth offered.

Aron swallowed hard. "Nah, don't worry, Beth. I'd probably drop him, or he'd pee or puke on me. Not something I will ever need to worry about, babies."

"So you've never wanted children?" Pauline asked pointedly.

"No, I've never wanted kids. I don't know how you cope with them, and there's all the worry. It's such a commitment having children. I'm not sure I could even cope with a pet. Perhaps I'm too selfish, but I've never understood the need to reproduce. And, from what I've seen, they grow up and hate you."

When silence greeted his words, Aron glanced around at the shocked expressions on his friends' faces. Had he said too much?

He raised his head only to meet Joe's stunned gaze. Time appeared to stand still while no one moved. Seconds later, Joe recovered himself and began to collect the empty plates.

"The scallops were wonderful," Aron managed to say.

Every person at the table sat still, glaring at him.

"The main course will be served in ten minutes, sir."

Aron shivered, almost able to feel the ice flowing through Joe's veins, the atmosphere now thick with uncertainty.

Throughout the meal, Aron picked at his food, even though it was delicious. His hand ached from gripping the knife and fork in anger and frustration at being put, he thought unfairly, in the wrong. But he couldn't get Joe's shocked face out of his mind. He needed to resolve this, but how and why? Joe should mean nothing to him. He'd met him at the side of the road and had built a fantasy around him. That had been safe, because they would never meet again, and what he'd said was the truth. He'd never wanted kids. He considered the other people at his table. Margaret and Harry's only child was halfway across the world in Australia, and he knew he'd become a surrogate son for them both. Pauline and Dai loved their kids, but found their choices hard to deal with. They worried about Rhodri and, Aron guessed, despite their stated support, secretly, they hoped he'd get over the gay thing. Evan and Beth had barely started on their parenting journey, and he knew they were both scared.

After dessert and the toasts, Pauline followed Aron into the kitchen. "He's gone, then," she said, gazing around the pristine room.

"Yeah, you'd never know he was here."

"Look, Aron, I may be speaking out of turn, but I couldn't help noticing how you both stared at each other at the beginning of the evening, then something happened, didn't it? The smile didn't reach his eyes later, and he seemed tense, and so did you. Tell me to shut up if I'm talking nonsense."

Had they been that obvious? "I don't know, Pauline. We met once, a while ago—bit of a story—I won't bore you with it. He was married with a baby on the way but…"

"You fancied him."

"Yeah, I guess I did. There's nothing wrong with window shopping."

"No, I suppose not, but that's not the end of the story, is it?"

"His wife died giving birth. He told me tonight."

Pauline's hand went to her mouth. "Oh, God. Poor man."

"I know. His little girl is a year old now. I can't explain this, but I touched his arm at one point tonight, before everyone arrived, and I swear there was a connection, then he heard me say that I don't like kids. That isn't exactly true. I'm just not comfortable around small children. They scare me. I don't know how people cope with the responsibility, never mind how they control your life."

"And he's a single dad. Hmm, tricky. He could be bi, I suppose, like our Rhodri, or fancied a walk on the wild side. And as for the kids thing—we're all scared, Aron. I still worry about Rhodri, you know, whether some man will take advantage of him. I worry about Melissa as well, now that she's away from home doing God knows what, with God knows who."

"See, I'm right. The worry never ends, does it? Anyway, it doesn't matter now. I'm not likely to see him again."

"Oh, Aron," she replied. "You need to get laid or something. Get yourself out there and mingle. I'm sure Rhodri could take you to a few places. I'd feel better if someone kept an eye on him."

Aron shrugged. "Nah, I'm too old for all that now."

"Oh, for goodness sake, you're in your twenties, not your fifties, and about to sign a deal that will make you a fortune, according to my husband. You are quite a catch, Aron Roberts, and you need to have some fun. You've done nothing but fiddle with little bits of metal for a year. It's time to fiddle with a warm body instead."

* * * *

When everyone had left, Aron sat nursing a glass of wine. Maybe Pauline was right—perhaps he did need to get laid. Trouble was, he'd been with Dan since he was sixteen, then briefly with Clark in America. Since his second split with Dan, he'd concentrated on work. He'd never been one for casual sex, but maybe he should try it. He laughed to himself. Pauline expected him to be Rhodri's gay guru, but maybe it needed to be the other way around. He put his glass down and went to lock up, leaving the key in the tray by the door. Turning, he noticed a faint glow coming from his bedroom at the top of the stairs. Puzzled, he made his way slowly toward the light seeping out from the slightly open door.

He edged it open. "Shit. Joe! What the hell are you doing here? I thought you'd gone."

Joe sat on the edge of the bed bathed in the glow from the bedside lamp. "We both know why I'm here."

Aron closed the door and stood his ground. Joe closed the distance between them in three strides, pinned Aron's arms to his sides and kissed him, hard, using his tongue to pry Aron's mouth open and probe inside. Raw and bruising, Joe's passion shocked Aron at first, but once he'd recovered his equilibrium, he gave as good as he got, pushing his tongue back to meet Joe's, neither of them willing to give way. Joe ground his groin against Aron's now hard cock. The delicious friction sent tingles of pleasure throughout his body. Aron licked his flesh and tasted blood from where Joe had chewed on his bottom lip. Absorbed in watching Aron's tongue, Joe let go of Aron's wrists long enough for the slighter man to take advantage and turn Joe around. He might be lighter than Joe, but he'd learned some moves of his own from handling a huge rugby player for many years. Aron removed his jacket, then Joe's, and threw both on the chest of drawers. He clutched Joe's shirt, intent on revealing the body underneath until Joe grabbed his hand.

"Work shirt. I can't afford to damage it." Joe lifted it carefully over his head in one move to reveal his chest with its smattering of dark hair trailing down to his stomach, and the abdominal muscles of a man definitely no stranger to working out. Aron made short work of Joe's belt, pulled down his zipper and fell to his knees. With a hand on each hip, he removed both trousers and briefs in one fluid movement.

"Oh my," he said, taking in the sight of Joe's erection surrounded by soft, jet-black hair. "You are gorgeous." He ran his tongue from balls to tip, taking in the taste of the man, desperate to feel the weight of Joe's cock on his tongue.

"Suck it!" Joe growled above him. "I want to fuck your pretty mouth."

Joe grabbed Aron's hair and held his head. Aron had no problem with that demand and opened his mouth wide, enveloping the whole shaft, showing Joe exactly how deep he could go. Aron winced as Joe pulled his head until his gaze met Joe's. He hoped his expression told Joe to do whatever he wanted. Aron would take it all and let Joe use his mouth however he wanted. He nodded, handing Joe the power. Every thrust hit the back of Aron's throat, but he didn't care. He wanted this. Joe's cock was thick, but not too long for Aron to manage. He stayed still as Joe drove into him, taking what he needed over and over, grunting with every thrust, until he stopped abruptly and dragged Aron's head up again.

Joe glowered at him, his green eyes now almost completely black. "I'm going fuck your sweet arse until you scream out my name." He lifted Aron's chin, kissed him then buried his face in Aron's neck, biting down on his shoulder while he twisted Aron's nipple with his fingers. Instead of backing away from Joe, Aron pushed toward him, seeking more.

"Where d'you want me?" Aron asked, needing to move on. The last thing he wanted was for Joe to come to his senses and walk away, leaving him high and dry.

"Over the bed, with your arse in the air."

Smiling, Aron removed the rest of his clothes and positioned himself, head down, arse up, totally exposed. The anticipation of what might come next was scary and exhilarating in equal measure. At that moment, he wouldn't have cared if Joe had taken him bareback with no prep whatsoever. He craved the pain, wanted the hurt, to apologize for his crass words said at the dinner table. He'd never allowed anyone to treat him this way, and he couldn't have explained why he did now, only that he wanted— needed—Joe to take him.

"Supplies?" Joe asked.

"Top drawer. They should still be in date. It's been a while for me." The scrape of the drawer as it opened at least told him Joe intended to take some care prepping him.

Joe spread his cheeks apart and Aron braced himself. He expected fingers at the very least. Instead, Joe licked the whole length of his crack then lapped at his hole. He squirmed under the man's probing, wet tongue. Every nerve ending in his body burned. A finger joined the tongue, followed by another. It had been a while, but obviously his body wanted this and he opened up easily. Joe kept licking, but removed his fingers. Aron waited for the telltale sound of foil being ripped. The discarded wrapper landed on the bed by his side and Aron shifted his position in anticipation of Joe's next move.

"It's enough," he said. "Fuck me. I need you inside me now."

He sensed Joe looming over him. His hot breath hit the back of Aron's neck.

"Just remember who's in charge here."

His dark tone made Aron shiver. Joe bit hard on the back of his neck. He knew he'd have so many bruises the next morning, memories of what had happened the night before, proof he hadn't dreamed the whole thing as he had on so many other occasions lying in bed with his cock in his hand.

"Fuck!" he yelled as Joe pushed straight into him without warning until he was full to the brim.

Still, Aron goaded him.

"Is that the best you've got?" he growled.

Joe withdrew then slammed back into him, forcing him into the mattress. Every time Aron pushed back to meet each thrust, steadying himself by placing his hands in front of him on the bed. One touch and he knew he'd come all over the duvet. He couldn't remember ever feeling like this. It was raw, but it was so good and he wanted more.

Joe stopped, still buried balls-deep in his arse.

Aron whimpered. No other word could describe the sound he made.

"Please," he said, afraid that Joe intended to stop and leave him there. "I'm so close." He waited for something, but not for the tiny kisses placed gently across the back of his neck and the feel of Joe running his fingers lightly down his spine. He lifted his body, needing to be closer, and met the weight of Joe leaning over him.

"I knew you'd be beautiful," Joe whispered. "From the moment we met, there was something."

Aron couldn't quite believe what he was hearing, his mind still a whirl of need, desire and confusion. Joe started to fuck him again, but this time with less urgency, each move slow and deliberate. He pulled out inch by tiny inch, changing his angle to make sure every thrust hit Aron's prostate. Joe clasped either side of Aron's waist. Aron wanted to hear more words, but Joe was silent now, except for his breathing. Aron didn't want this to end but he couldn't wait any longer and reached for his cock, unable to stop his orgasm hitting him any more than Canute could have turned back the waves. It roared into existence, sending streams of cum onto the cotton beneath him. His arse clenched around Joe, who followed him over the edge.

"Oh God," Joe said before he fell onto Aron, collapsing them both into the bed. Aron wanted to reach behind him, to stop Joe withdrawing, to stay like this forever, but without saying a word Joe pulled out. The condom made a small thud as it landed in the bin by the bed. He didn't want to turn around because he wasn't sure what he'd see on Joe's face. At some point Joe's anger had subsided, and Aron's greatest fear was that he'd see disgust in his expression instead. He lifted himself up. By the time he'd gotten off his front and turned around, Joe was halfway dressed. Aron ached inside and out, but he didn't care. When he finally screwed up the courage to raise his gaze, Joe stood staring at him, his eyes steely in the lamplight. Aron knew he should say something, but had no idea what words to use.

"I'm going now," Joe said. "Don't contact me. This was a one-off. I had an itch, so I scratched it. I saw the key in the tray by the door. I'll let myself out and push the key back through."

Aron wanted to tell him to stay, but there was no point. Joe left the room. His feet thudded on the stairs. The door banged shut, and Aron waited for the jangle of keys hitting the tiles in the hallway. He glanced at himself in the mirror. He'd just experienced the most incredible, overwhelming and confusing sex he'd ever had, and he'd never regretted anything more in his life.

Chapter Three

Joe yawned and stretched his arms. His head throbbed out a disco tune the Bee Gees would have been proud to have written.

"You still in bed?"

Oh hell, his father had arrived already. He gazed at the clock then checked again in an effort to make the blurs turn into numbers.

"Joe, I've brought Ellie home. I'm making tea. Get your backside down here!"

He groaned then remembered. When he'd arrived home last night, he'd downed the half bottle of brandy supposed to go into a tiramisu. His head hurt, and he was still dressed in his work clothes. He needed a shower.

"I'll be down in ten minutes, Dad. I need to get cleaned up. Was she all right?"

"Yeah, she was as good as gold, as always. You struck lucky with this one, didn't he, young lady? Your daddy was lucky to get you."

Joe smiled as he stood in the shower, letting the water wash away all traces of the night before. He was lucky.

He had his daughter and family, and he didn't need anything or anyone else, especially some dumb fuck like Aron Roberts.

"Forget it," he said, staring down at his cock. "That was a once-only deal. There'll be no plowing that particular furrow again. The guy's a douche bag — a self-centered prick." Jeez, he wanted to hit something.

He found his dad in the kitchen feeding Ellie. He peered up from where he'd settled the baby into her high chair.

"You look like death nobody bothered to put a light to. I made tea and toast. You need to eat something to absorb the alcohol. It's not like you to drink so much." He nodded to the nearly empty bottle. "Didn't last night go well?"

"Everything was fine," Joe said. He swallowed some tea then searched the drawer for painkillers.

"Eat the toast," his father said, pushing the plate toward him.

Joe sat at the table and watched Ellie eating her food without problems. He tried once more to find her mother in her face, but she was the image of him. Hair, eyes, nose, mouth — all him.

"Dad, I've a favor to ask you. I've got to have an hour at the gym this morning. Could you look after her?"

His father stared at him. "Feeling the need to hit something, Joe? Anything you'd like to share with your old dad?"

Joe shook his head slowly. "It's all right. I want to work off some frustration, that's all. It's been a long week, and tonight is the first Saturday I've had off in ages. I intend to lift a few weights, then I'm going to spend the rest of the day with my daughter. I promised her we'd go to the park to feed the ducks."

"Okay, son. I'll stay for an hour or so, but whatever's bothering you, you can tell me. I hope all my kids can talk to me."

Joe nodded. His dad had been made redundant several years ago, shortly after his mum gained promotion, so they'd decided he should stay at home and take care of the children, and he'd taken to the role like a pig in muck. Joe was close to his dad and he knew that without him, he wouldn't have survived those early days after Angie's death. He'd had no clue how to deal with a newborn but his dad had patiently shown him what to do. Still, how did he tell his father he needed to punch something because he was angry with himself for giving into temptation, for letting himself...

He grabbed a slice of toast and his gym bag, kissed Ellie's forehead and headed out. "Thanks, Dad. I owe you one—again."

* * * *

Jonno was bouncing from foot to foot in the corner of the large room, firing left and right hooks into the punching bag when Joe arrived. His trainer stood behind holding the bag, encouraging him to hit harder. Joe tapped him on the shoulder before going to get changed. Ten minutes later, Jonno joined him on the next bench as they lifted weights. He and Jonno had been best friends since they'd met on their first day in school. When Angie came along, they'd simply extended their friendship to the three of them, but since Angie's death, Jonno had been more distant. Joe told himself he was busy. Jonno now had several wins under his belt on the local amateur boxing circuit. He might be smaller than Joe, but he was as strong as an ox and bench-pressed way more than he did. Joe kept himself fit, but Jonno could outdo him at everything — press-ups, squat thrusts, chin lifts. Once Jonno got going, he was like the Duracell bunny, but with muscles. Fortunately, Joe had never fancied him, not his type, so there'd been no complications.

"You're quiet," Jonno said in between lifts. "Usually by now, I've heard all about Ellie's latest achievement, how your brother is being a dick about helping you and some new recipe idea you have for the greatest bread ever made. What's up?"

Joe had no idea how Jonno would react, but he had to tell someone about what had happened. Jonno had never been homophobic, and they'd been friends forever. He trusted him implicitly. He'd have trusted him with Angie and Ellie...

"I've got something on my mind, that's all," he said.

"Care to share?"

"Not here. Too many ears. Something's happened and if I don't tell someone, I'll go mad."

Jonno put the weight in its stand and sat up to look at his friend. "Not Ellie, is it?"

"No, nothing like that. I...I...did something stupid last night." He lifted the bar again. Maybe he'd been wrong. "It's all right it. Ignore me. It doesn't matter now." Heat rushed into his cheeks and he turned away.

Jonno dragged him back and grinned at him. "What? Did you get your end away last night, or something? It's about time. Hang on, weren't you catering a dinner last night?"

Joe nodded.

"Someone there? That's not like you, mixing business and pleasure. So, who was she?"

Joe pulled himself round so he sat on the side of the bench. "Can we throw a few punches?" They'd often sparred together when they were younger. "I've got some frustration to work off." He still had no idea what to say.

Jonno moved to face him. "Sure, I'll hold the bag for you. You can use my gloves."

The gym was an old-fashioned place, not like modern gyms with their banks of treadmills and other machinery. A boxing ring stood in the center of the room. They made their way around it, and Jonno held the bag while Joe punched.

"Come on, Joe, don't be such a wuss. You can hit harder than that. You're bound to feel guilty the first time after Angie, but you're only human, and Angie wouldn't want you to be alone."

"No, she wouldn't. She told me before she died."

"So you shagged some woman — what's the problem unless her husband caught you at it?"

Joe punched harder.

"He didn't, did he?" Jonno asked, holding onto the bag.

"There was no husband."

"So again, what's the problem? Shit! Don't tell me you couldn't perform."

Joe had a sudden vision of his cock pistoning in and out of Aron's arse. He punched the bag again. "No, nothing like that."

"So tell me then 'cause I don't get it. If the lady was willing and you were able, what's the problem?"

Joe stopped punching for a moment and breathed deeply. He drew back his arm and said, "It wasn't a woman last night, Jonno. It was a man." His fist connected with the leather just as he said man.

Jonno said, "What?" before he hit the floor.

"Jesus, Jonno, I'm sorry."

His friend lay on the floor, trying to get his breath back. Jonno shook himself. "It's okay. It's fine." He staggered to his feet and pushed past Joe without saying anything. Joe followed him to the locker room.

"Jonno, please talk to me." He put his hand on Jonno's arm, but removed it when the man flinched. "Please," he begged. "Don't walk away. I'm as shocked as you are." Joe sat on the bench. "It just sort of happened, and you can't tell anyone. For God's sake, Jonno, we've known each other over eighteen years. You're my best friend. I needed to talk to someone. I know you're probably disgusted but please…"

Jonno finally sank next to him. He slumped, his head facing downward. "I'm not disgusted." He reached into his bag then pulled on his sweatpants and shirt without meeting Joe's eyes.

"I'm not disgusted, Joe. I'm jealous. After all these years, all these years of being there for you, of doing anything to be near you, you go off and fuck some bloke you met last night."

Joe couldn't believe his ears. Stunned, he tried to stop Jonno leaving, but his friend jerked away from him.

"But, Jonno. I don't understand."

"For fuck's sake, Joe! Are you that dense? It's always been you. I've loved you ever since I can remember."

Unable to move, Joe stared at his best friend's back as he strode out of the room, unsure how his whole life had turned upside down in less than twenty-four hours.

Chapter Four

Aron stopped running. Breathing heavily, he leaned on his thighs, then staggered to a nearby bench and sat. He wiped away the sweat from his brow and loosened his T-shirt, now stuck to his chest. The morning air, despite the warmth of the sun, made him shiver.

Daylight had hit his face far too early, but then any time this morning would have been too early. He'd hoped the events of the night before were a particularly vivid dream, but from the smell on his sheets, the taste on his tongue, the feeling in his arse and the ache in his heart, last night had happened. The numbers on his alarm clock kept moving.

"Shit. Shit. Shit. Shit!" The one man he'd had any interest in over the last year had fucked the hell out of him but...

A woman walking her dog glared at him, and he realized he'd spoken out loud. I'm such a bloody fool. Joe was angry with him — that much was obvious when he served dinner and stopped smiling — but Joe had still wanted him, craved him. At least last night's activities had proved one thing for certain — Joe's undoubted bisexuality. And all right, the sex hadn't been pretty and tied up with ribbons and bows, but he'd taken everything Joe had given because he'd wanted it. After the comfortable pattern he'd fallen into with Dan, last night Joe had woken every one of his senses and had shown him in graphic detail—this is what I can offer you, but I come as a package deal and you don't do kids.

He needed to talk to someone about what had happened, but when he went through the list of possible friends, he realized there was no one with whom he could share his stupidity. Well, there was one person, an odd choice, but over the last year, they'd developed a friendship aside from the man they had in common. He called Iestyn.

"Hello."

"Iestyn, it's Aron, Aron Roberts."

"Oh, Aron. It's been a while. How are things with you?" The tone of Iestyn's voice told Aron how surprised he was to hear from him.

"Sorry," Aron continued. "Am I interrupting something?"

"No, I'm marking coursework. Dan is in France at an away match this weekend, in Toulouse, so if you wanted him…"

Aron had no wish to discuss his stupidity with his ex, now Iestyn's happily married husband. "No, it's you I want. Feel free to tell me no, but are you available for lunch today? I need to talk to someone." He hesitated for a moment. "Sorry, this is stupid. I'm sure you've lots to do."

"No, it's all right. Come on, Aron, I thought we'd moved past this. I know you didn't feel you could come to the wedding, but we're okay, aren't we? You've obviously got something on your mind, and I guess it isn't something you want to discuss with your other friends. Man trouble?"

"Yeah, you could say that. I did something stupid last night. Well, more than one thing."

Aron heard Iestyn take a deep breath. "Okay, sounds ominous. Meet me at the pub on Sully Beach? We can sit out there, and I can bring Charlie—he needs a run."

"Charlie?"

"He's our new dog. We got him from a rescue place after he failed his sniffer dog training."

Aron smiled to himself. Dan had finally got his pet then. He wondered how long it would be before they found a way to have a child. Dan had always longed to be part of a big family, and Iestyn's had welcomed him in with open arms. He doted on Iestyn's niece and nephews as much as their uncle did.

"I know the pub," he said. "I'll see you there abound twelve, and, Iestyn—thanks."

* * * *

Aron drove into one of the few spaces left in the car park at Sully Beach. He squinted in the sun and reached for his glasses. Families playing football on the beach below yelled at one another. Iestyn had grown up around here, so no doubt he and his siblings had spent time there searching the rocky coastline with their nets and jars. He locked the car and peered over the wall. On the stretch of sand, Iestyn threw a ball for an overexcited spaniel to fetch. Aron shouted down.

"Iestyn, you ready for a pint?" Aron sat on the wall and waited as the tall, dark-haired man with glasses put a lead on his dog and walked up the stone ramp. At the top, he brushed the sand from his feet and put his trainers back on, then he ran the brush through the dog's dense fur. He looked up, shielding his eyes with his hand, then offered it to Aron and dragged the man into a hug.

"Thanks for coming," Aron said, glancing around to see if anyone was watching. "There's a table over there. Let's grab it before it's taken and I'll get us those drinks and some menus." They got the formalities over, and Charlie settled between them, panting in the warmth of the midday sun.

"Dan got his way, then," Aron said, patting the dog's head. "He always wanted a dog,"

"Charlie was my idea. He keeps me company when Dan is away. The kids love him and he's ever so good with them, even when Megs pulls his ears. Now that we've got the new place, he has room to run around. But you didn't get me out here to talk about Charlie now, did you? What's up? I'm assuming this is nothing to do with work."

"No, work is fine. In fact, we're on the verge of signing a major contract, and we're working on new ideas. Aztechnologies has been going for a year now. We had a dinner last night to celebrate. The guy you had for the civil partnership catered it."

"Oh, Joe Welsh—wonderful food. He stepped in at the last moment when someone let us down. His brother, Idris, works at my school. He's one of the ICT managers, and a bit of a dick to be honest, but Joe was brilliant."

"Yes, Dan mentioned his company to me when I phoned him." Aron hesitated, not sure where to begin. Finally, he figured the beginning might be the best place. "You remember the pub we went to when you told me you and Dan were over and I said the guy I met after the car accident was the chef there?"

"I'm hardly likely to forget how you helped Dan and I get together, but I've only a vague memory about the accident."

"My car had broken down and another car nearly ran into me — well, that was Joe."

"Oh, yeah, I remember now. I got the feeling you fancied him."

Aron picked up his pint, not wanting to see Iestyn's face. "I did, and apparently I still do."

"But wasn't he married and expecting a child when you met?" Aron glanced up and met Iestyn's questioning gaze.

"You didn't try it on with him, did you? Surely, you're not that stupid or desperate. Sorry, that came out worse than I meant."

"No, I didn't try it on, and things aren't that simple. He told me his wife had died after giving birth to their daughter. He started the new business to give him more time to take care of her."

"Bloody hell — poor bloke! His brother didn't mention anything, but I did say he was a dick. So what happened last night?"

"We had a moment. I touched his arm and we stared into each other's eyes, frozen to the spot. Shit. I sound like something out of Mills and Boon."

"D'you think he's interested?" As Iestyn spoke the food arrived.

"Yes and no. How the hell do I put this?" He checked that no one was listening and leaned in. "He ended up shagging me senseless when everyone else had gone."

Iestyn halted in midaction, leaving his hand, with its food-laden fork, hovering in front of his mouth. He made no effort to hide his shock. "Nooo... But that's good, isn't it? I'd say shagging you showed he was interested, or were you a one-off experiment with the dark side? Is that what you're thinking?" He finally lifted the fork to his mouth then chewed the food slowly before swallowing. "What is it you want, Aron?"

"I don't know what I want. He was furious with me. We had angry sex, at least to begin with, but I'm not complaining. It's been a while for me."

A look of concern swept across Iestyn's face. "He didn't force you, did he?"

"Oh, no—absolutely not. I wanted him all right, but I'd said something stupid earlier in the evening about having children, and I guess his whole world is his daughter. I don't think he's out of the closet in any way. He told me I was an itch he needed to scratch." Aron opened his shirt to show the bruises from the bite marks.

"Wow!"

"There are more—in other places. It was mad and glorious, but I should never have let it happen. I don't know if we would have had a chance or if he even likes men. I'm damn sure he didn't like me much last night. I was a convenient hole, that's all, but I feel like I've lost something that could have been good if he didn't have the baggage."

Iestyn didn't say anything while he chewed on his sandwich. Aron hated the silence.

"You're thinking I got exactly what I deserved, aren't you? Maybe you're right. I've never wanted kids, or even a pet. How the hell do people feel grown-up enough to take on the responsibility?"

"But you have responsibilities, Aron. You're the boss of a new venture. Your success or failure pays people's wages."

"That's not the same. Children are an inconvenience. For me it's always been the bonus of being gay—no one expected me to procreate. Children tie you down, they get sick, they cost a fortune you can't spend on other things. How do people cope with the worry? Take Charlie there. You have to feed him, walk him, even in bad weather, take him to the vet, entertain him, clean up after him—and he's a dog!"

"But—"

"There is no but, Iestyn. Children are a burden I've never wanted. I know what it's like when…" He needed to get himself under control.

"Who are you trying to fool, Aron? The sex you had last night may have been fast and furious, but it meant something to you, didn't it? From what Dan told me, you're not a one-night stand sort of guy. This was the culmination of a long year of thinking about him and wondering, wasn't it?" He leaned in again. "And of long nights with your cock in your hand."

Aron swallowed hard as said appendage leaped at the thought. "All right, I hear what you're saying, but there's Ellie, his daughter. She's nearly a year old, and she is his world. I couldn't cope with her. And he's straight, so I don't want to deal with that either."

"Maybe he's not straight. You've no idea about his past, only that he was married and it sounds like you already have feelings for him."

Aron nodded. "It's madness, I know, and I've no idea what to do. Maybe I should put it down to experience, but I can't get him out of my head. You're right. I can't tell you how many times he's been there as some delicious fantasy. Now I find the reality is even better than my wildest, and I mean wildest, dreams."

"You've got it bad, haven't you?"

Aron nodded. "It's pointless, isn't it? But there's something about him, and now I find out he can fuck like that."

Iestyn frowned. "Maybe you should start by not thinking of his child as baggage."

Charlie's lead rubbed against Aron's leg, distracting him, and he looked over to see the spaniel sitting in front of a couple at another table. They petted his head as he sat.

Iestyn laughed. "Oops," he said.

"What is it?" Aron asked.

Iestyn lowered his voice. "He's a failed sniffer dog. When he smells drugs, he's trained to sit in front of someone, which is what he's doing now. He liked to play too much, so they failed him. Charlie! Here boy." The dog raced back over, jumped up onto Iestyn's lap and licked his face. "Good boy. Well done." Iestyn patted him, then he turned to Aron.

"You need to ask yourself if he's worth it, but you can't go on thinking of his family as baggage. You know what love is, Aron. You loved Dan, but you were strong enough to let him go. If this guy matters, then you've got to be strong enough to accept everything in his life — that is if he wants to be involved with you. You've no idea what pressures he might be under, and there's only one way to find out. Ring him. But the moment you put your heart on the line, you risk it being broken. Only you can decide if he's worth it and if he is, it won't be easy for either of you. It sounds as if he has a few demons of his own. If he's gay or bisexual, perhaps he's been living a lie. You might regret what happened, but he may have way more regrets than you do. Maybe you should try being a friend, and if that's all there is, or if there isn't even that, you need to put your feelings to one side."

Aron sighed. "I sound like a complete and utter selfish prick, don't I?"

"A bit," Iestyn said, smiling. "But at least you know you do. It's where you go from here that counts."

Aron gazed at the man in front of him cuddling and petting his dog. "Dan's a lucky man, having you."

"He is, but he's always been a lucky man, or perhaps he has impeccable taste," Iestyn confirmed. "You should come round to the new place sometime. He's planning to set up an LGBT community project in Wales and needs sponsors. It would be good to have someone from industry involved. Sport is still in the closet, despite his openness."

"I guess there aren't going to be any footballers rushing to declare themselves any time soon and it shouldn't be something you have to announce. Dan got it right by never being in the closet so he never had to come out. I always admired him for that." He smiled. "Amongst other things!"

Iestyn grinned. "Hey, that's my husband you're thinking about, but you're right. He does have a great arse!"

Chapter Five

Joe stared at the lists in front of him. Sometimes he thought his life was one long list, but he had to keep them or he'd be a mess.

List One — Jobs that week and beyond.
List Two — Who's looking after Ellie?
List Three — Food orders.
List Four — Food suppliers — any new products?
List Five — Plans for each day — work.
List Six — Plans for each day — household tasks.
List Seven — Finance — income and costs — two columns checked.

Now he faced another blank screen and started typing.

List Eight — Reasons why my life is a complete mess.
My best friend is dead.
My other best friend has told me he's in love with me.
I slept with a bloke I've met twice and loved it.
I have a daughter.

Joe stopped typing and gazed at Ellie playing happily with her blocks. Turning back to the screen, he added —

And he hates kids.
I'm in the closet.
I've been awake since three this morning.
I need someone to talk to.

He glanced up to see Ellie attempting to get to her feet again. It was hard enough keeping an eye on her and working at the same time now that she could crawl. He'd bought a large playpen for her to move around in, but she'd be walking soon. How the hell would he manage then?

"Oh, Ellie, your daddy is such an idiot. I wish your mummy was here. She'd know what to do." He smiled then went over to the pen. "Of course, if your mummy was here, I wouldn't have these problems, would I? Jonno wouldn't have said anything, and I wouldn't have slept with such a jerk." He placed Ellie in her highchair and put some porridge in a bowl. She banged the table in excitement and gurgled loudly, which was undoubtedly a comment telling him not to be so stupid.

"Yeah, yeah, and you're right, angel. You always are. I don't have to see this bloke again. And, yes, you're probably right to say that you're so cute he'd fall in love with you on first sight." He put the spoon into her mouth, once more glad she would eat practically anything he gave her. The outer door banged open.

"That'll be your auntie Gwennie come to help Daddy, even though she's a terrible cook."

"I can always go home. Eight-thirty on a Sunday morning — not my favorite time to be out of bed." The buzzer went off on an oven. Gwen sat next to Ellie. "Here, give me the spoon."

"The bread is ready," he said, getting up. "I've been experimenting with different flavors for the Friday sandwich delivery at Leggats and Payne. You're still all right to deliver it, aren't you?"

"Yes, I'm fine and I can help on Wednesday night."

He breathed a sigh of relief and went into the back kitchen built specifically for catering with money from Angie's life insurance. "That's great. Rob has this interview somewhere, but he's not telling anyone about it in case it jinxes him. You know what he's like. He hates serving anyway."

"Yeah, our brother isn't the most careful waiter. I hope he gets it. He's worried about money. So," she said, turning his laptop toward herself, "what's on the lists for today?"

"Shit!" Joe said, remembering the list he'd written. Had he closed it down?

"You all right?" Gwen asked.

"Could you give me a hand?" he said, hoping to get her away from the screen.

"Be there now. I'll put her in the pen." Gwen joined him in the outer kitchen.

"Can you put the rolls on the cooling racks?" he asked.

Gwen placed the bread while he removed the larger loaves out of the oven.

"These smell good," she said. "What are they?"

Joe breathed a sigh of relief. If she'd seen the list, she'd have said something. "They're cheese, potato, sage and caramelized onion. I'm also going to try goat's cheese with tomato and basil. I've made a few for our lunch to see what they taste like. We also need to make more batches of bolognese sauce, goulash and steak and kidney so I've got enough in the freezer. Mrs. Smith wants her meals delivered tomorrow. They're already frozen for her and her husband, but I'll need to do more once I've received her choices."

"If those diet meals take off, you're going to need to take someone on to work with you."

"I've considered getting an apprentice, someone from the local catering college, but I don't want to commit myself to more clients than I have at the moment."

"But if it works for her and the others and saves her time with her busy schedule, they could be a good little earner. I thought about trying them myself, but I think I need to do more exercise. Perhaps I'll come to the gym with you and Jonno. Dad said you went yesterday."

"Yeah, I needed to do something mindless and punch a few bags."

"How's Jonno? He's got a big fight next weekend, hasn't he? Are you going?"

"Not sure. I've nothing booked for the evening, but you never know when someone might get let down."

He pulled the last of the loaves out of the oven and set them to cool. He would freeze them ready to use later. Gwen came up to stand beside him. "So, are you going to tell me, or do I have to ask? I promise I won't say anything to anyone else."

Joe closed the fridge door and walked back into the family kitchen. Ellie had porridge around her face and had splashed the contents of the bowl on the floor.

"Come here," he said, lifting her from the pen. He wiped her face and hands and picked up the spoon. She ate the last mouthful and burped loudly. He placed her back in the playpen and examined the list on the screen. Gwen came back in the room and sat in the adjacent seat.

"Look, Joe, it's none of my business, but you're the only one of my brothers who isn't a complete dick. The way you've coped over the last year has been incredible. I'm not going to judge, but you said you needed someone to talk to."

Joe had no idea what to say when she put her hand on his arm. He loved his sister and the last thing he wanted to do was upset her.

"Okay, I'll ask you one thing, then I'll shut up and you can tell me whatever you want." For the first time, he met her gaze. Her expression softened, but her scrutiny didn't waver. They'd both inherited their mother's hair and eye coloring along with their father's stockier frame. People often assumed they were twins, but there were a couple of years between them. Joe was nearer Idris in age, but he'd always been closer to his sister.

He took in a huge breath. "Okay, ask away," he said, surprisingly relieved he had someone who might listen.

"You and Angie—that was always real, wasn't it? You loved her, didn't you?"

He stared at her for a moment. He supposed it was a fair question, given what he'd written about Aron.

"I loved Angie more than I can ever explain. She was my soul mate. We had no secrets from each other, Gwennie. I was never unfaithful, but she knew I liked men and women. Does that shock you?"

"I have to admit to being somewhat surprised. I've always had my doubts about people who claim to be bisexual. Is that what you are?"

"I suppose so, but I've never put a label on my feelings."

"And this bloke? Who is he? Not to mention Jonno, but I already knew about him."

"What! How?"

"Oh, come on, Joe. Anyone with a pair of eyes could see it. It was pitiful, the way he stared at you like a love-struck puppy. You really never saw it?"

"No, never. There were girls. Okay, he didn't go out with many for long, but he's always on about some girl or another he's met in a club. Was he so obvious? Have I been going around with my eyes shut?"

"I saw him in Swansea. There's a gay club the students go to sometimes. I went with Jamie and Jez and saw him there. I suppose he thought he'd be safe away from Cardiff."

"Why didn't you tell me? He's my best friend."

"It's not my place to tell you. I've always hoped he'd find someone and get over you. I guess he hasn't. I hope you let him down gently."

"I didn't exactly get time. I told him about Aron. I thought he'd be all right about it. Then he declared that he loved me and ran out. I've no idea what to do. I texted him, but he hasn't replied. It's a mess, Gwen."

She frowned at him. "And what about the other thing? You slept with this bloke, Aron did you say? That's big, Joey. Who is he?"

"His name is Aron Roberts. I catered a dinner at his place on Friday night, but we'd met by accident about a year ago, before Ellie was born. Neither of us was in a good place that night. He said something stupid...and... Hell, it's hard to explain."

"Let me see. It starts off with you thinking 'I fancy you', then the something stupid was said. You have hot, angry sex, because you're both desperate to feel the blood running through your veins again, but somewhere in the middle of fucking each other senseless, it becomes something else, and now you're not sure what to think."

"Bloody hell, you're a mind reader. What I was thinking. It seemed like a good idea at the time—like I was taking control for a change. I blamed him for making me want him and he wasn't her and I miss her. I've been numb for so long, and I wanted to live again, to have some power, but in the end, all I did was lose myself in him. I didn't expect to need him or to care how I treated him. I had to walk away and get out of there before I cried in his arms."

"No, come on, Joe. We've all been there."

"Really?"

"For God's sake, I'm not a virgin, Joe. Newsflash—I've had sex more than once—and it's not all sunshine and roses."

"You're careful, though, aren't you? No one's ever…"

"No, don't be daft, and this is you we're talking about, not me. Talking of careful, you used a condom, didn't you?"

"Yes, of course we did. I'm not stupid, although I don't think he's been with anyone since his last boyfriend. He said it had been a while for him, and I've only ever slept with Angie."

"So he's the first since Angie died. I can understand how no woman could replace her. Is that it?"

"Oh, I don't know, Gwennie. I've always fancied men. Angie and I used to give people points when we watched films. It was fun."

"You want to see him again, though."

"Doesn't matter what I want. It isn't going to happen. He doesn't like kids and I've got Ellie and she comes first."

She clicked a few buttons on the laptop. "Whoa."

"What now?" he asked

"His boyfriend."

"What about him?" Joe replied.

"I thought the name was familiar." She turned the screen to show him the images from her search. "He was with Dan Morgan, that rugby player whose civil partnership you catered. You know, to the teacher who works with Idris." She clicked a few more buttons. "It says he has a company called Aztechnologies and is quite the technical wizard. He's not bad looking either if you like them on the skinny side. He could do with a few of your steak and kidney pies. Seriously, though, is there a future in it?"

"Come on, Gwen, I told you he doesn't like kids, and I mean really doesn't. And what about Angie's parents? Can you imagine their faces if they found out I was seeing a man, not to mention Mum and Dad."

"They'd be okay, Mum and Dad. Well, all right, they'd be shocked, but they love you so they'd live with it, but I get what you mean about the Nashes, especially now they've discovered religion."

"They tried to take Ellie to begin with. They said I couldn't cope and that she'd be better off with them. I hate letting her see them, as who knows what poison they're dripping into her ears. Can you imagine what would happen if I was going out with a man?"

"Yeah, I see what you mean. Oh, Joe, it's a mess all round. Perhaps it's better if you forget this Aron, but you do need to speak to Jonno. You can't leave it as it is."

"I know I can't. Come on, let's get some work done, then I'll make you lunch. I should have told you in the first place. I'm glad we've had this talk." He reached over and hugged her tightly.

"Yes, you should have, but you have now." She grinned at him, turning her head slightly. "So, did you top or bottom?"

Chapter Six

Aron buried himself in work, desperate to take his mind off Joe, if only he could get his body to stop wanting him. His cock had developed a mind of its own. He'd even tried to distract himself with porn, but nothing worked. Every set of eyes became green, every face developed a smattering of freckles, and every moan reminded him of the sounds Joe had made when he'd come. He'd been dreaming of him too—wet dreams at his age—ridiculous. And these bloody plans wouldn't work, either. He needed coffee, and he needed to get out of the office.

"Arrgghh!" he said, throwing up his hands, sending the mouse clattering on to the floor.

"What's up?" Margaret asked as she came into his office. She put a large mug of coffee on the desk beside him then picked up the mouse.

"How do you do that?" he asked.

"Because I'm good. A good PA always anticipates her boss's needs." She placed a file in front of him. "These are the details for the Germany trip next week. I've forwarded them to your computer, but I know you like to have a paper copy."

"I'm trying to organize the presentation. Trouble is, it's simply an idea at the moment. We have the basic tech worked out, but there's a big difference between planes and cars." He picked up his coffee and swallowed. "Oh, that hits the spot. You're a marvel." He pushed his chair back from the desk. "I've had enough of sitting here. I'm going to drink this then go to see Dai. I need to do something practical to take my mind off the in-situ tests tomorrow. The prototypes have got to be spot on. If they don't perform as our model promised, then I'm back to the drawing board. I wish I had a plane of my own I could use."

Margaret smiled and tidied the papers on his desk—again. "Yes, but where would you keep a jumbo jet? Come on, they're confident, and they're offering a fortune for exclusive use. If you can save fuel with this gadget, then more firms will want it. And if you can do something similar for cars, well…"

"I know, but it all depends on these tests tomorrow. It's going to be a long few hours."

* * * *

The next day was indeed a long one. In the morning they ran the tests on the engines then in a real plane. As the information appeared on his screen, Aron placed a tick next to every item on the checklist.

Dai gripped his arm. "It worked, Aron. It bloody well worked. The figures show a real terms reduction in fuel used for the same distance. You did it, Aron!"

He couldn't speak. He checked the information on the screen again. People gathered around him, slapping his back and shaking his hand.

After a long return drive to Cardiff, with awful traffic jams on the M4, Aron stopped to drop Dai at his house.

"Come in, boss, and have a drink with us. We can celebrate getting the contract. You can't go home on your own."

It was true, Aron didn't want to go home to his empty house. He'd never missed company before. He told himself it was better to have no distractions but now… "Yeah, that would be good," he said.

Dai put an arm around his shoulder and they walked toward the door. The narrow opening forced Dai to let go so Aron followed his manager inside.

"Well?" Pauline asked nervously when they entered the main room. She knew how important the day had been.

"It worked," Dai said. "We got the contract, and there will be bonuses for everyone!"

Pauline jumped up. Dai picked her up and swung her round.

She screeched. "Let me down, you idiot." Back on the floor, she put her arms on his broad shoulders and her head on his wide chest, and they held each other tightly.

Aron heard a noise and turned toward the stairs.

"What's going on?" Rhodri asked. He grinned when he saw Aron. "Does this mean I get a new car for my eighteenth next week, then?"

Dai glared at his son.

"Yeah, I know I'm a mercenary little shit, but you taught me, Dad. You always said if you don't ask, you don't get, and taught me to aim high in pocket money negotiations. You've only got yourself to blame."

Aron couldn't help grinning at the exchange between father and son, especially when Dai reached out and mussed his son's carefully organized hair.

"We'll see, but you need to find something sensible to buy and get yourself a job this summer to help pay for the insurance. Oh, and is that mate of yours still fighting on Friday?"

"Yep, Stevo's fighting early on the bill. Jonno Johnson's the headliner. Some people reckon he should have gone professional, but he's probably too old now." He turned to Aron and smirked. "Fancy coming, Mr. Roberts? Lots of beefcake to stare at, if that's still your taste." He finished by batting his eyelashes flirtatiously. "I know you like them big."

Dai glared at his son. "I'm sorry, boss."

Aron laughed. "It's all right, he's trying to be an annoying little bastard, aren't you? I don't think I've ever been to a live boxing match, so why not? It'll make a change to get out, and he's right. I'm not averse to a bit of muscle."

"Honestly," Pauline said. "I don't know which one of you is worse. Now, I've curry and beer, so sit at the table and I'll serve."

* * * *

Over the next couple of days, Aron didn't get much time to think of Joe. Getting the contract meant spending time sorting out all the legalities, but at least it had given him time to apologize to Evan about the crass comments he'd made at the dinner party.

"D'you really hate kids?" Evan asked him. "Hate is such a strong word."

They'd spent a few hours checking every word of the contract. Aron had the design. He understood the value of his idea and that it would make him a rich man. If he and Dai and the small team he'd gathered around him could do the same thing for other engines, then who knew what the future would hold.

Aron put down the papers and stared at Evan. His friend was a good bloke and an unlikely looking solicitor. Like Dai, he had no neck and his ears showed the signs of abuse common in rugby prop forwards. Never comfortable in a suit and tie, he constantly fiddled with his collar.

"I don't exactly hate kids, and I'm sorry if what I said sounded...inappropriate? Can you apologize to Beth for me? I've never seen myself being involved with children. How do you cope with the responsibility and the worry? I worry enough about my designs and if I can keep paying people. I feel responsible because my little company helps to keep families in their houses, but you and Beth have a life in your hands, especially now when Scott is so small and depends on you for everything. And you're supposed to love your kids, but what if you don't? What if you can't? What if you get this human being, who totally depends on you, and you find you don't like them, or they come to dislike you?"

"There are no guarantees about anything," Evan said. "Sometimes you have to take a chance, I guess. No one is perfect. Beth and I will make mistakes. She worries all the time, but her mum has been great and Scottie is as strong as an ox—you should feel his grip. Look, why don't you come over and meet him? Scottie won't bite. He doesn't have any teeth yet."

Aron smiled. Evan wouldn't take no for an answer and it would be good to get over to their house in St. Andrews.

"Come to lunch on Saturday. If the weather's good, I'll do a BBQ. You can practice holding Scottie if you want—or if you don't—it doesn't matter. I promise to make sure he doesn't poo or puke over you, although he peed all over my shirt last night. He lay there and this great arc of liquid headed toward me. I think he did it on purpose because he giggled his head off afterward. Beth said it was wind, but I'm not convinced." He stopped and looked at Aron. "Sorry, I'm doing it again, aren't I?"

Aron nodded.

"You can tell me to shut up. Now, I think that's everything. This deal is going to be rather lucrative, and it won't do my profile with the firm any harm either. I may be a newbie solicitor, but I want to make partner, or have my own firm." He gathered the papers together and put them in his briefcase. "I'd better get going. We've the in-laws around tonight. You doing anything?"

"I'm off to a boxing match," Aron replied.

"Boxing? You? When were you interested in boxing?" He stopped and smirked.

"I was asked to go," Aron protested.

"So nothing to do with half-naked men with washboard stomachs then, or is that a bonus?"

"Maybe. I'm going with Dai and his son, Rhodri. A friend of Rhodri's is fighting in one of the junior bouts. Top of the bill is Jonno Johnson, the welterweight."

"How big is that?"

"No idea, but it'll make a change. Dai thinks I can be a source of advice for Rhodri."

"Is he interested in technology, then?"

Aron snorted. "No, he's recently finished his first year of catering after giving up on A levels. He announced that he's bisexual and Dai is finding it hard to understand. I don't think he gets that if Rhodri likes girls, why doesn't he stick to them, why complicate things?"

"Do you think he's going for shock value?" Evan asked.

"No, Rhodri is one of those people happy on both sides of the fence as long as he finds the person interesting. I'm not sure how much experience he's had — probably more than me!"

"Yeah, we were both caught young, weren't we?"

"Hmm, but not everything lasts forever, does it? In the end, me and Dan turned out not to be the person either of us needed. He's much happier with Iestyn." He decided not to mention that he'd seen him recently.

"Maybe you'll see someone who catches your eye at the boxing tonight. Your eyes might meet across a crowded room."

"Does Beth know you're such a soppy old romantic?" he asked.

"Oh, yeah, she knows."

Chapter Seven

Dai and Rhodri stood talking next to their car when Aron pulled into the space next to them in the already crowded car park.

"Let's go inside and find the best seats," Rhodri said excitedly.

"Not on the front row, though," Dai said. "I'm not risking getting covered in sweat, spit and blood. If you want to sit there, sit with your mates when they arrive, and no drinking. You're not eighteen until tomorrow."

Rhodri pouted then turned when three people waved at him from the door. "I'll see you later," he said as he ran toward them.

"I can't believe he's going to be eighteen tomorrow. I swear, he was a baby yesterday and now look at him. I hope he's being careful."

"Rhodri is a handsome boy — takes after his mother — popular with everyone. Despite his devil-may-care attitude, he's got a good head on his shoulders and he knows what he wants. If he can't sew a few wild oats at his age, when can he?"

"I know, but he's nothing like Melissa. Pauline always said she'd let Mel go to Cardiff on her own when she was ten, but she's not sure she should let Rhodri now. Mel's going to be home from Bristol next week for the summer before she goes to Germany on placement next term. Did I mention she's expected to get a first?"

"Once or twice," Aron replied. He followed Dai into the sports hall and they found chairs on the far side. Banks of seats had been placed on all sides around the ring for the occasion, and they sat at the end of the third row. Rhodri and his friends waved from their position in the front row of seating opposite them. Aron couldn't help smiling at the boy sitting next to Rhodri. His purple hair spiked with gel seemed out of place at a boxing match. Dai caught the trajectory of his view. "That's Butch."

"Butch?" Aron questioned, thinking the boy appeared to be anything but, draped as he was all over Rhodri.

"Yeah, I blamed him for influencing Rhodri to begin with. Stupid, I know. They've been friends for years. His dad's a butcher, hence the name. Rather ironic as he's camper than a row of tents. Came out when he was twelve, apparently, but according to Rhodri, he was never really in. Stevo, the one they've come to support, is his boyfriend."

"Really?" Aron replied, glancing over at the young man again.

"Yep," Dai confirmed. "It's a brave new world out there and although I may not understand it, I think it's good to see more sportsmen being courageous enough to be themselves."

Aron nodded. "Dan was the same. It's one of the things I most admired about him and look at him now — captain of the Welsh Rugby Union team."

The hall filled up, and eventually the announcer stepped into the ring. He explained there would be five matches, culminating in the championship match between Jonno Johnson and Neil James.

The first two fights were decided on points. Aron went to the vending machine and bought a couple of cans. The night was warm and lots of people crowded into a smallish room made it warmer. As he walked back to his seat, he saw a familiar face and stopped. Joe was on his own, making his way back to the seats behind Rhodri. Aron didn't know what to do. He wanted to go over to Joe to speak to him, but had no idea what to say. The next bout was announced, and Aron hurried back to his seat. He needed time to work out his plan and hoped to catch Joe on the way out.

Stevo Jones stepped into the ring to whoops of support coming from the front row. Joe sat behind them, and for a moment their gazes locked across that crowded room. Even at that distance, the shock clearly showed on Joe's face. No doubt he'd never have expected to see him in this particular place. Aron guessed he must be there to see someone and hoped Joe wouldn't bolt.

The bout went to a third round — the boxers evenly matched. Stevo finally caught the other boxer with a right hook. After a count of ten, the referee held up Stevo's hand and declared him the winner. He immediately jumped out of the ring and grabbed his boyfriend, swinging him around. Aron heard a few comments around him, but put his hands together and clapped with the rest.

Eventually, they announced the final bout. Jonno Johnson bounced into the ring. He turned to stare in Joe's direction. It was hard to see his expression, but he didn't look happy, and neither did Joe. Aron glanced back to where Rhodri sat with a rapt expression on his face, his gaze not moving from the shapely sight provided by the boxer in the blue corner.

Both men got several good punches in early on, but Dai assured Aron that Jonno was winning on points after two rounds. Jonno was the local boy and had the most support. With a minute to go, he caught his opponent with a right uppercut, sending him crashing down. James tried to get up, but he obviously had no idea where he was. The referee held up Johnson's arm. On the other side of the ring, Joe was his feet cheering and Aron wondered about the nature of his relationship with the victor.

"Good fight," Dai said. "Did you enjoy your first live boxing tournament?"

"I did, but I don't think it'll be a regular thing for me. I think I'll stick to watching rugby and playing chess — much more my style."

Dai smiled. "I'll go and get Rhodri and meet you back in the car park," Dai said.

"No, you go to the cars. I'll get him." Aron hoped he might be able to spot Joe, but he'd lost him in the crowd of people making their way out, so made his way to Rhodri.

"Your dad has gone back to the car. I've come to fetch you."

"I want to get Jonno Johnson's autograph," Rhodri explained. "Tell him I won't be long."

Aron turned to Stevo Jones, who had joined them. "Good win," he said. "I hope you don't mind me saying, but I think you two are so brave." The guy didn't look too happy for a moment until Rhodri introduced him.

"This is Aron Roberts, Stevo. He used to go out with Dan Morgan, the rugby player." Now all of them stared at him.

"Sorry, I didn't mean anything bad. I admire any sportsman prepared to be out of the closet." He put out his hand, and Stevo shook it warmly.

"I'll tell your dad you'll be along in a few minutes, then. Remember what I said, Rhodri."

He made his way back to the car and gave Dai the message. They waited for fifteen minutes until Dai could wait no more and called Rhodri on his phone. Aron heard the conversation and smiled.

"Give me a couple of minutes, Dad. I want to get Jonno Johnson's autograph. I might get into boxing."

Or into that particular boxer's shorts! He was still hoping to spot Joe, although he had no idea what he'd say to him if he got the chance.

A couple of minutes later, a disappointed Rhodri tramped across the tarmac to the cars.

"Maybe next time," Aron said.

"He's over there," Rhodri said. Before anyone could stop him, he ran back to the door, leaving his father with a mixture of concern and annoyance battling for supremacy on his face. He took a step forward.

"Leave it, Dai," Aron warned.

"But it's obvious Rhodri fancies him, and he's a boxer who punched a guy into the floor tonight. What if Rhodri says something out of turn? The bloke might break his nose or worse."

"He's a big boy now, Dai, and he's got to learn the boundaries for himself. You can't protect him forever." However, the boxer wasn't alone. Behind him, trying to get his attention, stood Joe.

Joe waited then followed Jonno out. He put his hand on the boxer's arm. "Jonno, wait up. We need to talk. Come on, we've been friends for too long."

Jonno stopped and turned around. "Yeah, I thought we were friends. I thought we knew each other. Goes to show how wrong you can be. I need some time to think, Joe."

"That goes both ways. We all have secrets, Jonno. After what you told me, I talked to Gwen." He stopped, unsure whether to say anymore. A young fan hovered close by. Joe edged nearer to Jonno. "She saw you in a club in Swansea." His friend blanched under the lamplight. "As I said, you've kept some things from me as well. We need to talk."

Joe gazed over Jonno's shoulder as the boy offered a leaflet for the boxer to sign. He glanced up and spotted Aron across the dark space, standing next to another man. He'd assumed Aron would be gone by this time. Sound echoed across the empty car park and he heard Aron tell the man to wait in the car, then he headed in his direction. Shit. Not now. Not here. Not in front of...

"I'll call you, Jonno," he said and set off in the other direction toward where his car stood alone in a darker part of the area. He didn't get there quickly enough.

"I've nothing to say to you," he said.

"Please, Joe, let me at least apologize," Aron pleaded.

"What for? We both wanted it." He held Aron's gaze and lowered his voice. "What's the matter? Want some more, do you? Want me to pound that arse of yours until you scream?"

Aron swallowed hard, making his Adam's apple bob up and down. His gaze raked Aron's body. Even in the semidarkness, the bulge in his jeans stood out. Unable to stop himself, Joe grabbed Aron's cock through the material and massaged it under his palm. "Don't deny that you want me because this tells me all I need to know. I could keep doing this and make you come in your pants, couldn't I?"

Aron breathed what Joe thought was a yes then glanced over Joe's shoulder.

Joe turned his head but kept his hand in place. "Your friend is staring at us," he whispered. "And he doesn't look pleased." Joe stopped what he was doing then turned his head once more and saw Jonno frozen to the spot. Aron grabbed his arm.

"Come home with me," he said.

"You'd like that, wouldn't you? Another quick fuck with no strings, but sorry, I've got someone waiting at home for me." He moved away, and before Aron could reply, he ran across the car park to Jonno.

He'd been tempted to go with Aron—his cock as hard as steel. Something about Aron turned him into this stranger he didn't recognize. He'd never been an aggressive man, or bad tempered, and he couldn't work out who he was most annoyed with, himself or Aron. He caught up with Jonno at the man's car.

"Who was that?" Jonno asked.

Joe didn't know what to say, but his face must have revealed all.

"Was that him?" Jonno asked. "The bloke you shagged?"

"This isn't the place, Jonno. Come round on Sunday night. I'm working tomorrow—got a dinner party in Roath."

"Better not shag the host at that one, then," Jonno said, pulling open his car door.

"Please, Jonno." Tears streamed down Joe's face. He wiped them away with his sleeve. Jonno had been his friend for so long, the thought of losing him…

Jonno climbed into the driver's seat and slammed the door. Joe waited, unable to walk away.

Finally, Jonno lowered the car window. "All right, I'll be there Sunday, but no secrets, right. Cards on the table."

"No secrets," Joe agreed. When he turned to his own car, he spotted Aron talking to the young autograph hunter.

"Found yourself a fan?" Joe said.

Jonno removed the piece of paper from his pocket and waved it at Joe. "Maybe," he replied. "I'll see you Sunday."

Chapter Eight

He turned off the engine. The sound of a baby crying inside the house didn't inspire confidence. Evan and Beth lived in the suburbs in a tidy, semidetached, red-brick house with bay windows. The front garden had been paved over and turned into a driveway. He waited in his car for a few moments, psyching himself up to get out of the car. The door opened to reveal a large blond Welshman.

"Well, are you simply going to sit there?" Evan questioned.

Aron grabbed the bag containing wine and a present for the baby and got out of the car. At the doorstep, Evan pulled him into a hug. "It's all right, Scottie was hungry — that's all. Beth's upstairs feeding him now." Aron stepped through the door, handed over the bag then followed Evan into the main living room.

"Oh, good wine choice," Evan said, opening the bag. "Dan and Iestyn will be here soon, as well as Hayley and her partner, Matt, and…Emrys has invited himself. Sorry."

"Emrys is coming?" This day was getting better and better.

"Yeah, I know he has a tiny little crush on you, but I've warned him. I'm hoping having Dan here will distract him. He's harmless, really. He came out because of you and Dan. He told me he wished he'd been able to at school. The old ladies he visits on the geriatric ward love him. Are you're sure he's not your type? You do have form for liking big men!"

"Your brother's lovely, but he's like Tigger on crack. I've never met anyone with so much energy and optimism. To be honest, he scares me. He'll need someone with more patience than me, Evan. It'll be good to see Hayley again, though. It's been a year since Mac and Julie's wedding."

A sudden wail made them turn. Beth stood in the doorway. Aron stayed rooted to the spot, despite Beth's reassuring smile.

"Evan told you Emrys is joining us, then? Don't worry, Scottie here will distract him." She gazed at the baby in her arms. "Your uncle is totally besotted with you, isn't he?"

His stomach churning, Aron tensed immediately. Panic threatened to overwhelm him. Why had he ever agreed to come? The baby seemed so tiny in Beth's arms. She put Scott into his carry cot and sat next to Aron on the sofa. At least she hadn't tried to get him to hold the child.

"I'm sorry about what I said at the dinner last week," Aron began. "It's just..."

Beth put a hand on his arm. "It's okay. The first time I held Scottie properly, I was terrified I'd drop him. So was Evan. It's natural to feel that way. We'd created this little person who was totally dependent on us for everything. I wonder if I'm doing the right thing all the time, and if I'll be a good mother and, boy, can he scream when he wants something. But he can't tell you what he wants so you try food, a nappy changing or hugs — anything you can think of to soothe him."

The sound of a motorbike arriving interrupted their conversation.

"That'll be Emrys on his new toy," Evan explained. "I think he's hoping the leather look might work on you!"

"Oh God," Aron whispered. Between the baby, his uncle, his ex and his new husband, Aron feared he wouldn't survive the day.

Evan and Beth abandoned him to greet Emrys at the door.

"Hi, bro. Hi, Beth. Where's my main man, then?" Emrys's deep voice boomed from the hallway.

"Asleep," Beth said. "So if you could…"

"Where's the fun in that? So, bro, what do you think of the bike, then? Isn't she a beauty?"

"I'm sure it's perfect for the mean streets of Cardiff," he replied. "Beer?"

"Oh, yeah, I'll just have the one. I'm parched."

They entered the living room. Aron got up and prepared himself for what would happen next.

"Aron — as hot as ever I see. Shit, those jeans must hug every inch of your arse. So, do I rock this leather outfit, or what?"

Aron braced himself as he was bear-hugged to within an inch of his life by the enormous man in front of him.

"God, man, there's nothing to you, is there? I could pick you up and swing you around except I'd break the furniture, and not for the first time." He kissed Aron's cheek and let him go. "Ah, there he is, the eighth wonder of the world. Isn't he the most gorgeous thing you've ever seen — other than that guy in *The Normal Heart*? Man, he is so hot. Right, I'll get these leathers off.

It's going to be a hot one today. We setting up this barbecue then, bro?"

Aron breathed a sigh of relief as Emrys followed his brother to the kitchen. Beth patted his arm. "I know he's an acquired taste, but he means well, and there's not a bad bone in his body. I wish he could find someone special. He'd make such a great dad."

The doorbell rang, and Beth got up to let in the rest of the party. Aron was hugged in turn by his ex, Dan, and his partner, Iestyn.

"The company's doing well, I hear," Dan said, letting him go.

"Yes, it is. We've recently signed a fantastic deal. Good news about the World Cup. You must be made up being named as captain so early."

"The powers that be thought it would be good for the team. I'd better go and say hello to Scottie."

Dan moved away to join the others in the kitchen. Their split had been amicable, but there was still some awkwardness between them.

"How's things after last week?" Iestyn asked while the others talked.

"I have news," Aron said, dragging him to one side. "I saw him last night at a boxing match."

He jumped as a pair of female arms slid around his waist from behind.

"Surprise."

Aron pulled away and turned, knowing full well whose arms they were. Hayley hadn't changed. Her gorgeous red hair cascaded in long curls around her shoulders over a colorful maxi dress that showed off her figure.

"You look beautiful as ever," he said. "It's been a while. How's life in London treating you?"

"Life is good. I've been lucky. This is Matt."

Aron put out his hand to the tall blond man in front of him. "We sort of met at the wedding last year."

Scottie chose that moment to wake up, and they all turned toward the noise.

"Can I?" Dan asked.

"Sure," Beth replied, glancing at Aron. She lifted Scott from the cot and put him into Dan's arms. Iestyn tickled the baby under the chin and both men made noises Aron supposed meant something. The others gathered around as well.

"I'll go and see Evan and Emrys," he said. The sight of the man he'd once loved cooing over a baby with his husband... He couldn't deal with that now.

Outside, Evan and Emrys were arguing over the best way to cook the mountain of meat set out on trays next to the huge gas-powered machine. Still, at least they wouldn't be arguing about wood versus charcoal or other such nonsense. He sat in a chair and stared out across the garden bordered either side by tall fences. He liked the idea of having a garden, but not the job of tending it himself.

"So," Iestyn said, sitting next to him. "I've left Dan in there talking to Hayley about old times. They're up as far as telling Matt about the prom and someone called Spike. I thought I'd leave them to it. So what happened?"

"Bloody hell, Iestyn. He was at this boxing match I went to last night. We sort of confronted each other. I can't control myself around him. Just being near him made me... Well, you can guess, and he noticed and grabbed my crotch. I nearly came in my pants. I asked him to come home with me, but he walked away and went back to his friend. Last night I had the most vivid dream and woke up covered in... I'm sure you can guess. Who has wet dreams at my age?" Heat rushed into his cheeks, and he stared at the crazy paving.

"I get it," Iestyn said, putting a hand on his arm. "What are you going to do? I have to say it sounds as if he doesn't know what he wants, either, and that's why he's got all this pent-up aggression."

Aron shrugged. "There's still the baby thing. I saw you and Dan with Scott and I had to get out of the room. You're so good together, and Dan would make a great dad, while I'm a bloody freak. Evan invited me today partly so I could hold Scott and get used to the idea, but now I've no idea what to do."

"I only know what I'm doing with babies because of my niece and nephews. Megs adores Dan and he adores her. She can twist him around her little finger, even though she's three, and the twins jump all over him."

"I'm scared that if we did manage to get to the stage when we weren't angry with each other, I'd find I really didn't like children, as well as being bloody terrified of them."

The noise of the others coming out onto the patio shut him up and he sighed in relief that the baby wasn't with them.

"He's having a nap," Beth explained, putting the baby monitor on the table. "Listen out while I go and get the rest of the food sorted, if there's anything left that isn't burnt to a crisp after those two try to cook."

The rest of the afternoon was one long round of eating and talking. Once or twice Aron caught Dan glancing at him and wondered if Iestyn had said anything to him. After a couple of hours, tiny grizzling noises came from the monitor.

Evan stood. "He probably needs changing. I'll go."

Aron got up as well. "I'm going to pop to the loo."

He followed Evan inside and ran up the stairs, glad to be on his own for a few moments at least. When he came down, Evan was doing up the poppers on Scott's outfit.

"He loves the mobile you bought him. We put it over his cot at night and the music lulls him to sleep."

Aron peered at the blond little boy. He appeared so tiny next to his father.

"Why don't you try holding him now while the others are outside," Evan said. "Sit back on the sofa, then you won't worry about dropping him. Babies bounce anyway."

Aron plonked himself down and held out his arms. He could do this.

"That's it, support his head. You can put your arm on the arm of the sofa. There, your first time holding a baby and no one died."

Aron searched his feelings. Maybe it would be different if this were his child, but that was never going to happen. He had a small, warm, helpless creature lying in his arms, but that was all. Should he make those goo-goo sounds others seemed to do? He didn't know what to say or do while Evan stood there staring at him, obviously expecting something. All he wanted to do was give the baby back to his father and pass the responsibility to someone else.

"Oh, hell," he said when Scottie started to cry. "I'm sorry, I'm so useless at this. You'd better take him."

Evan leaned over and took Scott back.

"See, he cries when I hold him too. Time for the magic powers of Uncle Emrys. Come on, it's all right. If at first you don't succeed, you can always try again. You might get used to it, and this bloke's child is nearly one, isn't she? She'll be crawling at least, and they develop a personality then. Don't give up if he matters to you."

Aron followed Evan back into the garden.

"There he is, my little man," Emrys boomed. "Aww, stop this grizzling and come to Uncle Emrys."

Evan handed over the baby to his brother, who waltzed around the garden singing at the top of his voice. Scottie stopped crying immediately.

"He should hire himself out," Beth said as Emrys danced across the garden. "It never fails. A few times, I've considered asking him to move in when Scottie won't settle at night and I'm afraid that the neighbors will complain."

His face must have revealed his fear.

"It's not for everyone, though. Being a parent is not everybody's dream. Perhaps, when there aren't so many people around, you could come back."

So Evan *had* talked about their conversation. Who was he trying to kid? He may as well forget about Joe now. Why had he thought there might be any future with him? One shag did not a relationship make.

Chapter Nine

Joe closed the oven door and turned to pick Ellie out of her playpen. He carried her into the living room, closing the gate to the kitchen behind him, and set her on the floor. Immediately she crawled toward him. He got the box of blocks and set them in front of her, along with her plastic eggs and the glockenspiel, which she hit with enthusiasm. He smiled as she giggled, and a warmth filled his chest. Soon she would be walking. She'd already tried to get to her feet and all too soon there would be boyfriends, or girlfriends, or even both. For now, she remained his little girl with shining green eyes and dark curls, just like her father. She stopped banging and lifted those eyes to meet his gaze. He couldn't believe she would be one next week. Where had the time gone? It would also be a year since Angie had died.

Ellie lifted her head and gurgled. She loved making noises and often talked to herself, moving her hands and fingers as she did.

"Did you say Dadda, clever girl?" He wasn't sure, but the noise sounded as if it could have been Dadda. Tears welled in his eyes and he brushed them away. A car pulled up outside the house, and Joe got up to look out of the window.

"Your uncle Jonno has arrived. Make sure you give him your best smile as he and Dadda have a lot to talk about. I've made him his favorite cottage pie, even if it is warm out."

He went to the front door and opened it, making sure he'd closed the gate behind him. Now that Ellie was crawling, he had learned to be careful, and there were gates everywhere. Stairs led up off the narrow hallway and the door to the main living room which had once been the front room. Joe had turned the middle room into a dining kitchen by knocking down the wall between that room and the kitchen, giving the room more light. They'd had a long garden, so he'd taken some of it to build the extension and put in the working kitchen with its stainless-steel fittings. The room gave him enough space for the extra ovens and freezers he needed for a professional operation, and everything in it was moveable in case the business did well and he decided to open a business premises.

He waved to Jonno when he got out of the car. Ellie rattled the gate. "Yes, don't be so impatient."

He stood back and let his friend come in. Jonno reached over the gate and picked Ellie up, holding her in midair then blowing raspberries on her stomach.

"How's the prettiest girl in the world? You being a good girl for your dadda?" He didn't wait to be asked and sat with the baby on his lap then tickled her until she giggled uncontrollably. For a moment, Joe allowed himself to wonder what it would have been like to be in a relationship with Jonno. He was so good with Ellie, but he'd never had romantic feelings about his best friend.

"Something smells good," Jonno said.

"I made your favorite—cottage pie with lots of veg and sweet potato on top." He sat at the other end of the sofa, keeping a distance between them. "You did well on Friday night knocking Neil James out. Are you likely to get another fight soon?"

"I don't know, Joe. I'm not getting any younger, and I'd rather go out winning than losing. Jimmy has asked me to do some coaching with the younger ones, especially as we've a few girls who want to learn now that it's an Olympic sport. I can fit it around work as it's mostly nights and weekends. It'll be good. I like working with the kids and being a binman is hardly a stimulating occupation."

"No, but someone's got to do it."

They were avoiding the elephant in the room, but he didn't know where to start. Jonno beat him to it.

"Joe, about what I said last week after you told me about that bloke. I shouldn't have said anything. It's no biggie, all right? I don't want you to think I'm pining for you or something and that you're the only man for me, or some such nonsense."

Joe looked him straight in the eye. "You told me you loved me, that you'd always loved me. I'd say that was quite big. Why didn't you tell me you were gay? We've known each other since we were four. How didn't I realize you had feelings for me?"

"Angie knew."

"What?"

"She told me it was all right, but hoped I'd find someone who would love me back. It helped talking to her. That's when I decided I had to get over you and get out there."

Why wasn't he surprised? It was typical of his wife. "She knew I fancied men and women as well. Angie and I had no secrets — well, I didn't think we did, but I guess you were a big secret. You didn't say anything after Angie died."

"Aw, come on, Joe. What was I supposed to do? Declare my undying love and imagine I could replace Angie? Shit, no one knows about me being gay except you and your sister. Oh, and the one or two blokes I've had sex with over the last couple of years, trying to make myself get over this teenage fantasy I've had of you and I setting up home together." He blushed bright scarlet.

Ellie squirmed in his arms and he put her on the floor. She crawled quickly toward her blocks then sat picking them up and putting them down again, talking to herself.

"She said Dadda earlier," Joe said. "At least I think she did."

"Sure it wasn't wind? She'll be one next week. How did that happen? She'll soon be walking and talking and bringing home her first boyfriend."

"Or girlfriend," Joe said.

Jonno grinned. "Or girlfriend. I'll bring her present around on the day, if that's okay."

"Of course it is. We're having a family party, but you're more my family than some of them so you'd better be there. Nothing has changed as far as I'm concerned. You're my best friend, Jonno, and I hope you always will be, I just…"

"Don't fancy me. I understand, and that bloke was a skinny thing unlike me. I guess he's not a thick binman either." Joe stared hard at him.

"Sometimes you can be such an annoying dick. I don't care if you're a binman — you're also a champion boxer and a great friend. I wouldn't have got through the last year without you and my family — obviously not all of them because my brothers are idiots, but the rest, and you, have kept me sane and helped with Ellie, and look at her. She's happy, and she's healthy, and that's all that matters."

"What about this bloke, then?"

The buzzer sounded on the oven.

"Come through to the kitchen and I'll serve. Bring her, would you?"

Jonno picked her up and sniffed. "Hmm, smells like someone's made room for her dinner. Want me to sort her out?" He put her back on the floor and went to the cupboard to find a nappy.

"Come on then, little lady, be a good girl for your uncle Jonno and don't wriggle too much."

By the time Jonno had finished, disposed of the nappy outside, and washed his hands, Joe had put the food and plates on the dining table. He strapped Ellie into her highchair and put some mashed-up meat, potato and vegetables in her bowl. She banged her spoon excitedly.

"Give it a minute to cool, Ellie," he said, blowing on it.

Jonno banged his fork as well.

"You can get your own," Joe said laughing. Jonno did as he was told and spooned a huge pile of food onto his plate. He sniffed it then dug in. "Man, this stuff is gorgeous."

"Try to taste each mouthful," Joe said, as forkful after forkful disappeared. Eventually, with the plate more than half empty, Jonno stopped.

"So, you never answered me — this bloke?"

"You sure you're all right talking about him?" Joe asked as he spooned food into Ellie's mouth.

"I guess we'll find out. You need someone to talk to and I'm your best friend — that's what best friends are supposed to do."

"His name is Aron Roberts. He has his own company, Aztechnologies. They make something technical — not sure what."

"Cute name."

"The dinner was to celebrate the company's one-year anniversary. I'd met him before, though, when the brakes failed on that damn death-trap of a car I used to own. He was the guy I nearly hit on the hard shoulder."

"Oh, yeah, I remember. A stupid cop thought you'd done it on purpose, didn't he?"

"That's the one. Aron's PA booked me after I'd done the party for Dan Morgan's civil partnership."

Jonno looked at him strangely. He got out his phone and tapped at it.

"What is it?" Joe asked.

"I thought the name seemed familiar. I have a thing for names, as well as rugby, and I'm a big fan of Dan Morgan. Is this the bloke?"

"Yeah, that's him, and yes, he was Dan Morgan's boyfriend. Gwennie showed me pictures from a magazine. He told me that he'd been in school with him. He didn't tell me he was gay."

"Perhaps he thought it might scare you off. I think we can say he definitely fancies you, although you're nothing like his ex, are you? So if he fancies you, and you fancy him, why all the drama between you? I mean, I get that your family doesn't know, so that might be a problem, but if you just wanted some sneaky sex… What am I missing?"

"We had a moment." Jonno raised his eyebrows.

"A moment?"

"Yeah, yeah, I know, but he put his arm on mine, and I can't explain it—heat rushed through me. I was half-hard from that."

"And?"

"But then during the dinner, I overheard him say he doesn't like kids because he was too selfish to bother with them, and… It made me so angry."

"Angry or disappointed? Sounds to me like you fancied him and allowed yourself this little fantasy, then realized it wasn't going to happen because of Ellie. But you still had sex with him, didn't you?"

Joe wiped Ellie's mouth and looked down at the table. "I'm not proud of what I did, and please tell me if this gets too TMI for you. I waited for him upstairs rather than leaving."

"You did what?"

"I've no idea what I was thinking. I'm not sure I was thinking at all. When he came upstairs, I pinned him against the wall. We kissed and groped and I ended up fucking him over the bed."

Joe watched as Jonno swallowed hard and dismissed what might have been his instant comment. "You did use precautions, didn't you?"

"I'm not that stupid. Jeez, I was angry, but he was *so* hot. He wanted me fuck him. It was fast and furious at first, then I slowed everything down. Oh hell, Jonno, he's beautiful. Afterward, I walked out and told him not to contact me. I didn't expect to see him again."

"But you wanted to."

"There's no point. I don't get why he talked to me last night. I've got a baby and he doesn't like kids. There's no future in it. I suppose we could shag like rabbits with no strings but…"

"That's not your style. There's never been anyone else for you but Angie, has there?"

"No, he's the second person I've ever had sex with, which I guess is odd for someone my age."

"Maybe if he meets Ellie, it might be different. Perhaps he's never had anything to do with kids. You don't know. He deserves a chance — doesn't he? — if you like him."

"Help yourself to more. I made an especially large portion, knowing you were coming, and there's apple pie to follow if you've room."

Jonno spooned more onto his plate. "When do I ever not have room for your cooking?" By now Ellie had started banging the tray with her spoon.

"I'll get her some of the apple purée I made. She loves the stuff."

"Joe, don't change the subject."

"Okay, let's say you're right and he hasn't had anything to do with kids — there's also the other stuff. Can you imagine how the Nashes would react if they found out I was seeing a man? They'd be at the lawyers again, saying I was unfit to take care of her."

"As if any judge would think that seeing at her. You're a great dad."

"Maybe I'll simply have to put it down to experience, as Dad would say. The next thing I have to do is organize this little one's birthday. I don't want to be sad on that day. I'm going to have the family here for her party. Hopefully the weather will hold and we can have a barbecue."

"Count me in — especially if there's food on offer."

Joe remembered something from the night before. "Did that lad give you his phone number?" he asked.

"Yes, as it happens, he did. I'm guessing the man Aron was with is his father."

"He was at the dinner with his wife. He works for Aron. Will you phone him? I'd say the way his tongue hung out showed he's interested."

"He's a bit young, but yeah, perhaps I will. Can't go on mooning after you now, can I?"

"Please get that image out of my head."

Jonno hunched his shoulders and stuck out his lips. "My arse not good enough for you, then? I've been told it's one of my best features."

"Well, maybe the twink will think so!"

Jonno grinned. "Hmm, maybe he will. Now, where's my apple pie?"

Chapter Ten

"Thanks for coming over to help me with the cooking," Joe said as his dad removed more sausage rolls from the oven.

"It's all right. You know what this lot is like when they get together, gannets all of them. I assume the Nashes will be arriving at some point to bring a cloud of doom and despondency to the proceedings."

"They wanted to bring Ellie her presents as well. I know they aren't my favorite people, but Angie was their only child, and no parent should have to outlive their child." He glanced at Ellie playing contentedly in her pen, bashing away at the glockenspiel and making noises a lot like singing. "I can't imagine having to deal with that."

"You're a good man, son. Today will be hard for you as well, but this little one deserves all the attention she's going to get lavished on her."

Joe lay his head on his father's broad shoulder as Andy wrapped his arms around him, and thanked his lucky stars he had such parents.

"Andy? Joe?" His mother's voice echoed from the hall.

"In the kitchen, Mam."

"Ah, there you both are. We've brought the drinks. Andy, would you fetch them for me while I hug my baby boy? Gwennie has the presents."

"I hope you haven't gone over the top, Mam."

"Nah, just a few little toys and some storybooks so you can read to her. You know how important that is, and some clothes and things. Times may be difficult in the public sector, but the Welsh parliament can't function without me."

They made a strange pair, his parents. She tall and always elegant whether dressed in a T-shirt and capri pants as she was today, or in one of the suits she wore for work. His father shorter and broad chested, like the typical mining stock from which he was descended. His dad had taught him to cook. The arrangement had suited them both.

"Now, there's my little granddaughter, and isn't she gorgeous in her party outfit?" His mother waited until Andy had left the room then put her palm to her son's face. "You all right, Joey?"

"I'm fine, Mam. I sat with the photo albums this morning and showed Ellie all the pictures and told her what a wonderful woman her mother was and how proud she would have been." He stopped and choked back tears. "I'm sorry, Mam. I shouldn't be doing this. She needs me to be strong for her."

"Don't be so stupid. What you and Angie had was special, and between you, you produced this wonderful child. Now, when are they coming so I can prepare myself? I swear that man thinks I'm some sort of painted whore because I dye my hair, wear heels and put makeup on my face—not to mention working for a living while your dad stays at home. If he says anything about a woman's place, I swear —"

"Penny said they'd be here about three this afternoon. Bill has a function at the church and Penny is helping out."

"So long as he doesn't try to sermonize here. I've no idea how that lovely girl you married turned out the way she did."

"I don't think they were as bad when she was young, and her nan was a bit of a girl by all accounts and Angie spent lots of time with her. Bill has become more involved in the church since her death. You know how it is with some people, Mam. I can't blame them needing something, and I have Ellie."

The noise of voices came from the front room. "I guess the rest of them have arrived. Jonno is coming as well."

"Has he got himself a girlfriend yet?"

"No, you know Jonno. He likes to keep his options open." Joe didn't want to say any more.

"And what about you, Joe? Angie didn't want you to be alone. Time you got yourself out there. All work and no play makes Joe a dull boy, and we'll always babysit Ellie for you."

Joe leaned into the playpen and picked Ellie up. She was good with people, but a lot all at once could spook her.

"Where d'you want this lot, then?" his brother Idris asked, putting a crate of beer on the table.

"I made room in the fridge," Joe explained. "I hope you got soft drinks as well, and please, Idris, watch your mouth when Angie's parents arrive."

"I will be as good as gold," his brother replied, winking as he stole a mini pork pie from the side. "Hmm, these are yummy. That's what I like about coming here." He tickled Ellie under the chin and went back into the other room. Joe gave his mother an appealing glance.

"I've told him," she confirmed.

"Hey, little bro, good to see you. Work going well, I hear."

Rob, his eldest brother, looked like his mother. He was smiling, which was something Joe hadn't seen his brother do for some time.

"Yeah," Joe replied. "I've had a few good jobs lately, and I had a phone call yesterday about doing a birthday bash. It's a week Saturday. I will need some help with that one."

At that moment, Rob's wife and kids appeared. "You look good, Joe, and my, Ellie, aren't you the pretty one in that frock. You two, go and play football in the garden, but try not to get muddy."

Some hope of that. His five-year-old twin nephews were a handful. He watched as they raced through the French doors into the garden and kicked a ball around. At least they didn't kick hard enough to break his windows yet, he hoped.

"About helping you," Rob began.

Joe noted Mandy had put her arm through her husband's and was smiling as well.

"You got the job," Joe said, slapping his brother on the back.

"I did. The interview was great, and they seem like a decent bunch of people. I haven't met the boss yet, but the manager's a good bloke, and they're expanding their workforce because they've achieved a major new contract. My induction phase starts the week after next."

"I'm so glad for you, Rob. So what's this company called?"

"Strange name — it's called Aztechnologies. I'm told the boss likes to be hands-on and work on the shop floor as well. His PA was a bit fierce."

Joe didn't know what to say. His brother was going to be working for Aron. Had he realized they were related? No, he couldn't have. Welsh was a common name. First the dinner, then the boxing match and now this. Something appeared determined to bring them together.

* * * *

Later, as they sat around the table eating and drinking, Joe gazed over at the photograph of Angie on the wall. She'd been nearly nine months pregnant and complaining about being the size of a house. His father caught his glance and put a hand on his arm.

"Hello, Welshes," Jonno shouted from the other room. "I come bearing gifts and I hope you locusts have left me something to eat."

Joe got up and hugged his friend. "You're as stunning as ever, Mrs. W. Still keeping the country going then? Mr. W — missed you at the fight, but I guess someone had to take care of this one so her dad could go gallivanting."

"You had a good win."

"That I did, but I think I'm going to hand in my gloves now and train the youngsters. Did Joey tell you they want me to work with the girls? Interest in the sport has taken off since the Olympics. I can't wait to get stuck in."

"You'd better behave yourself then, Jonno. If you try anything on with those girls, you'll get punched," Idris said, laughing.

"I think they'll be safe with me." He gave Joe a strange look. "Oh and, Joe, you were right about phoning Rhodri. We're going out on a date next week."

Joe had never seen as many mouths fall open at the same time. Only he and Gwennie remained the same. He had to admit if you were going to come out, it was certainly one way to do it.

"That's good," Joe said to end the silence. "Rob landed a job working with Rhodri's dad at Aztechnologies."

"Wow, small world, isn't it?" Jonno said as if nothing major had happened. "Typical Cardiff, mind you. Now, presents for the birthday girl."

Gwen came up and put her arms around Jonno. "Well done. That took guts." She kissed his cheek, and he blushed. "I figured it was time to be honest, so I told Mam and Dad. They were fine about it—shocked, but fine. Dad said, 'But you're a boxer,' so I said, 'And Dan Morgan is a six-foot-six rugby player.' I wanted to tell you lot next because, well, you've been a second family to me."

Joe's mother joined her daughter in the hug and mouthed a 'did you know?' at her son. He nodded and began to open the presents for Ellie. He laughed when he saw the Glamorgan Giants rugby kit. "Never too young to start being a fan," Jonno said.

After his mother and sister had let Jonno go and his brothers had slapped his back, Joe hugged his friend.

"See," Jonno said. "I told you they'd be all right. Life's too short, Joe. Sometimes you've got to grab it by the tail. I'll always love you and be here for you, no matter what, and they will be too—even that dick, Idris."

The doorbell rang. "Oh hell," Sue said. "The doorbell of doom. Everyone—best behavior!—and perhaps they won't stay long."

Joe went to the door and brought his in-laws through to the kitchen. Bill Nash was a large man with a beard that gave him the appearance of an Old Testament prophet. His wife, Penny, looked like a doll when she stood next to him, a doll with mousy hair, pale skin and pale blue eyes. It didn't matter how many people there were in a room, Bill Nash dominated it. No one could deny the man had presence. Joe had always been rather scared of him, even before he'd taken to preaching fire and brimstone from the pulpit. He put out his hand.

"Bill, thanks for coming." The hand that shook his was as large as the body in front of him. He kissed Penny's cheek then bent and picked up his daughter and handed her to her grandmother. With a child in her arms, she became alive and her eyes smiled as she bounced Ellie on her hip.

"Who's beautiful in her new dress?"

Ellie giggled on cue, making even her grandfather smile.

"We've brought her a few presents," he said, putting the bag down on the table.

"I'll bring her over tomorrow morning," Joe said. They planned to take Ellie to the family plot in the local parish church. Most of Angie's ashes were buried there, and they visited every week, rain or shine. Joe had taken a small portion of them to their favorite place and scattered them into the wind and waves. He liked to think her heart was where it belonged, in the beautiful scenery of Three Cliffs Bay.

Joe's mother brought the teapot to the table, and they all sat. His brothers had stayed in the garden out of the way with Jonno and the children while his father hovered ready to jump in if necessary. Sue poured cups for everyone, and Joe opened the presents, handing the small books to Ellie to look at. Penny sat her on her lap and told her about the animals in the ark as she pointed to each picture.

"Next year she'll understand more of what's going on," Sue said. "I can't believe she's already a year old." Bill opened his mouth to say something, but was distracted by a commotion behind them.

"Aw, come on, gay boy, hand it over, or d'you want me to feel you up trying to get it?" They all turned to see Idris attempting to remove a football from Jonno's clutches with the twins racing around them. Joe muttered something under his breath and hoped his in-laws hadn't heard, or wouldn't understand the reference, but one glance at his father-in-law's face told him that wasn't the case.

"I'm sorry about Idris," Sue said. "He does tend to speak without thinking."

"He's lucky he didn't get a punch in the face for the implications of his statement, especially as Jonno is a boxer. Not everyone would be as tolerant and rightly so. Homosexuality is an abomination."

Joe's heart sank. He saw Jonno drop the ball and stand in the doorway. What the hell was he supposed to say? His parents and Gwen glanced at one another. Gwen went to open her mouth first, but Jonno beat her to it.

"Mr. Nash, I'm aware that you see yourself as a God-fearing man, and I have no problem with that, or your beliefs, but I am gay and Idris is an idiot. I loved your daughter. She was my friend. I don't want to argue with you on this of all days, so I'm going to get my coat and leave. Joe, I'll see you soon."

"I'll walk you to the door, son."

Joe knew his dad had chosen his words carefully. He reached over and retrieved Ellie from her grandmother.

Trying to keep his voice on an even keel, he said, "Jonno is my friend, and he was Angie's friend. My daughter will be brought up to accept all people, and I would appreciate it if you wouldn't say such things in front of her." He held his head up and met the older man's gaze.

"But the Bible says..."

"The Bible says many things, Bill, as you know, and I'm not going to get into a theological argument now. Ellie is my child, and I expect you to respect my views. I will bring her to see you tomorrow and collect her in the afternoon. Ellie needs all of her family and I don't want to deprive her."

Penny gave her husband a look of panic. "Ellie is God's creation as well, and she deserves to know about His love," she said quietly.

"I have no problem with love, Penny, but I won't have her taught to hate."

Bill stood, taking his wife's arm. "We will be ready at ten in the morning," he said.

"She'll be there. I'll show you out." He passed Ellie to his mother and followed his in-laws to the door. When they'd gone, he leaned against it until his father came to get him.

"You did well, son. I'm proud of you for standing your ground."

"Angie would have hated to hear him use those words with the Bible as his defense."

"I know, Joe. Come on, there's still some of your delicious food to eat and I've got an idiot of a son to deal with. I swear I'm going to stick a ball gag in that young man's mouth."

"What!" Joe said, uncertain he'd heard his father correctly.

Andy grinned at his youngest son. "Trouble is, knowing him, he'd probably enjoy it too much."

Joe put his arms around his dad and hugged him. "I love you, old man," he said.

His father patted his back. "And I love you too, son. Now, I need a beer and a sausage roll, and more time with my family. Let's get back to the kitchen."

Chapter Eleven

After nearly two weeks flying around parts of Europe, living out of suitcases, Aron was more than simply happy to fall into bed—his own bed. In the shower, he'd washed off the dirt and grime of the trip then sank his naked body on to the cool, crisp sheet slept in by no one other than himself. It might be eight in the evening, but he intended to close his eyes and sleep the sleep of the dead. Of course he didn't, because he noticed his answering machine blinking at him, so he picked up the handset and pressed the button. The last message was Pauline Morris inviting him to a surprise birthday party for Dai's fortieth. Aron sighed—he hated surprise anything, but this was for Dai. He texted Pauline to let her know that he'd be there. Pauline replied immediately.

Soz 4 the late notice. Trying 2 keep it secret is mare. Be there at 7 OK.

With his eyelids dipping, he struggled to read the message. When he opened them again, the alarm clock read seven, and he was desperate for the loo. After cleaning his teeth, he pulled on his sweats, found his running shoes and hit the pavements of Cardiff. After two weeks of meetings in suits, every pace sent adrenaline coursing through his veins, the freedom of moving his body again thrilled him. He headed toward his usual haunt, the park not far from his house, intending to do a few circuits. Once there, he allowed himself a brief rest, drinking water while sitting on a bench watching the ducks and swans on the lake. It was going to be a hot day.

* * * *

Back home, he showered, got dressed and made himself a pot of tea and some toast, then set about catching up with his post and emails while sitting on his patio.

Later, having a rare free day, he spent time playing chess online. It had been ages since he'd played and he'd missed the intellectual stimulation chess provided. Deeply competitive, he hated to lose, but chess wasn't enough to fill his time. He picked up his phone. Running might get his body going, but he needed more. He needed to fly.

"Mike, it's Aron. Any slots available next week?"

"Aron, it's been ages."

"I know, work has been mad, but I need to get up there. You know what it's like."

"I do. Let me check. We've got lots of these flying experiences booked as the weather's been so good, but I can do Wednesday afternoon. You bringing anyone?"

"No, only me."

"You can use the Extra then, or the Cessna. We'll have her fueled up and ready for you. Maybe we can have a drink afterward and a catch up."

"Yeah, that will be great. I'll see you mid-afternoon, then."

Wednesday couldn't come fast enough for him, but first he had a party to get through. He didn't mind parties, but Dan had always been better at them than he was, and Dan had always been the one people wanted to talk to. Now, he'd be the sad one on his own. For a moment, he thought about ringing Joe.

"What are you going to do?" he asked himself. "Invite him out on a date? Yeah, like that's ever going to happen."

Later, he chose his clothes carefully. He figured his black jeans and pale blue shirt would do. He added a black waistcoat and socks and shoes and tried to do something with his hair. Finally, he was ready to go. He'd give it a few hours, for appearances sake, then come home again.

The taxi dropped him outside the parish hall. Rhodri and his sister, Melissa, stood at the door. He waved.

"You came," Rhodri said. "Nice outfit." Rhodri moved right up into Aron's personal space. "Hmm, you smell good too."

His sister made a noise impossible to describe. Aron took a step back.

"It's good to meet you again, Mel. Your dad tells me you're doing well. Have you found out where you're going on your placement yet?"

"I'm hoping to go to Cologne, but I'm not sure yet. It would be good to get your view of the place if you've time later. Mum says we've got to get everyone in before she brings Dad here."

Rhodri grabbed his hand. "Come on, I'll introduce you to my date for the evening."

Aron allowed himself to be dragged through the doors. He gazed around the highly decorated room full of people and spotted Margaret and Harry in the corner. Before he could move, he found himself in front of a face he recognized. The face did not look pleased to see him.

"Aron, this is Jonno Johnson, the boxer we saw at the match a few weeks ago. Jonno, this is Aron Roberts, my dad's boss."

Jonno put out his hand. "It's good to meet you. Joe's told me all about you."

Aron wanted to turn on his heel and run. He reckoned he had a chance of outrunning the man glaring at him. Instead, he grasped Jonno's hand and shook it. The grip exerted by Joe's best friend suggested Jonno wanted to crush every bone Aron had. Then, just when he thought the evening couldn't get more complicated, he saw a familiar face among the crowd talking to a girl at the far side of the hall. Jonno followed his line of sight.

"Oh, didn't anyone tell you Joe is catering tonight? That's his sister Gwen with him."

Aron shook his head. "No, I've been away for a few weeks on business and got back last night. Is he all right?"

"Do you care?" Jonno asked pointedly. "He told me what happened between you. Joe's my best friend, and I won't be responsible for my actions if… He's been through a hell of a lot over the last year, and doesn't need the likes of you trying to get into his pants. His daughter is the sun, moon and stars for him."

Aron didn't take his eyes off Joe as he moved around the tables, making sure they were ready for the buffet to be set up later. His cock stirred in his pants until it was half-hard from the vision of the man. What the hell was it that attracted his whole body like iron filings to a magnet? He held on to the edge of the table, fearing if he let go his body would fly over and attach itself like a limpet mine to the other man, waiting for the explosion that would inevitably follow.

"I know he has a daughter. It's all right, it's just..." What the hell did he say? "I guess he had a mad moment or something. These things happen. Someone wonders what it might be like if... I get it."

Jonno pulled him around to face him. "What? You think he's a straight guy who wanted to walk on the dark side for a moment, and now *you're* complaining you've had *your* feelings hurt? Really? Joe is the nicest guy you will ever meet. He isn't like that. You have no idea how lucky you are, and how much I want to punch your lights out."

Aron glanced downward and noted Jonno's fist curled ready to strike. His brain tried to work with several pieces of information at once. So Joe wasn't necessarily straight, and Jonno loved him, but was here with Rhodri. He backed away. "It's been good to meet you, Jonno. I'm going to go and talk to my friends over there now."

Aron ducked around the back of the crowd so Joe wouldn't spot him, finally finding his way to Margaret and Harry and taking a seat next to them.

He tried, he really tried to stay out of the way. He didn't dance all night and remained at the other end of the hall from where the buffet was served, even when the food was set out and his stomach rumbled. He sat at the table and nursed a bottle of beer, and kept his head down, not daring to drink too much, watching the people dance. In truth, he didn't know many people there, and anyway, most eyes were on Rhodri and his new boyfriend as they danced among the other couples.

"You've been a bloody wallflower all night." He glanced up to see Rhodri in front of him. "Time you got up and danced, boss man. Did I tell you how sexy you're looking tonight? I have a thing for men in waistcoats. Come on, Jonno's abandoned me to dance with the girl who did the catering. Anyway, I want you to dance with me."

Rhodri's somewhat drunken declaration made a few heads turn their way. He glanced around the room, but Joe had disappeared. Aron guessed he'd be in the back room kitchen tidying things away.

"Just the one, Rhodri, and no hands all over me. I don't think your date likes me." He allowed Rhodri to pull him onto the dance floor. So much for no contact as Rhodri turned his back and rubbed himself up and down.

"You said no hands, but there was no mention of arses," he shouted over the music. Aron pushed him away, and Rhodri continued to dance around him. A little way to his left, Jonno leaned in to talk to his dance partner, who immediately glanced in his direction. She moved them closer then tapped Aron on the shoulder.

"Care to swap partners?" she asked. "I believe you've met my brother."

Rhodri grinned and pulled Jonno away with him.

"Perhaps we'd better sit as I guess you have something you want to say to me," Aron said. She nodded then followed him back to his seat.

"My name's Gwen. You slept with my brother, Joe."

Aron was dumbfounded. She was certainly direct. "Slept may be the wrong word."

"Okay, but you had sex with him, didn't you?"

"Umm, yes, but I'm not sure I should be talking to you about it."

"You're aware that his wife died a year ago, that he was married and has a daughter."

"Yes, that's been made crystal clear."

"So, d'you want to sleep with him again?"

"What? Sorry?" Aron shook his head, unsure he'd heard correctly.

"I said do you want to sleep with him again. I probably shouldn't be telling you this, but men can be so stupid. He's bisexual. He told me Angie—she was his wife—that Angie knew. He comes across as all hard, but he's soft on the inside, and I don't want him to be hurt. He's lonely and maybe he needs someone in his life other than Ellie and us."

Aron struggled to process all he'd been told. "I'm not sure what to say. Has Joe said he wants to see me again? I didn't think that was on the cards when I spoke to him last. Look, I've no idea why I'm telling you this, but I said some stupid things. It wasn't exactly…"

"Yeah, he told me that too."

"He did?"

"Joe and I have always been close—our other brothers are dicks. He said you hate kids."

Aron sighed. Joe *had* told her everything. "I don't hate them, exactly. I've no experience with them. They scare me."

She laughed. "Is that all? I remember those first days after Angie died and Joe had to cope with a baby. He was bloody petrified he would do something wrong. Every sniffle, he raced her to the hospital, terrified that she was going to die. He's still overprotective and he worries so much, but he's learning to let go, even though the whole house is as child proofed as possible. I can understand how you feel, but if you've never had anything to do with kids, you've never experienced the good side either. You should see them together, him and Ellie. Sometimes, when they're both shattered, she falls asleep in his arms and they both end up snoring. He loves the bones of that kid. He's her daddy, and that isn't going to change any time soon."

"This isn't making me feel any better."

"Do you like him?" she asked.

"Yes, I think so."

"Think so?"

"All right, yes, I like him."

"And you fancy him?"

"Is that a statement or a question?"

"Does it matter?"

"Yes, I fancy him. Shit, I might as well have sent a letter off to some teen magazine's problem page."

"You're welcome. And my answer would be that you need to deal with his daughter. He and Ellie come as a package deal. You don't get one without the other. So tell me, are you scared of kids because you've never had anything to do with them, or is there something else?"

No one had ever asked him before and he didn't want to open that thorny question here.

"I wasn't expecting to deal with them myself—you know—gay."

"I can understand that, but if you want to talk to him, he's in the back now. You won't find out unless you try, and maybe this time try asking him out somewhere rather than staying in and shagging. Shagging can be the easy bit, talking is much harder." She looked over toward the door. "Go on, nothing ventured, nothing gained."

He examined her face for a moment. She was a lot like Joe, same dark hair and same green eyes.

"What do you do?" he asked.

"I'm at Swansea studying organic chemistry, why?"

"If you ever want to work in sales, come and see me. I'm sure you'd be able to sell sand to the Saudis."

He got up, ran his fingers through his hair, straightened his waistcoat and drank the last few mouthfuls of his beer. "If this goes pear-shaped, I'm blaming you," he said.

"Well, you'd better get it right then, hadn't you?"

The walk across the room lasted forever. He pressed the door open. Joe stood at the sink with his back to him.

"Finally, you turn up when I've nearly finished," Joe said, expecting to find Gwen when he turned around, but the body stood in front of the door definitely didn't belong to his sister.

"Gwen told me to come and speak to you."

Joe rinsed and dried the last of the containers then put it in the box on the table. "I wondered where she'd disappeared to. I might have guessed she'd be interfering again. Where were you? I didn't see you out there."

"No, I hid in the corner. I wasn't sure you'd want to see me, but Gwen said —"

"Gwen always has a lot to say, especially when it comes to interfering with my life." He couldn't help but wonder what the hell Gwen thought she was playing at.

"She told me to ask you out," Aron said, stepping closer.

Joe had no idea what to do. Killing his sister was an obvious choice, but he couldn't deny being more than a little pleased to see Aron. No matter how hard he tried to deny it, he wanted something from the man in front of him, but this time he wasn't going to be led by his cock, or let his anger and disappointment overwhelm him.

"She did, did she? Did she tell you where to take me on this date?" He noticed Aron had again moved closer and was attempting to lean nonchalantly on the table. Joe unfolded his arms and leaned back against the sink, waiting to see what would happen.

"Would you like to go flying with me on Wednesday afternoon?" Aron asked.

Well, that wasn't what he'd expected. A movie and dinner was more usual. He couldn't help but be intrigued.

"Flying? Like in a plane?"

"I've a pilot's license and I'm a member of a local flying club. I could show you how to fly the plane if you want. We'd have to run through a few safety issues first, but the planes are set up for those flying experience days. We'd be able to fly over the coast. If you don't want to, we could go out to dinner."

"Is the plane one of those little ones for two people?" he asked. "And you can actually fly on your own?" How often would he ever get a chance like this?

"Yes, so it would be me and you up there. I love it and don't get to go as often as I'd like. So what d'you think? Interested?"

"I'll have to get someone to look after Ellie. You remember I have a daughter, don't you?"

"I remember. I can't say it doesn't worry me, but maybe if we get to know each other more..."

Joe's stomach practiced somersaults now that Aron stood right in front of him having moved like one of those cats on the Internet getting closer with every shot. He could smell his aftershave. Every hair on his body rose, as if they were trying to get nearer.

"I'd like to kiss you," Aron said softly.

Joe waited, rooted to the spot. When Aron ran a hand over his chin, he shivered in anticipation. His breathing increased along with his heartbeat, and his stomach filled with fluttering wings once more. Aron leaned in and brushed his lips against Joe's mouth. Stubble rasped against Joe's skin, and a warm body pressed against his.

"More?" Aron asked, putting his hands either side of Joe's head.

"More," Joe replied. The feel of Aron's mouth on his sent tremors throughout his body and suddenly everything was on high alert. Joe opened his mouth to Aron's tongue. He allowed Aron to slip his hands around him and pull him closer before he shifted his own hands to cup Aron's arse. The kiss was warm and wet, but still gentle, as if it was asking a question and he wanted to answer yes.

Aron leaned back after a minute or so. "That was wonderful. I could get used to kissing you."

Embarrassed at the realization that his hands still clasped Aron's arse, Joe moved them up to his back but didn't let go.

"So do you want to come flying with me?" Aron asked. "I'll pick you up about two if you can manage it, and if you give me your address."

"I'll ring you. Let me put your number in my phone." Joe didn't want to let go, but he reached into his pocket and pressed buttons as Aron gave him the number. They heard a cough behind them and jumped apart.

"I see you two have talked — or something," Gwen said unable to keep the smile from her face.

Aron moved toward the door.

"I'll ring you," Joe said.

"I'll be waiting." Aron closed the door behind him, leaving brother and sister staring at each other.

"Can you babysit on Wednesday afternoon and possibly longer?" Joe asked. "I'm going flying."

Chapter Twelve

Aron picked him up at his house in a hybrid Lexus. In the dark of the boxing club's car park, Joe hadn't been able to see which type of car Aron drove, but then he'd been looking at the man, not the vehicle. The fact that he drove a hybrid didn't surprise him, especially after the man spent the drive to the flying club telling him about Aztechnologies. Considering the tension in their recent meetings, conversation flowed, and Joe couldn't help enjoying how Aron's face came alive when talking about his work, like all people who had a passion. Joe guessed he must look the same describing a new recipe.

"So how come you got into flying?" he asked.

"We lived near the airport, and I used to watch the planes going over. My parents often flew all over the world and I used to badger my father about the planes, so one year, for my birthday, he arranged for me to go up in a plane like the one I'm taking you up in today. He couldn't be there, of course, but I fell in love with the feeling and begged for lessons. It made me feel free up there among the birds and the clouds, flying over the coast and seeing all those places you can only see from above. The Welsh coast is beautiful."

"So can you do all those maneuvers? You know, loop the loop and rolls and dives?"

"Yep, we can do all those. I'll show you how to do them yourself. The planes have duel controls. You might feel sick because of the G-force, but it passes quickly."

They pulled up in front of a large hangar. Several small planes stood inside and a man waved to them when they got out of the car.

"That's Mike Bayliss. He runs the place, and he's the man who taught me to fly." They walked toward the tall, blond man in the gray flying outfit. Joe waited as the pair hugged each other.

"Been too long," Aron said. "This is Joe, a friend of mine."

Mike scrutinized him from head to toe, and Joe wondered if the pilot was more than a friend too. He grasped Mike's hand and shook it.

"Good to meet you."

"You too, Joe." He turned back to Aron. "I've sorted the Extra 300L for you. She's fueled and ready to go. I've cleared the usual flight path over the coast down to Swansea, but you know what you're doing. Make sure you go through all the safety stuff."

Aron made a noise.

"Yes, I know I sound like I'm teaching Grandma to suck eggs, but you don't usually take people up with you, do you? This is a first as far as you're concerned."

Joe, surprised by that particular piece of information, noticed Aron shrug.

"Right, then, let's get you kitted out and you can show Joe around the plane."

They followed him to the changing room. Aron opened a locker, pulled out a blue outfit and put it on over his clothes.

"This should fit you," Mike said, handing Joe a similar outfit in red.

He stepped into it and zipped up. "I expected a leather flying jacket and those jodhpur–like trousers at the very least, and big boots. Oh, and a scarf and dark glasses. Don't I get any of them?" Joe asked.

"No, but you get one of these," Mike said, handing over a parachute. Aron helped him secure it then ran through the instructions with him before putting on his own. "Health and safety insist on these things. Okay, let's go. The quicker we get out there, the quicker we're up in the air."

Aron showed Joe around the plane. It was painted red and had white wings and a propeller and appeared so small compared to the planes Joe had been in before.

"It's going to be a tight fit in there," Aron explained. "And you'll feel strange because your legs will be above your feet. You're in the front seat, and I'll be right behind you."

Joe wriggled into the cockpit, glad he wasn't any taller. He pushed his legs into the two narrow channels either side of the control stick. He could only sit once his legs were fully extended. Aron clambered in behind him and closed the cover. Now, it was merely the two of them in that small space.

"You okay?" Aron asked.

"I think so. You were right about it being a tight fit."

The engine roared to life and suddenly the propeller spun. A shiver of excitement and fear ran through him.

"Last chance to change your mind," Aron shouted above the noise as the plane began to move forward.

The control stick moved in front of him, and seconds later, the plane rose into the air.

"Oh, my God, this is wonderful," Joe said as the ground got farther away. The day was perfect for flying, with a slight breeze and hardly a cloud in the sky. The larger planes at Cardiff airport below got smaller and smaller as they headed out to the coast.

"We'll get over the sea, then I'll show you some tricks," Aron shouted. "Hold the stick lightly and you'll feel every move I make. Don't grab it too hard, though, and keep your hand in one place. Don't rub it up and down." Joe wanted to turn around at the obvious innuendo. He took a firm hold while the stick moved. As he gazed through the clear plastic windscreen, he was able to imagine what it must be like to be a bird. Everything appeared so small as they flew over fields and houses toward the Bristol Channel. He knew he was grinning like an idiot. Aron touched his shoulder.

"So what d'you think?"

"I'm not sure I have the right words. I mean, I've been in a plane before, but this is so different, you feel part of it up here. In an ordinary passenger plane, you're with so many others and it's like being in a sardine can. In this, it's like you can reach out and touch the birds and the sky. Is that Barry Island down there?"

"Yep, we'll get out over the water and I'll show you how to do a loop. First, have a go at flying in a straight line."

"What, actually fly the plane?" Joe had to admit that the thought scared the hell out of him.

"It's simple. Keep the stick pointing forward and try to keep it level. Don't worry, I've got control as well. Okay, over to you." Joe held on a little bit tighter, worried the plane would immediately fall out of the sky.

"Fucking hell. Am I really flying this thing?"

"You are. That's it, easy does it," Aron said. "You're a natural. Okay, I've taken control back. We're going to do a steep climb then loop. Brace yourself."

The plane pulled up. Joe's body became heavier as the G-force kicked in. He'd been on rollercoasters, but nothing compared to this. Suddenly, all he could see was sky. The land had completely disappeared from sight and he had no idea where he was, especially when the plane rolled as well. Then he felt lighter than air as they plunged down toward the sea only to pull up again and resume their course.

"Bloody hell, that was incredible. At one point I thought I would fall through the plane, I was so heavy, but then I had to hold on to stop myself floating away. You rolled us as well. Would it be all right if we stayed level for a bit? You're right about the nausea."

"There's a bag in the pocket on your right if you need it. I'll fly straight for a while."

Joe studied the coastline with all its little coves and bays people would never visit.

"Ready to take over again?" Aron asked.

Joe nodded and resumed control.

"Try pulling her up slightly," Aron said.

Joe pulled at the stick and they climbed again. "I can't believe I'm controlling the plane. I'm sorry, it's mind-blowing."

"We'll head down to the Gower then turn around. Fancy another maneuver? This one is called a lazy eight." The plane began to turn as they flew up and down. They were climbing again then falling as if the plane had no power and was going to nosedive into the sea until it pulled up again and leveled out.

"Shit, are you trying to kill me?" Joe yelled.

"I can go a lot nearer the water than that. Perhaps next time I'll show you if you want to come up with me again."

Joe thought for a moment. "I'd love to come up again."

Aron patted him on the shoulder. "We'll head back now. D'you want to take the controls again?"

"Yes, please."

"Okay, follow the coast until we get to Barry, then I'll take over and guide us back. I'll warn you now the landing can be bumpy in these planes because they're solid fiber glass."

Joe took the controls and concentrated on following the curves of the coastline below. On such a sunny day, the water appeared blue to match the sky. Confident of what he was doing now, he'd stopped feeling so scared and he wanted to show Aron that could manage on his own. All too soon the sands of Barry came into view.

Aron guided them back inland until they flew over the airfield once more. "This is the tricky bit," he said. "I can't see in front so I have to look out of the side to judge. Don't worry I've done it before."

Joe remembered Aron usually flew by himself. "Are you sure?"

"Yes, it'll be fine if a little bit bumpy as I level the wings off." Joe braced himself, but in the end it was easy and they taxied to the front of the hangar. Once out of the plane, they pulled off their helmets.

"So how was it for you?" Aron asked. Without answering, Joe pressed him back against the fuselage. He couldn't have explained why he did it, but he had to be near the man in front of him. He shoved Aron backward and kissed him hard, needing to touch as much of him as he could, wanting to feel skin, but all he had was Aron's face, so he placed a hand on both sides and pulled him forward into the kiss. Joe pushed his tongue into Aron's willing mouth. This time there was no anger, just need. It was so different and so much better. He sucked at Aron's lower lip, taking it between his lips, then pressed his tongue back in once more. The sound of a cough made him stop and pull away. Behind them, Mike looked distinctly embarrassed.

"Sorry to interrupt," he said.

Aron grinned and held his hand. Joe didn't move it. That simple act sent warmth coursing through his veins. He wanted those fingers gripping his. In fact, he wanted those fingers gripping a lot more than his hand. His cock was half-hard already.

"Sorry, Mike, we got carried away. Joe wanted to thank me for taking him up. You know what I was like that first time you took me."

"I don't remember any kissing," Mike said, returning his grin.

"Aw, sorry. Do you want one now?" Aron asked.

"Get away with you. I think you need to take this one home. Give me the overalls and I'll put them back for you. Will I see you soon?"

"What do you think?" Aron asked Joe. "Want to go up again?"

"You know I do. Will you take me home now? Ellie is at my parents. I'm sure they won't mind having her overnight if you want." Maybe it wasn't the most sensible thing to do, but he didn't want to go home alone, not after this. The adrenaline still pumped through his veins.

"Are you sure?" Aron asked.

"Positive."

They stripped the overalls off and passed them to Mike. Forty minutes later, after spending the journey reliving the flight, Joe stood facing Aron in his bedroom.

His initial excitement had faded now he was face to face with reality. He'd dragged Aron upstairs and now, he couldn't recall ever feeling as nervous, not even that first time he and Ellie had sex. Should he be thinking about that when he'd just pulled another man up the stairs and into the room he and Angie had slept in for over a year, in that same bed?

He sat on the edge and put his head in his hands. "Oh God," he muttered.

Aron came and sat beside him. "Angie?"

Joe nodded.

Aron pulled his hands away from his face.

"It's all right if you don't want to…you know. I understand how difficult this must be for you, and I don't have to stay, although I'd like to. I want to stay more than anything else, even if we simply go downstairs and drink tea." Aron stroked down his face and wiped away the tear attempting to make its way down Joe's cheek. That simple gesture made Joe's skin tingle. He leaned forward and kissed Aron gently as they breathed each other in, fingers moving tentatively, lightly, just enough to know that they were there. Joe broke away first, reached for the edge of his T-shirt and pulled it over his head in one stroke. Aron ran his fingers over Joe's chest, exploring every inch, moving from freckle to freckle almost, over every ridge, every muscle as if he was checking for something. He stopped at the scar that ran down the left side of Joe's stomach.

"That looks serious," he said.

Joe tried to organize his brain to form words. "It was. Idris pushed me through a window and I got glass stuck in my side. They had to leave it in until the paramedics arrived so I wouldn't bleed as much. I ended up having a shed load of stitches. Idris got grounded forever. In fact, he's still supposed to be grounded."

Aron leaned in and licked around Joe's nipple. The cold moisture on the man's tongue made it harden immediately. Joe groaned in response as Aron flicked it over and over then blew softly.

"I want to see you too," Joe said quietly. Aron lifted his top over his head. Joe put out a hand and ran his fingers down the hairless chest and over the ridges of Aron's abdomen. His pale skin suggested Aron didn't spend a lot of time in the sun. He leaned forward and kissed Aron's shoulder toward his neck. Aron bent his head back to allow Joe to kiss across his Adam's apple over to the other side. Joe reached his hands around and buried his face in the join of neck and shoulder while moving his fingers so they danced down Aron's back, feeling each vertebrate. He lifted his mouth away from Aron's skin. "I'm going to have to cook for you. I bet you eat rabbit food all the time or takeaways, or even worse, those shit-awful protein drinks that are a funny shade of green."

Aron's body vibrated as he laughed. "But I like my seaweed shakes!"

"For fuck's sake! No one can possibly like drinking seaweed shakes! In the morning, I'm going to make you my famous eggy toast and bacon breakfast." Joe pulled away and edged himself up the bed until his head hit the pillow. He undid his jeans then said, "You will stay, won't you?"

"If you're sure? I can't think of anything I'd rather do." Aron scooted up so he knelt between Joe's legs. Joe lifted his hips invitingly and Aron clutched at the jeans and briefs until the man lay naked before him.

"Should we lose the socks as well?" Joe said, grinning. Aron sat back on his heels and gazed him. "You look like you work out with those strong arms, wide shoulders and muscular chest." He ran his hands up the full length of each leg then bent down and licked the bead of liquid that had formed on the tip of Joe's now erect cock. Shivers made Joe's hair stand on end. It was the first time he'd seen Aron fully naked and he liked what he saw. Aron opened his mouth and engulfed Joe's cock, relaxing his throat.

Joe stared at the sight of Aron firm lips enclosing his cock. When he leaned back, the cock leaving his mouth made a popping noise.

"You have a real talent for that," Joe said, grinning widely. He levered himself up and wrapped Aron's cock in both hands. "Hmm, you're quite a big boy for your size, aren't you? Not quite Frank Sinatra but enough for me to get my large hands around."

"Frank Sinatra?" Aron questioned.

"Someone asked Ava Gardner why she married him as he was so skinny and she said something like he may weigh a hundred pounds but ninety-eight pounds of that is cock!" Aron fell forward and kissed him again. Joe loved the skin-to-skin contact and the feel of Aron's weight on him. He kissed back with enthusiasm once more, running his hand over Aron's back and feeling their cocks sliding together. The sensations were delicious.

"I want you to fuck me," he whispered into Aron's ear.

The man shot up, lifting his body away, and Joe whimpered in protest.

"You don't have to. I mean I'm happy if you want to fuck me. I've not topped much and well, you haven't before, and it can hurt the first time and…"

Joe reached up and put a finger to Aron's lips. "What makes you think it would be my first time?" Joe couldn't help chuckling at Aron's puzzled expression.

"Look in the top drawer." Aron leaned over and pulled on the handle. "Oh my God!"

Joe smirked at the shock on the man's face. "As I said, not my first rodeo." Aron picked up the black dildo and ran his fingers over it. Then he noticed something else in the drawer and pulled out the straps.

"Shit! You and Angie. She fucked you?"

Maybe Joe should have been embarrassed, but with Aron he felt no shame, only excitement about what might happen next. He leaned back and opened his knees wide, knowing Aron would be able to see his hole. "Condoms and lube are in the second drawer," he said.

Aron raised his eyebrows. "All right, you got me. I bought supplies." Heat rushed to his cheeks. "I'm honored, but I too have a confession."

He coughed and Joe wondered what his secret could be.

"I'm a bit nervous. I'm more of a bottom than a top, but I have to say your arse looks inviting."

Joe, his confidence growing, decided he'd needed to get the ball rolling and seized the lube from Aron's hand. He slicked up his fingers then pushed one then two inside himself. Aron licked his lips. "Maybe you should try *that* in *me* first," he suggested gazing at the dildo. "You can angle it so it hits that magic spot." He reached over to pick it up, but Aron stopped him.

"No, let me." Aron picked up the dildo and ran his fingers along the ridges, then he put more lube on it and pushed against Joe's hole. Joe's arse burned with the slow intrusion. He arched his back and clutched at the bedsheets.

"Are you all right?" Aron asked.

"Don't stop. I want you," Joe said. "And don't treat me like I'm made of porcelain either." He heard Aron whisper something to himself.

"Come on, fuck me. I need to feel you inside me. I'm ready."

Aron definitely looked more nervous than him, judging by the way his hand was shaking while he put on the condom before lining himself up. Joe nodded and braced himself.

Aron bided his time and pushed his cock slowly inside. Once fully embedded, he then thrust in out.

"That's it," Joe cried. "Just there, don't change your angle. Oh God, this isn't going to take long."

Aron kept up the momentum, practically bending Joe over to get deeper inside every time. All Joe could do was surf the wave as his orgasm hit. He fisted his cock, sending streams of white liquid over his stomach and chest. Aron rose above him, pushed back in, and Joe felt the warmth of his cum pump into the condom until Aron fell over him.

They both breathed hard. Aron reached back and removed the condom.

"Give it here. I'll sort it and get a towel to wipe us up," Joe said. "We should get something to eat as well."

"No," Aron protested. "Don't want to move. Too tired. Want to sleep." Aron moved to position himself so his head was on Joe's chest. Joe leaned over and dropped the condom in the drawer. Aron yawned making Joe yawn in response. Maybe he was more tired than he thought, even though the clock showed it was hardly late and it was still light outside. Aron sighed contentedly in his arms, and Joe knew he was sleeping when his body relaxed. He reached over and grabbed his T-shirt, giving his body a wipe-over. He stroked

Aron's hair and closed his eyes then slept longer than he had done in months.

Chapter Thirteen

Joe moved his fingers, flexing them to check the warm flesh underneath. Tentatively, he stroked the smooth skin, dancing his fingers over muscle until he reached the hardening nub of a nipple. For a moment, he was confused. Something wasn't right. This body felt hard and had no swelling of soft flesh around the tip. He opened one eye. Short, dark hair filled his vision, but the smell was all wrong. The body spooned into his groaned in response to his fingers and pushed back against him. Now he opened both eyes and pulled back slightly, allowing his erection to spring forward into the space he'd made. He gazed down and saw the slight curve of a cute arse and some interesting red marks on his own chest. It had been a while since he'd woken up in bed with anyone. What was he supposed to think about this development? Was he meant to wake up happy, or scared, or annoyed, or pleased, or eager to get rid of this man? Man, this was a man. He was in bed with a man. He had a hard-on currently attempting to push its way between the cheeks of a man's arse. He searched for a name and found one. Aron Roberts — the man who didn't like children. Yes, they would have to deal with that, but not now. Instead, Joe wanted to follow where his cock obviously wanted to go. He ignored the niggling thought at the back of his mind, the one that said having Aron in his arms the night before had left him feeling content, not the same as it had been with Angie, but right. And he didn't want to fight this feeling. Oh no, he wanted to embrace it, wallow in it, and let it overwhelm him.

"Do you have any plans for that thing poking into my arse?"

Joe leaned in and kissed the back of Aron's neck. "I'm not sure if *I* have any plans, but my cock would like to bury itself in your bubble butt."

"My what?"

"Oh, come on, you've got to admit it is sort of a bubble butt, sort of perfectly round and muscular." Joe moved his arm and scrabbled about on the bedside cabinet until he found what he was looking for. He squeezed the lube onto his finger then reached down to part the other man's pert cheeks and slowly inserted a finger.

"Mm, feels good."

Joe added more fingers until he'd established a rhythm and Aron pushed back against him. "Haven't got all day here. I've got to go home and get dressed and get ready for work. Fuck me already."

"You are such a greedy bottom."

Aron turned his head and smirked at him. "You'd better believe it."

Joe kissed him, opened a condom, rolled it on and pushed inside. "God, that feels good. You're so warm and tight. I'm going to take this slowly."

He began to move, not nearly withdrawing every time but pulling away from Aron's prostate then hitting it again. He reached around and gripped Aron's cock in his fist. Gradually his orgasm started to build. Tingles traced their way to the bottom of his spine. He breathed in the aroma of Aron's shampoo and aftershave mingled with sweat as he panted heavily.

"Close," Aron murmured. Joe caressed the now heavy balls of his lover. He squeezed gently and Aron bucked in his embrace. "Oh hell, that's wicked."

Joe grinned into Aron's neck and bit down somewhat less gently. Aron tensed then Joe heard him gasp. Suddenly warm contractions of muscle surrounded his cock and sent him over the edge, and Aron spurted warm liquid over his hand.

"God, I'd love to feel you come in my arse with no barrier between us," Aron said. "I've been tested."

"Angie and I only ever slept with each other."

"So... Maybe next time we can do without."

"What, you want to have my cum in your arse all day—kinky bugger," Joe said, laughing as Aron blushed bright scarlet.

"Sadly, I've no butt plug. I suppose I could buy one if we're going to make a habit of this." Before Aron had a chance to respond, Joe pulled out, removed the condom and levered himself so he was sitting at the edge of the bed. Aron rolled over to face his back.

"You all right?" he asked.

Joe turned and caught his breath. The man was stunning. His brown eyes now almost completely black, his hair stuck up on end and his cum splattered all over his stomach. "Why don't you grab a shower while I make us breakfast? I promised you my special eggy bread and bacon combo."

"You did."

"There's a spare toothbrush under the sink. They're always doing BOGO offers on toothbrushes. Let me use the loo then it's all yours." He skipped out of the room, paid a quick visit to the loo then ran down the stairs, hoping he'd closed the curtains at the front. Once in the kitchen, he found his apron and tied it around his bottom half. Today he planned on making the food for a lunch buffet on Saturday. Gwennie would be over to help and bring back Ellie. He tried to put that huge complication out of the way for now. Perhaps he'd been stupid to sleep with the man, but he'd needed it, and he had to admit he was attracted to him.

He got the eggs and bacon out, sliced the bread then dipped it in the beaten egg. He placed the bacon under the grill and the bread into the hot fat, then water in the kettle and teabags in mugs. Finally, he reached for his iPod, put it in the dock and turned it onto random. The sounds of *Carry On My Wayward Son* filled the air, and he sang as he worked, shaking his naked arse to the music.

"I didn't figure you for a lover of American soft rock."

Joe turned, spatula in hand, to see Aron sitting at the table. "Sorry, I didn't hear you come down."

"Love the outfit," Aron said. "You'd make a fortune if you hired yourself out dressed like that."

Joe placed two slices of toast and a few rashers of bacon onto a plate and brought it over to Aron who sniffed the food and smiled.

"There's nothing like bacon in the morning." Joe put more on a plate, picked up the mugs of tea in one hand and the plate with the other and sat next to him.

"Seriously, though, Kansas? How does someone our age listen to a group like Kansas?"

Joe watched as he tucked into the food. Having someone like his cooking was important to him. He waited for Aron to comment.

"Oh wow, this is wonderful, and I'm still waiting for an answer. No getting out of it. And that's AC/DC?"

Joe smiled. "It must be on the *Supernatural* mix."

Aron looked puzzled. "Sorry, you've lost me."

"I can't believe you've never watched it—the TV show, *Supernatural*. Two sexy brothers and a cute angel hunt demons and other creatures."

Aron shook his head. "Nope."

"Well, that's going to have to change. The actor who plays Dean was our other." He saw the surprise on Aron's face. "You know, someone who you'd let into your bed for a threesome, though we'd have had the guy who plays the angel as well." He reached over to the laptop and pulled it open. "Here you go."

Aron raised his eyebrows at the image on the screen. "What? They do this in the show?" he asked, looking at the seminaked pictures of two attractive men entwined in each other's arms.

"No, sadly not, that's wishful thinking. The music is part of the soundtrack." He picked up the plates and got up as *Eye of the Tiger* blasted out. They both sang as Joe wiggled his bare arse once more while placing the plates under the tap.

"What the..." Joe turned and hit the stop button. "Shit! Dad, I wasn't expecting you."

Andy Welsh glanced from one man to the other. "I gathered that."

Panic seized every part of his body. He needed to gather his thoughts, but how the hell could he explain this to his father who was currently frowning at him with his granddaughter in his arms. She wriggled and held out her hands. "Dadda."

Joe grabbed a pair of boxers from an ironed pile of clothes, put them on quickly then retrieved his daughter out of her grandfather's arms.

"This is Aron, Dad. Aron, this is my father, Andy. Gwen said *she'd* be here after nine." He would murder her later.

"I've an airport run so I said I'd bring Ellie on my way. I didn't realize you'd have company. Gwen said you were working, a sudden job."

"Umm, no, not exactly." What the hell did he say? He carried Ellie over to her playpen and placed her inside. Aron got up.

"I'd better go and leave you two to talk unless you want me to stay," he said quickly. Joe shook his head.

"No, you've got work." Joe needed to talk to his father alone. Having Aron there would complicate an already complicated situation.

Aron stood next to him. "Call me. We need to talk." Joe wanted to kiss him, but he couldn't with his father there. "Yeah, all right, I will." He followed Aron's movements, but didn't go with him to the door.

"He's not the only one who needs to talk." His father stood with hands on hips obviously waiting for Joe to explain.

Joe gulped. "I'm sorry, Dad. I know you're probably shocked but I'm not exactly certain what's going on myself."

"Well, whatever it is, I'm going to have to wait to find out. She's been fed and changed. I'm due to pick this bloke up in ten minutes. I'll be back when I've finished, all right?"

Joe stood totally dumbfounded. What the hell was he going to say to his father? There was no way he could say nothing was going on, not as he'd been caught dancing bare-arsed for Aron's entertainment.

"Yes, all right, Dad. I'll see you later." He watched his father go out of the room then collapsed onto a chair.

Ellie began bashing away at her glockenspiel, making her usual noises.

"Oh, darling, Dadda's gotten some explaining to do. Now if only I can figure out what the hell to say to your granddad."

She peered up at him and gave him one of those smiles that melted his heart.

"Sadly, I don't think that's going to work on your granddad if I try it," he said, reaching over and ruffling her hair. He had some time before he needed to start work. He picked Ellie up, carried her to the hall and put her in her buggy. "Let's go to the park, shall we?" The noise she made could have been a no, but they went anyway.

* * * *

"You've sat there, staring into space for nearly twenty minutes now," Margaret said, as she put a letter in front of him to sign. He picked up a pen and signed it without looking.

"Are you okay? You've been rather distracted this morning. The others will be up here in a few minutes for the debriefing about the European trip. I assume you want me to take notes. I've set up the drinks next door and some pastries. You know what this lot is like."

Aron nodded and mumbled, "Thanks."

"It's no bother. It's my job and I worry about you. Someone has to around here. If there's anything I can help with…"

"No, I'm fine, Margaret. Just thinking about a few things, but thanks for the offer."

"Well, the offer is there. I've printed copies for everyone and the AV equipment is ready if you want to go through and set up your laptop."

"Yes, I'll go through now." He gathered his laptop and a few papers and made his way to the meeting room next door. Like his office, it had windows on both sides and one set overlooked the workshop downstairs. Dai stood to one side, talking to the small team who worked with him on the practical aspects of the technology — putting models together and making the prototypes ready to test in situ. He needed to share the details of his conversations with the various firms in Germany and Italy. He could have all the ideas in the world, but unless they worked in practice, there was no point. These men helped him do that. He connected his laptop then scrolled through the images.

"Oh good, pastries," Dai said when he came into the room. "Don't tell Pauline, though. She says I need to take better care of myself now that I'm forty."

Aron noticed the new member of their team standing behind Dai along with Neil, the plastics expert in the team. He stood and put out a hand.

"Hi, I'm Aron. We haven't met before." The man held his hand. His grip was firm and there was something familiar about his smile. He looked more than a little nervous standing there in his green overalls.

"It's good to meet you." A local voice, but more valleys than Cardiff.

"I assume you have a name," Aron replied with what he hoped was a reassuring smile on his face.

"Yes, sorry, I'm new here. My name's Robbie Welsh. I used to work for Mackintosh and Rees until they closed. It's good to be back to work again."

The men sat, and Aron examined Robbie's features. Could Robbie be related to Joe? Welsh was a common enough name, and Aron had no idea about the full extent of Joe's family.

"I don't suppose you're related to Joe Welsh, are you? He's in catering and did a dinner for me and Dai's birthday party."

Robbie looked from Dai back to Aron. "My little brother is called Joe, and yes, he is in catering. Wow, it's a small world, isn't it?"

So that's you, a sister and there's another brother who works with Iestyn. Robbie had a ring on his finger. "And d'you have any children, Robbie?"

"I have twin boys aged five who are quite a handful. We were all over at Joe's recently for his daughter's birthday. It's mad when we're all together."

Aron swallowed hard. The Welshes were obviously a close-knit bunch. He wondered how they would take finding out that their brother was in a relationship with a man—if that's what it was. The thought of it made him feel uneasy about the whole thing. He and Joe needed to talk.

"All right, we'd better get started. Good to have you on the team, Robbie."

Chapter Fourteen

Joe wiped Ellie's favorite meal of mashed banana from her face with a shaking hand when he heard the front door open and his dad shout his name.

"In here, Dad." He turned back to Ellie and put another spoonful into her mouth then wiped the mess away again as food dripped down her chin. He then crossed the room and switched the kettle on.

"I thought you'd be back before this," he said. His father had taken a seat and was spooning another mouthful of banana for his granddaughter.

"I did a few more jobs. No point in turning away money. And I've more time on my hands now, in between babysitting for you and your brother. Rosie's on nights so the twins are coming over later."

Joe poured them a mug of tea each and sat opposite his father. *I may as well get this ball rolling.*

"Dad, about this morning. I'm sorry you had to…" His father raised a hand and he stopped speaking.

"Joe, you're a grown man, and who you spend your time with is your business. I may be your father, but you don't owe me anything. However, I'd like to feel you're able to talk to me about it. I'm not going to judge, but I can't say I'm not concerned."

"His name is Aron Roberts."

"Hang on, haven't I heard that name recently?"

"Yes—that new job Robbie got with Aztechnologies—that's Aron's company."

"Did you help Robbie get the job?"

"No, Robbie didn't tell anyone about the interview, did he, and Aron was in Germany at the time."

"So, you and him? I'm guessing it's what it looked like with you being dressed as you were. How long has it been going on?"

"Not long—last night was the first time he's been here. I met him at a dinner I catered a few weeks ago." There was no need to explain how they'd first met the year before.

"This is difficult for me, son, so you'll have to forgive me if I say something stupid, but have you always, you know…"

"Liked men?"

"Yeah, I suppose that's what I'm asking."

"I'm bisexual, Dad, but this is the first time I've ever…" He picked up his own mug and swallowed. Ellie agitated to get down, so he put her on the floor, having first checked the gates were closed. She immediately turned over and crawled toward her toys. "I loved Angie. She knew about my sexuality and accepted it. I was never unfaithful to her if that's what's worrying you. I thought we'd be together forever, so it didn't matter if I fancied men. She was everything to me, and I miss her more than words can say. No one will ever be able to hold a candle to her."

"So is that why you're sleeping with him because no other woman could ever measure up to Angie?"

Joe thought for a moment. *Is that it?* "Gwen asked me the same thing and the answer is that I don't know, Dad."

"But you like him. You've never struck me as the sort of man who sleeps around, so I'm guessing this wasn't a one-night thing and you intend to see him again."

"It's complicated."

"Isn't it always?"

Joe looked down at Ellie reaching up to the chair, trying to pull herself up. "She'll be walking soon. She keeps trying to get up now." His father settled a hand on his. Comforted, he swallowed hard and glanced up. "Aron doesn't like kids."

"Ah."

How could one small word speak volumes?

"Maybe like is the wrong word. Let's say he's not comfortable with them. He's gay, Dad, and I don't think he expected to have anything to do with children. He's an only child from what I've found out, and kids simply scare the hell out of him. You remember how I was to begin with, worried about everything, imagining every sniffle was going to kill her and take her away from me like her mum was taken away. I didn't want to pick her up or get close to her, I was so worried I'd drop her on her head."

"I suppose it depends on whether you think there's any future in this. If it's only been a couple of weeks, then maybe you chalk it up to experience and walk away. Your daughter has to come first."

"I know that, Dad, and she does, but I have to admit I've been lonely, and there's something about him. People can change, can't they? And although I admit I might be somewhat biased, who couldn't learn to love her?"

"Look, son, I can't say this development is easy for me to understand. I've spent the last few hours trying to get my head around you and him and... But all I want is for you to be happy, like I want all of you to be happy, even Idris. You must realize that if you carry on with this relationship, you're going to face comments galore, and not just from your brothers. There's so much to consider, Joe. Although people are more accepting, and gays can get married now, there's an awful lot of prejudice out there. I know I can't protect you from every hurt, but do you have to go out and make life more difficult for yourself?"

Joe sighed. He understood his father's concerns. "He's the first person I've met in the last year who I feel something for, Dad, and whatever other people think is up to them. I need to find out if there's anything in this, and if it doesn't work out, then I haven't lost anything. These things happen, and at least Ellie's still too young to understand what's going on. So we're all right, then?"

"We're fine, son."

"Will you tell Mum?"

"If you want me to. She'll be here like a shot. Then she'll want to have him round to dinner at the weekend so she can meet him and find out everything there is to know about him, even if it is a few weeks in. You've always been her baby boy."

"I'm not sure we're at the meet-the-family stage. I'm going to ask him if he wants to take Ellie out for the day to Longleat or a zoo, so we can spend time together."

"Okay, I'll leave talking to your mother until after then, but not for long — I don't like keeping secrets from her. When were you planning to go?"

"Sunday. I'm catering another party on Saturday."

"It sounds as if the catering is doing well?"

"Word of mouth, Dad, and catering Dan Morgan's civil partnership didn't do me any harm. The one on Saturday is for one of the Giants as well—an anniversary party for a player's parents at the club. I've been wondering about taking on an apprentice as well to give me a hand. I can't expect Gwennie to help me all the time, especially not when she's back at university." A small hand touched his thigh and he glanced down.

"Oh my God, Dad, she's on her feet."

His father got up and came around the table in time to see Ellie fall back down onto her bottom. She checked them both, giggled and began to crawl off exploring the room once more. Joe had tears in his eyes as he immediately thought of how much Angie would have loved to have seen this. He wanted someone with whom he could share his daughter's achievements, but he had no idea if Aron would ever be that person.

"She's going to be forward that one, like her mum," Andy said. "She'd have been so proud of you and how you've coped." His father wrapped his strong arms around him and pulled him into a hug.

Joe wiped a tear from his cheek. "You know I would never have coped without you and Mum. I couldn't bear it if you thought badly of me."

"Never have any fears about that, Joe. You're our son, and we love you and your little girl. Be careful, that's all. It's a big decision you've made, and I'd say the same about a woman as well. Now, before I get too sentimental, I'd better get off. I'm sure you've work to do."

"I'm making bread for tomorrow's sandwich run. We've another firm on the estate expressed an interest, so I've got to give them some samples. I'm going to contact the catering department at Cardiff College as well and see if they have anyone wanting practical experience."

"Right, I'll let myself out. I'll need a rest before the dynamic duo arrive. I'll be round on Saturday to pick her up. Let us know when."

"Will do, Dad, and thanks."

After his father had left, he put Ellie in her pen for a few minutes while he checked on the dough in the other kitchen. Satisfied the loaves were ready, he put them in the ovens then settled back at the kitchen table once more to update his lists.

* * * *

"Shit! I must have fallen asleep." He wasn't sure what to deal with first, the timer for the bread, the phone or Ellie. He grabbed the phone first then went into the other kitchen and turned off the oven. Ellie grizzled in her downstairs cot. *Damn, she needs changing.*

"Could you give me a minute?" he said to the person on the phone. He got a nappy from the cupboard along with a fresh towel, talc and baby lotion, and somehow carried them, the phone and Ellie to the kitchen table.

"Sorry," he said picking up the phone again. "I've got a baby who needs a new nappy. Could you give me your name and I'll get back to you as soon as I can?"

"Joe, it's Aron. I thought I'd ring to find out how you were after this morning. Ring me back when it's convenient." Joe heard the phone click. *Damn.*

"All right, Ellie. I know you're uncomfortable. Give Daddy a minute to sort, will you? And stop wriggling so much. Jeez, you smell." He sorted her out as quickly as possible and sat her up in front of him.

"That's better, isn't it? All the stinky stuff gone until the next time. Now Daddy's going to call Uncle Aron."

Hmm, Uncle Aron might be pushing it. "You be a good girl and play with your blocks." Once he'd settled her, he picked up his phone and called Aron.

"Sorry about that. A full nappy waits for no man."

"You're okay, then? You sound okay."

Joe allowed the trace of a smile to cross his lips hearing the concern in Aron's voice.

"Yeah, I'm fine. Me and Dad talked, and although I doubt he'll be hanging out rainbow flags anytime soon, he didn't say he never wanted me to darken his door again either. He wants me to be happy, and he worries about me getting hurt. You know what parents are like."

Aron sighed at the other end of the phone. "I'm glad," he said. "I was worried. In other news, I met your brother Robbie today. Did you know he had a new job with my company?"

"Yes, he mentioned it last week, but he didn't tell us the company name until he got the job. He'd been out of work for a while and was afraid he'd get knocked back again. Robbie's a good worker, Aron. When we were young, he used to take things apart to find out how they worked. Perhaps I shouldn't mention that he didn't always successfully put them back together again."

Aron laughed. "I was the same. I remember when I took apart Trude's Walkman to discover how it worked. She was not pleased."

"Trude?"

"Our *au pair*, when I was young. Mum and Dad were doctors—worked long hours. She taught me to speak German, which proved useful later on with so much scientific research being in that language."

"Do you see them much now?" Joe asked.

"A couple of times a year, usually. They live in the south of France near the border with Spain. So when can we get together again?"

"I wondered if you fancied going out somewhere on Sunday."

"Sounds good. What do you have in mind?"

"I thought we might take Ellie out for the day to the Ark Project. It's over the bridge near Bristol. She loves animals."

"Oh, right. I see."

Joe could almost feel the tension coming through the phone aware he'd set Aron a test. "If you don't want to I understand. Better to stop now before things get too…"

"No," Aron interrupted. "I'm being stupid. I want to see you and I know you and Ellie are a package deal. A day out sounds good."

"Is it okay if we use your car?" Joe asked. "I'll bring mine to your house and leave it there if that's all right. I can put Ellie's seat in yours as well." Also it would mean the neighbors didn't get to wonder about the shiny new Lexus parked outside his house again.

"Yes, that'll be fine. Will she be all right driving that far?"

"She's a great traveler. It's me you'll have to worry about puking over your leather interiors. I'll see you at nine."

"Yeah, good, nine's good."

"You sure you're okay with this?" Joe asked again.

"Sorry, I'm apprehensive. It's been a while since I've done going out, and I told you I'm no good with kids. Aren't you at all concerned what people will think when they see us together?"

"People can think whatever they want. I shouldn't imagine it'll be the first time two men have taken a baby to a zoo."

"I haven't been somewhere like that since I was eight and came back with chicken pox."

"You can tell me the story on Sunday. Madam here is banging her spoon, which means she wants feeding. I'm looking forward to seeing you again." He deliberately lowered his voice, hoping the rasp would have an effect.

"Um, yeah, me too. The forecast says it's going to be a warm."

"I'll pack us a picnic." Ellie made her presence known. "Gotta go," Joe said. "Bye."

"Bye."

Joe put the phone down and turned to his daughter. "Well, Dadda's done it now. You and I are going on a date."

Chapter Fifteen

Aron glanced at his watch—again. Joe was late. All right, it was merely fifteen minutes past the hour, but he was nervous enough already. What if Joe had changed his mind? He'd nearly rung him a few times to say he'd been called somewhere in an emergency, but he couldn't think of a plausible reason. He heard the sound of an engine and a red van pulled into the other space in the driveway at the front of his house. Immediately, he grabbed his jacket and opened the door.

"Sorry, last minute nappy change," Joe said as he got out of the van. "Still that's a good thing, believe me. The boot's open. Can you get the picnic box and her buggy while I get her seat out?"

"Sure," Aron replied, clicking the buttons to open his car. "I'll put them in my boot and you can put Ellie in the back. Will she be all right there?"

"She'll probably go to sleep. Dad takes her out in his taxi when she's restless. He swears she goes to sleep then. Bloody hell, I hate these fiddly straps."

"Can I help?" Aron asked after stowing the food.

"Grab the bag on the floor, would you?"

Aron picked up the bag, wondering what it contained.

"Sorry, babies don't travel light," Joe explained. "There's a lot of just-in-case stuff involved. Are you sure you're still up for this?"

Aron wasn't sure at all, but he wasn't going to admit that now. He couldn't keep his eyes off Joe, especially the smattering of dark hair revealed by the open-necked white cotton shirt he wore tucked into beige, three-quarter-length cargo pants. Aron's gaze was drawn to Joe's firm calf muscles covered in downy dark hair as well as his bare toes. He pushed away the thought of sucking on each and every one of them in turn. Since when did he have a foot fetish? Or maybe he simply had a Joe fetish. Joe needed a shave as the same dark hair had created a very sexy stubble on his chin. It made him appear more dangerous and oh so sexy. Aron wanted to kiss him there and then, not to mention do a whole lot more, but he could already see curtains twitching next door. He got into the car and turned to glance at Ellie. She smiled at him while playing with the row of little soft toys attached to a bar in front of her. She was the spitting image of her father, dressed in blue cotton trousers with a pink and blue T-shirt, all dark curls with the same smattering of little freckles across her cheeks. Aron guessed her eyes were green as well.

"All done," Joe said, closing the door. "We'd better get off. At least the traffic shouldn't be too bad on a Sunday." He got into the passenger seat next to Aron.

"Luckily," Aron said, smiling as Joe's thigh touched his own. "This beauty has air-con. You're sure she's clicked in safely?"

Joe put a hand on his leg and warmth shot through him. "Yes, I'm sure, Aron. I do this all the time. Stop worrying."

Aron knew this was true, but he couldn't help himself. Being responsible for their safety was a heavy burden. Part of him wished Joe was driving.

As if he could read his mind, Joe said, "We're going to have a perfectly lovely day out together. I'll deal with Ellie, but you can get to know her a bit. Talking of which, I haven't introduced you two. Ellie, this is Aron, Daddy's friend. Can you say hello, Aron?"

Aron thought Ellie looked distinctly unimpressed before she turned away.

"Say hello, then," Joe said.

He turned back. "Hello, Ellie."

"Run."

Joe beamed. "There, she remembered your name. I told you she's learning new names every day."

Aron turned back to face the front and nervously grasped hold of the steering wheel. He needed to get his act together.

"Right. Okay, if you're sure she's strapped in properly, we'll get going. I'm sorry if I sound impatient, I've never had a baby in here before, but I guess you know what you're doing. I've programmed the route into the satnav, so hopefully we won't end up on some country lane. The zoo, here we come."

When they got to the M4, Joe said, "So, some music? I've no idea what you like."

"If you brought your iPod or phone, you can plug it in there. I listen to all sorts of music."

"Hmm, driver choses the music and passenger shuts his cakehole was always the rule with me and Angie."

"There's a few CDs in the glove box. The latest *Elbow* CD is there."

"I haven't heard that yet, but I like their music. I thought you might like some godawful rap stuff."

"No, I prefer something with a tune."

"So, Aron Roberts, while I have you captured, tell me what else you like. I want your top ten musical choices, film choices, books and TV shows. But before that shag, marry, throw off a cliff?"

"Really? We're doing that?"

They bantered names back and forth for a while until the suggestions began to get more and more outrageous. "Can't I throw them all off the cliff?" Aron asked. "I mean, at a push I'd shag the *X Factor* judge, but the other two, no way."

"Have to agree with you there. Right, okay, films then. What's your favorite?" Joe asked.

"This is difficult, but if I had to be pinned down..." Joe sniggered.

"How old are you?" Aron asked.

"Old enough." A shiver ran through Aron, as he remembered their previous encounters.

"You were saying if you had to be pinned down," Joe reminded him.

"I was, well, I'd say *The Empire Strikes Back*, but I love the first three. It's going to be interesting to see what happens with the new ones."

"Interesting — so favorite character?"

"Easy — has to be Hans Solo. So what about you?"

"You might be surprised," Joe said. "I bet you're expecting me to say some action film, or horror, or something like that."

"Maybe. You're not going to tell me you're a big fan of romcoms or musicals, are you?"

"Not exactly, but my dad's a big fan of old black and white movies like the Marx Brothers, Abbot and Costello, the Fred Astaire and Ginger Rogers films and screwball comedies, but his favorite actress was Katherine Hepburn, so my favorite film is *Bringing Up Baby*. It's about a woman who has a leopard."

"I've seen that one. Cary Grant's in it as well, isn't he?"

"That's the one. It makes me laugh and their timing is immaculate. I've always thought she was kind of beautiful and strong-minded. She had balls. All right then, it's time for favorite books now. You give me one and I'll give you one."

"Really?" Aron said, raising his eyebrows. "Are you doing that on purpose?"

Joe reached over and lightly brushed his hand over Aron's groin.

"Shit! Don't do that."

Joe smiled until he saw the look of panic as Aron gripped the steering wheel tighter.

"It's okay," he said removing his hand. Aron maintained his position staring straight ahead. "No, it's not. Your daughter is in the back of the car and I'm on the bloody motorway. I can't believe you did that!" His voice woke the baby and she began to grizzle.

Joe turned around so she could see his face. "It's all right, Ellie. Daddy's here."

"Is she okay? We can stop at the services over the bridge if you want, although we'll be nearly there by then," Aron said.

"Might be an idea—if only to check on her and give her a sniff, though we'd have probably smelled her by now."

Ellie pulled at the toys again and giggled when they jingled on the bar.

"I'm sorry," Joe said quietly. "I didn't mean to worry you."

Aron allowed himself to relax a moment. "I guess I'm a little wound up about today."

"Before you said you hadn't spent much time with kids. You haven't any siblings?"

"No, no brothers or sisters, and my parents are both only children as well, so no cousins or anything, but I didn't mean Ellie. I meant all this. It's been a while since I spent a day out with someone. All I've talked about recently are work and you." He could almost hear that information being processed.

"You told someone about me?"

Aron hesitated before replying. "Yes, after what happened that night I needed to... Look, we're at the bridge. It feels so much safer on here than it did on the old one. Always makes people laugh that you have to pay to get into Wales." The satnav told him to go onto the M49. "Only about thirty minutes now," he said.

"Who did you talk to?" Joe asked.

"This is going to sound strange, but he and I are friends."

"Now you've got me interested."

"You catered for Dan Morgan's marriage, didn't you?"

"You talked to your ex about me."

"You know he's my ex?"

"Yes, Gwennie showed me the pictures of you and him."

Taking that information in, Aron continued to explain. "I spoke to his partner, Iestyn. He's a good listener, and this may sound even stranger, but I helped them get together."

"Okay... Paint me confused now, but what did he tell you?"

"He told me I needed to work out what I wanted, and that I needed to face my fears." The satnav spoke again, and Aron turned off the motorway.

"So today is you facing your fears?" Joe asked.

Aron swallowed hard and thought about the man sat next to him and his baby in the rear seat. "I guess you could say that. It's a test for both of us, isn't it?"

Joe turned and check on Ellie. "Maybe."

For the rest of the journey to the zoo, the only sound came from the disconnected voice of the satnav.

* * * *

After a promising start, Joe began to wonder whether today had been such a good idea after all when an uneasy silence descended. They pulled into the zoo's car park and Ellie started talking to herself and wriggling in her seat.

"In a minute, angel. Daddy needs to get your buggy out of the back."

"I'll get it," Aron said. "You get her. She obviously wants out of there."

Joe noted Aron was still obviously tense. This might be a long day. He got Ellie out of the seat and placed her on his hip. At the back of the car, he found Aron trying to work out how to set up the buggy. "There's a knack to it," he explained, taking it with one hand and using his foot to stop it moving. A couple of adjustments and clicks and it was ready. "Can you grab the bag from the front? I'll take out what we might need."

A few minutes later, Joe had put all he needed in the net under the buggy or in his ample pockets. Aron's head moved from side to side as if he was watching a tennis match, taking it all in.

"These pants are useful with a baby, but I have to wear the belt. I didn't once and they fell rather low down on my hips." He deliberately bent to make sure everything was secure, knowing that Aron would look. "You're imagining me with builder's bottom, aren't you?" he said, grinning widely as he stood back up. He pushed the buggy, giving Aron time to pull himself together. Joe leaned toward him. "You're sexy when you blush," he whispered, then grinned again as Aron knocked his arm.

"You are going to be trouble, aren't you, Joe Welsh?"

"Oh, I hope so. I think you might enjoy some trouble in your life, someone to shake you up and blow away a few cobwebs."

As they walked to the entrance with other families around them, he wondered if he should be more bothered about the fact that they were two men out for the day with a baby. Maybe these days people didn't look twice anymore. Aron paid the fee and they immediately walked to the petting zoo part of the park with the baby animals. When they got to an open area with goats and sheep walking around, they sat on a bench and watched as larger children fed the lambs and pygmy goats. Joe undid the security belt in the buggy and lifted Ellie onto his lap.

"Sheep," he said, pointing at the animal in front of them. Ellie attempted to copy the sound and reached out to the ewe and her lamb.

"They must get them to give birth later than normal," Aron said, "for them to be so small now." When the sheep was near enough, Ellie reached out and touched it on the head. Joe pulled out the packet of wipes in his pocket.

"You have to be careful around animals," he explained. "She puts her hands in her mouth, so I'll give them a wipe if she touches anything."

"You want to go down?" Joe asked as Ellie squirmed in his arms. He put her down and grabbed her reins. She immediately began to crawl in the grass after the sheep until she was distracted by a tiny baby goat. They almost met on a level, and could have head-butted each other. "Goat," Joe said.

Aron watched father and daughter explore the small area. Joe showed an infinite amount of patience. Ellie moved hesitantly at first then almost dashed when she saw something interesting. When Joe picked Ellie up and held her above his head before carrying her back to the bench, Aron studied his strong chest and arms. His cock stirred appreciatively, and he wished he'd worn jeans with more wiggle room in them. He pulled his T-shirt lower.

"Come on," Joe said. "I'll carry her for a while if you push the buggy." They walked past the meerkats and wallabies and onto the arena where one could hold the smaller animals. Aron pushed the buggy, feeling somewhat self-conscious. He'd never worried people might think he was gay, because he was gay, but this was different. There was every chance people might see them as a family — him, Joe and *their* little girl. They sat on a bench and peered around. An assistant came up to them.

"Would you like a rabbit for your daughter to pet?" she asked, glancing at them both. She had a little black and white rabbit in her arms and handed it to Joe.

"She'll want one of these now," Joe said as Ellie stroked the rabbit in his lap.

Aron noticed how gentle she was even though her smoothing technique was a little clumsy.

"Bunny," she said and Aron watched Joe's whole face light up.

"She's picking up new words all the time." The pride in her achievements reflected in his shining eyes. "Come on, babycakes—more to see."

They wandered past the lemurs and gibbons where Joe did a totally charming chest-thumping monkey impersonation and finally arrived at one of the picnic spots. Joe lifted Ellie up and smelled her bottom.

"I'll go and get her changed. Can you go to the car and get the picnic box? I'll meet you back here."

Aron strolled back to the car. So far things had gone well, not that he'd had interaction with Ellie, but at least she didn't mind him being there and hadn't screamed blue murder at the sight of him. The image of her father, she had his sturdy build and coloring. She didn't appear to be demanding or clingy and was quite happy to go off on her own given the chance, but what did he know? He had no comparison for this. Today would be the longest he'd ever spent with a child other than when he was one himself, and he'd been significantly older, and in infant's school before he'd mixed with other children. Until then, he'd been by himself except for Trude.

He'd met Dan when he'd moved to his junior school. On the face of it, Dan and Joe had little in common in the looks department, but they were both wide-chested and had strong arms, arms that made him feel safe and loved. Both men were people you'd want on your side in an emergency, strong, capable and physically fit, with devastating smiles that went all the way to their eyes. He got a sudden vision of muscular thighs. Maybe they did have a few things in common after all.

He opened the boot and withdrew the cool box. When he returned, he found Joe sitting at a picnic table with Ellie sat on the table in front of him, her legs dangling over the edge. He watched as Joe clapped her hands together and sang to her, making her smile and laugh. Aron imagined the look on his face — joy, pride, love — all mixed together. He didn't want to interrupt father and daughter, but he walked up behind Joe and placed a hand on his shoulder.

"Someone's having fun," he said, putting the box on the table.

"Run," Ellie said, gazing up at him.

Joe positively beamed. "That's it, Ellie — this is Run. You remembered, clever girl." He opened the box and removed plates and cutlery. "I made sandwiches and there are sausage rolls and homemade coleslaw and salad with little sausages — she loves them. Yes, yours is coming, Ellie. She gets excited when there's food on offer — much like I do."

Aron lifted out a bowl and removed the lid. He picked up sandwiches and groaned as the flavors hit his tongue. "This is great — no seriously." He took another bite and let the flavors dance across his tongue.

"It's cranberry and rosemary bread with a brie and pancetta filling. Here, try the dressing on the salad."

Aron poured some over his mixture of different lettuce, onion, tomato and carrot then chewed a forkful. "What's in the dressing?" he asked. "It's to die for."

"Nah," Joe said, shaking his head. "I'd have to kill you."

Aron continued eating, moaning every so often as he took another mouthful of the array of food Joe had provided.

"She's a good eater," Aron said, watching how Ellie grabbed at the spoon covered in pasta.

"She is, but then her daddy does make her great-tasting food, doesn't he, angel? The trouble is, it comes out of the other end and it's not so lovely."

Aron couldn't believe he was about to ask this when he was eating. "Did you find somewhere to change her all right?"

"Yes, thankfully the changing place was in the disabled toilet and not the ladies. That can be a bugger when you need to change her. So many places assume babies get changed by their mothers. I've had a few strange looks sometimes, I can tell you, but if they don't provide facilities, what am I supposed to do?"

"I never thought of that," Aron said. "There must be a few times and places when that's the case."

A woman stopped at their table. "Aw, she's cute," she said. "How old is she?"

The hairs on the back of Aron's neck rose, and he had a strong desire to reach over and take Joe's hand. The woman ignored him completely. She used Ellie to bat her eyes at Joe as if he wasn't there.

"She's just had her first birthday," Joe said affably.

"I'm here with my sister and her two little ones. It's a great place to bring them. Have you been before?"

Aron couldn't stand it any longer. "No, this is *our* first time," he said, watching as Joe failed to suppress a chuckle.

Sudden realization crossed the woman's face, and Joe coughed behind his hand, his eyes dancing with barely contained amusement.

"Oh, I see, you two are… I'd better get back to my sister. It was nice to meet you."

"You too," Joe said.

They watched her go, then when she'd said something to her sister, both women looked their way.

"Bloody cheek! She was hitting on you with me sat here as if I was no one. I might as well have been invisible." Joe stood, put Ellie on the grass, reached over and deliberately put his hands on either side of Aron's face and kissed him. Aron checked all around to see if people were staring at them, but other than the two women, no one glanced their way.

"There," Joe said. "I think they know we're together now."

Little hands touched Aron's leg.

"Joe, look, she's standing." They both watched as Ellie moved around the bench using it to keep herself upright until she could manage no more and plonked back down on her bottom.

"Don't seem worried," Joe said. "Smile at her."

Aron smiled and Ellie smiled back at him then reached out her hands.

"Run. Up," she said.

"She wants you to pick her up," Joe said.

Aron panicked. "I can't. I don't know how."

"Reach down and put your hands under her arms, lift her and put her on your lap, then you can give her some pieces of strawberry and apple. She loves them, and I have some for us as well. Have you ever tried strawberries with black pepper or balsamic vinegar? They taste incredible. Go on. She obviously wants you to."

Aron swallowed hard then reached down, put his hands under Ellie's arms and lifted her, trying not to shake. He put her on his knee and pulled the bowl of fruit toward them. She dipped her hands in and put a strawberry piece into her mouth. Her eyes lit up as she tasted the juice and she made a strange *nomming* noise. It all seemed totally surreal.

"Here," Joe said, reaching over with a strawberry in his hand. "Taste this." Another dip into surrealism — being fed strawberries, by another man, in a public place, with a baby on his knee. Never in his wildest of dreams had he ever thought this would happen and the taste...

"Oh my God. How the hell does that work?" The flavors exploded in his mouth, hot and sweet. There was no way it should work, but it did.

"No idea. Here, try it with the balsamic."

Again the flavors pirouetted on his tongue. "Oh, wow, you do realize I'm going to have to marry you now I know you can produce food like this. I'm going to have to do a lot more exercise as well because..." He stopped when he realized what he'd said, and that Joe was staring at him.

"Sorry, it was just a figure of speech. You know what they say — the way to a man's heart and all that. Joe, say something."

The man came out of his trance. "Yeah, sorry. Let's eat up, then we can go and see the rest of the animals. She'll probably fall asleep in the buggy." He stowed everything back in the box then carried the rubbish to the bin.

Aron suddenly registered Ellie was still sitting on his knee. How the hell had he forgotten that fact? "I think I might have surprised your daddy," he said, lifting her back into the buggy.

"Run," she said, gazing at him through her father's green eyes.

"That may be good advice, young lady," he told her, but he didn't want to run, at least not away. As Joe strolled back to them, the only way Aron wanted to run was toward him.

Chapter Sixteen

"I'll take her upstairs and get her settled. At least she should sleep after being so busy today," Joe said when they got back to his house. Aron had followed Joe in his own car and parked it down the road from Joe's house to avoid, in Joe's words, the curtain twitchers.

"Order what you want. I usually have a Chicago pizza, cheese garlic bread and wedges."

Aron made the call and gazed around Joe's house. One section of wall displayed photographs of his family. He spotted a wedding photograph among them. Angie had been rather boyish with her pixie haircut and he suspected the wedding dress wasn't her thing. Next to her, Joe looked so handsome and so proud to have her on his arm. Others showed Ellie at various stages. A few frames stood on the mantle. He picked one up, shocked at the wave of emotion that overwhelmed him seeing mother and daughter.

"It's the only one I have of them together," Joe said, coming up behind him. Aron turned around and closed the space between them. He wanted to take Joe in his arms and hug him so much. Joe took the photograph out of his hands.

"Everything went to hell minutes later."

Aron watched spellbound as Joe wiped a finger across the image.

"She would have been a great mother. I worry Ellie has missed out on so much not having Angie in her life."

Aron shifted from one foot to another. "D'you want me to go?"

"No, don't be silly. We have food to eat when it arrives. Come and sit on the sofa with me." He placed the baby monitor on the table next to them and Aron sat, leaving a gap between them, more than a little conscious of the monitor and what it meant.

"She's worn out and went off to sleep straight away. We can pig out on the sofa and watch an old film if you want." As Joe edged toward him, closing the distance between them, Aron shoved his shaking hand under his thigh.

Joe reached out and touched him gently. "And make out a little."

Aron loved the feel of Joe's hand on his now burning cheek then the rasp of stubble that brushed across it as Joe leaned in to kiss him. He loved the caress of those surprisingly soft lips on his own. This kiss was the antithesis of the first one they'd shared in his bedroom. He opened his mouth when Joe probed with his tongue, touching Aron's, then Aron moaned as Joe held his bottom lip between his own and sucked gently. Joe wrapped his arms Aron's back and pulled him forward until he lay on top of the man, grinding himself against the body underneath him. The sounds coming from Joe as their bodies moved in synchronization filled Aron's cock as well as his senses. He breathed in the smell of aftershave mixed with the sheen of sweat on Joe's neck as he bit down on the place where neck met shoulder, not hard enough to leave a mark, even though Aron wanted to darken that faintly tanned skin. They jumped at the bang on the door.

Joe sprang up and dashed to answer before there was another knock that might wake Ellie. He put the boxes on the coffee table and went to the kitchen to get plates. "I've salad we could have with that if you want," he said, placing the crockery down in front of Aron.

"Nah," Aron replied. "I'll do an extra-long run tomorrow to burn it off."

Joe patted his stomach. "Yeah, I need to find time to go to the gym, and I want to find out the news from Jonno now he's come out. You know this lad, Rhodri, don't you? What's he like?"

"Young, confident, and full of himself, but he's basically a good lad. He's in your line, doing catering at college. I suspect he's rather young to be seeking anything long term, but you never know, it does happen. I suppose it depends what Jonno is after as well. His parents are supportive, even if they find it all mystifying." He picked up a piece of pizza and bit into it, chewing slowly. "You were right. God, this is good."

"I would have made us some. Another time, perhaps?"

Aron grasped Joe's free hand. "I'd like that. I've enjoyed today, being with you."

"And Ellie?"

"Give me time, all right?" Gazing at Joe's concerned face, Aron decided he needed to say something positive. Holding Ellie had been scary and more than a little awkward. "She's the spitting image of you."

"She is. I wish there was more of Angie in her, but like many daughters, she's cursed with taking after her father."

For a moment, Aron wished he had a fringe to peer out from under. "It's not a bad thing to look like you."

Joe shifted in his seat and muttered, "Thanks."

"I mean it. That bit of stubble suits you. You could grow it. Beards are all the rage now." Joe shivered as Aron reached out again and ran a finger down one cheek then over his chin. Aron could have sworn the air crackled with electricity between them, setting the nerve endings in his fingers on fire. He needed to step away before he pounced on the man and demanded he take Aron there and then. "Talking of fathers, yours was okay with us, then?"

Joe breathed out and the tension that had simmered between them dissipated. "My dad and I are close. He basically brought us up."

"What about your mum?"

"Mum will be all right with it, but I asked Dad to let me tell her. She'll insist on you coming to the house for dinner or something. She's very strong and determined, always organized and doesn't suffer fools, although she says she works for a few."

"What does she do?"

"She's a top civil servant in the Welsh Parliament. She and Dad are a strange mix I suppose, but they complement each other. My grandparents threatened to boycott the wedding, but gave in when Mum refused to give Dad up. They thought Mum had married beneath her. What about your parents? You haven't mentioned them."

Aron shrugged. He had no desire to talk about his parents, but he had to say something. "I don't see much of them now that they've retired."

"You're not close, then?"

"No."

Joe recognized a conversation shutdown when he heard one. Obviously, Aron didn't want to talk about his parents. He needed to say something as a dark cloud had settled over Aron's head and he was staring into space.

"So, we never finished our conversation earlier. We did film, but what about books and TV?"

Aron came out of his trance.

"I'll start with TV shows," Joe continued. "Mine isn't what I'd call a favorite, but it did influence me, and that's *Ready Steady Cook*. I used to come home from school and watch it every day and beg Dad to buy the ingredients so I could see what I could do with them. My family had to suffer a lot of my experimental efforts. So what's your favorite?"

"I'm going to sound like a total nerd, but it has to be *Star Trek*. Space travel has always fascinated me. Flying up amongst the clouds is awesome, but I'd love to go into space and see what the Earth looks like while I'm floating above it."

"*Star Trek* and *Star Wars*—you are a sci-fi geek, aren't you?" Joe teased. "I don't suppose you have a pair of pointy ears?" He leaned forward. "We could do a little role-playing. I could be Captain Kirk to your Spock." Joe was gratified to see Aron squirm, not to mention the bulge that appeared in his jeans. He moved closer and kissed him, sucking his bottom lip while pushing his hands under Aron's T-shirt, touching his chest and tweaking a nipple. He moved the shirt up and added his tongue and teeth to his arsenal of weapons as he licked and nipped, moving down toward Aron's belly button.

"Shit, that tickles," Aron said between groans.

Joe undid Aron's belt and lowered the zipper then nuzzled the cotton fabric of his white briefs already damp with pre-cum. When he pulled the cotton material down, Aron's cock sprang free, almost hitting him on the nose.

"Hmm, someone's eager." Joe encased the tip in his mouth and swirled his tongue languidly around the head then held the base and moved his hand up and down. Without warning, he enveloped the whole shaft into his mouth, remembering to relax his throat. He gagged a little and withdrew.

"Sorry, I don't have much experience at this."

"Believe me, it doesn't show. Shit, you're good."

Joe welcomed Aron tugging his hair and pushing his head back down. He dipped again and captured it all, enjoying the feel of Aron's hand on his head, encouraging rather than insisting. He was no expert, and other than a brief abortive attempt with a lad he'd met at a Pontin's holiday camp, before he got together with Angie, this was the single time he'd given head.

"I'm not far away," Aron warned him.

Joe continued to stroke his hand up and down Aron's cock while still sucking the tip. Aron stiffened under him, and he prepared himself, opening his mouth to let the cum drip onto his tongue. When it came, Joe managed to messily milk Aron's cock until he was totally spent and lying in a heap underneath him. Joe lifted his head, and Aron greeted him with a huge smile.

"Come to bed with me," Joe said. "I want to take my time, but I want to fuck you."

Aron's skin prickled with nerves, and the hairs on the back of his neck stood at attention. He loved the thought of Joe fucking him but... "What about Ellie? Does she sleep in your bedroom?"

"Yeah, but she won't know anything," Joe assured him.

Aron sat up and turned around. "Yeah, but I will. I realize people do, but she's not mine, and we might scare her. I couldn't imagine keeping quiet with you. What if she cried while we were, you know. I'm sorry."

"It's all right. I understand, and you're right. It didn't cross my mind. I'm so used to her being there."

Aron breathed a sigh of relief. "You're not angry with me."

"No, I'm sure there are other parents who wouldn't want to either. I'll go up and check on her, then maybe we can use the sofa instead, if you still want to, because I still want to."

Aron let Joe take his hand and put it on the bulge in his pants. "Hmm, so I feel."

They both turned when they heard slight grizzling noises coming from the monitor. "I'll go up now. Don't go anywhere."

Aron took a few deep breaths in an effort to calm his nerves after Joe disappeared out of the room. He liked Joe a lot, and he knew he needed to get his act together. There was no getting away from that fact that Joe was first and foremost a parent. Nothing else in his life mattered as much and his body was certainly on board with the plan. A distressed shout pierced his musings.

"Aron, there's something wrong – she's burning up." He was off the sofa in seconds and running up the stairs. Joe shouted again. The sight that greeted Aron sent shock waves through his whole body. Joe stood next to the cot with his shaking daughter in his arms.

"She's having a fit. What the hell do I do? We need to get her to the hospital now."

Aron put his hand on Ellie's head. "She has a temperature," he said. He could see that the twitches were subsiding. "Get her clothes off. We need to cool her down as best we can." He was amazed he remained so calm, as Joe fell apart in front of him.

"We need to get her to hospital. What if she dies? I can't lose her, Aron."

"You won't. There, she has stopped shaking now, but she has probably got an infection. Febrile convulsions are usually caused by high fevers. Get her something light to wear and we'll take her in my car, then you can go straight into A and E."

Joe grabbed a pair of cotton pajamas. Ten minutes later, they were heading for the hospital with Aron trying to assure Joe that Ellie would be all right.

"How the hell did you know what to do?" Joe asked from the back of the car.

Aron put his foot down, hoping there were no police cars about. "We had first aid lessons in school and there was a section of childhood illnesses and how to spot them. Febrile convulsions can seem scary, but as long as they don't fit for too long, they usually recover quickly. Children can suddenly get them. They'll check her over, see whether there's an infection and give her antibiotics, I expect."

Joe talked to Ellie all the way there. Aron pulled up directly outside and let Joe out. "I'll find you," he said.

Standing at the reception desk after running all the way from the car park, he discovered the first problem of finding out what was going on—he wasn't a relative, so to begin with they wouldn't tell him anything. I'm a friend sounded so weary, but at this stage that was all he was to Joe. How did you define a relationship in the early stages? Sure, he knew some important things about Joe, but this was the first time they'd experienced

everyday life together and look how that had ended —
stuck in A & E in the early hours of the morning. He
glanced around the waiting room, taking in all the
posters mentioning various services and giving advice
about this and that. Fortunately, the waiting area only
had a few occupants.

Finally, after what seemed like forever, Joe pushed a
now sleeping Ellie out of the curtained area to his left.
His face was still gray with worry and lack of sleep, but
his demeanor much calmer than it had been when
they'd arrived. He sat next to Aron and sighed heavily.
Aron wanted to take his hand, but he wasn't sure how
Joe would react in public.

"You were right," Joe said wearily. "She has a high
temperature and an ear infection. They've given me
antibiotics and told me to check her temperature,
because if she's susceptible to infection, it can come
back. I need to keep her cool and take her back to my
GP to check her if I'm worried. She's quiet now and
likely to sleep, they said, which is more than I'll
manage. Can you take us home now?"

Aron managed a smile. "Of course I can. Come on,
let's get out of here."

They didn't say much during the drive back to Joe's
house. Aron glanced back every so often, noting Joe
kept totally focused on his daughter, checking her
breathing and feeling her forehead and hands. Doubts
seeped into Aron's thoughts. He'd been right to be
worried. How did you cope being responsible for such
a small human who was totally reliant upon you for
everything? Had he and Joe had moved too fast?
Should they slow things down? They definitely needed
to talk.

He pulled up outside the house and waited until Joe
had sorted Ellie out. He didn't want to make any

assumptions about going back into the house, so he wound down his window and waited. Joe leaned in the passenger side.

"I've been thinking," Joe began.

Aron remained silent, suddenly nervous about what was coming next.

"We need to knock this on the head, before we get too serious. I don't have room for anything else in my life. I have to concentrate on my daughter and my business. And you said yourself you don't like children, then there's all the other stuff. I was naïve to imagine I could manage a relationship, and let my cock lead me on, and I can't afford to do that. I can't do what I want. I'm not free to do what I want. Don't get me wrong, Aron, I like you and it's been good, but I have to live in the real world, not some romantic fantasy, and you're not saying anything."

"You don't interrupt when someone is trying to explain themselves." He wasn't surprised. Everything Joe said made sense, but he couldn't help feeling they'd missed the chance at having something good. He could see Joe desperately wanted him to agree with all he'd said. He wanted Aron to make this easier for him, to reassure him he was making the right decision.

"You understand, don't you? I just can't."

"It's all right. I get it," Aron said quietly. "You'd better get her in and try to get some sleep yourself." He wanted to tell him it had been good. He wanted to say maybe some time in the future. Instead, he started the engine and closed the window as Joe stood then turned and pushed the buggy back into his house. With a heavy heart, Aron moved off slowly, not allowing himself to imagine what might have been.

Chapter Seventeen

Joe wasn't sure where the last few weeks had gone. Ellie had taken her first few wobbly steps, holding on to the furniture to help her. There'd be no stopping her soon. He held out the spoonful of porridge, but she grabbed for the handle again, wanting to feed herself. This morning, however, he couldn't give her the time she needed, so he made sure she ate all she wanted from the spoon. The doorbell rang. He lifted her up and carried her to the door.

"It's all right, I'll give you the rest in a minute." He still found it hard to leave her on her own after what had happened, but he didn't want to remember that night, because if he did, he thought about Aron, and he didn't want to go there either. Aron occupied his dreams often enough without thinking about him during the day as well.

He opened the door and was greeted by a young man with a cheery smile. He hoped he'd made the right decision, allowing Jonno to talk him into this arrangement.

After Ellie's illness, he'd found it hard to carry on with work. To begin with he wouldn't trust anyone else to take care of her. He'd rung his father the morning after and arranged for Gwennie to deal with a couple of straightforward jobs. He'd expected his father to appear that morning. Instead, his mother had appeared.

She'd sat at the table and fixed him with a concerned stare. "Your father told me what happened. He also told me about this Aron. You could have told me. I know I haven't always been there for the day to day stuff like your dad, but you're my son, and all I want is for you to be happy. I needed to know that you and Ellie were all right. The government will survive without me for a few days."

"You took leave?" Joe had asked.

"Is that so surprising?" He heard the hurt in her voice. When Angie had died, she'd been there for him. At times, he hadn't been sure how she'd managed. There was no person who he admired more. Angie had been like her in many ways, both strong and confident, and not afraid to say what she thought.

"No, Mum, I didn't expect it, that's all, but I'm so pleased you're here."

"So tell me what we need to do. Gwennie said she'll be over later to help. Your dad's got a Heathrow run this afternoon, and he's babysitting after the twins until Rosie picks them up later. I can mind Ellie while you work."

"It was so scary last night, Mum."

She stood and put her arms around him. "I know, love, but these things happen to little ones. You had a couple yourself when you got infections. She'll be fine and at least you weren't on your own. I'll make us a mug of tea then you can tell me about him."

"There's nothing to tell now. I knocked it on the head for a few reasons. I need to be here for Ellie. She's always going to be my number one priority."

They'd both glanced over to where Ellie was amusing herself trying to put different shapes into the right holes.

She reached over a hand and took his. "You deserve a life as well. If you like this bloke, you know your father and I don't care about the sex of the person you're with." He'd noticed she opened her mouth then thought more of it and finished making the tea.

"What?" He hadn't been able to resist asking.

"It doesn't matter." She'd put the mugs on the table, but stupidly he hadn't been able to let it go.

"I did sometimes wonder about you and Jonno. I saw the way he stared at you, but then Angie came along and she was it for you. You looked at her as if you couldn't believe anyone so perfect had walked into your life. I wasn't sure you'd ever see anyone in the same way again. I worry about you being on your own, love, and Angie wouldn't have wanted that for you. Ellie won't always be this age. I swear, it's only five minutes since I had the four of you running around at home."

"Aron and I…" He sighed. "It's complicated, Mum."

She'd fixed him with a look which said, 'Isn't it always?' "Well, whenever you need to talk or anything else, remember your dad and I are here for you."

Everyone had rallied around him afterward. Work had been busy and Jonno had come up with this suggestion to help him and despite the fact that the lad knew Aron, Joe had to admit he needed assistance, and so Rhodri Morris stood on his doorstep, waiting to be asked in.

The way Rhodri gazed up and down, Joe couldn't help but feel he was being assessed.

"Hi, I'm Rhodri, and you are gorgeous."

Joe smiled when Rhodri's face flushed.

"Sorry, I meant your daughter. Shit, not that you aren't good looking as well and oh hell, sorry, I shouldn't have sworn in front of her." His whole body sighed. "Could you close the door then open it again as if this never happened? I guess I'm nervous."

The grin he broke into would have charmed anyone. Joe guessed Rhodri used his boyish charms to get his way over lots of things. He cocked his head and peered out from under his dark fringe with huge chocolate-colored, puppy-dog eyes. Ellie wriggled in Joe's arms and reached toward Rhodri, who in turn held her hand.

"I think she likes you," Joe said, laughing.

"She's obviously got remarkably good taste. So can I come in?"

Joe stood back, smiling to himself as Rhodri sashayed through to the kitchen. God help Jonno, because his lad had confidence written right through him like a stick of Barry Island rock.

They worked all morning prepping for a dinner party that night. Thankfully, Rhodri had received training in waiting on tables. No doubt he would work his magic on the guests as well as Ellie, who was already in love. Whenever Rhodri went near, she raised her arms and demanded his attention.

"I have a way with babies and old ladies," Rhodri said as he bounced Ellie on his knee during their break.

"You have a way with lots of people, from what I've heard," Joe said. He'd already noted the T-shirt displaying the colors of the bisexual awareness flag. "I don't think anyone would describe you as shy." He thought of Jonno and wondered how the hell he coped with such an obvious flirt, but he had to admit that Jonno appeared happier than he'd ever known him, and he guessed a lot of that was down to Rhodri.

"My parents believed in letting me make my own mistakes and encouraged my sister and me to be who we wanted to be. They may not entirely get everything..." He stopped for a moment, as if considering what to say next. "But you'll know how difficult it is for some people to understand how you can fancy the person not the gender."

Joe swallowed hard. "Have you seen Aron recently?" He wanted to ask if he was all right. Was he missing him? Had he gone into a decline? Was he pining away and not eating?

"No, not for a while. We're not in each other's pockets. Jonno told me what happened."

Jonno had been round the next day and virtually every day after that. He gave no opinion of Joe's decision to stop seeing Aron. In fact, he was the same as he'd always been, keeping Joe company watching bad films and boxsets, and amusing Ellie.

Rhodri continued when Joe nodded slowly. "Dad says he's working all hours and driving the rest of them hard too, but your brother is working for him, so you must know that much already."

"Robbie hardly mentions his work, and I don't see him often. He's my brother, but we're not tight. I'm closer to my sister, Gwen."

"Do you want to talk? Jonno told me to keep my mouth shut. He's very...um...protective of you."

There was something ironic about seeking advice from an eighteen year old with more experience than himself. Joe wasn't sure how much Rhodri knew. "He is. We've been friends for years. He's dear to me too." Of course, there was a silent 'so don't piss him about and break his heart too badly' at the end of that sentence.

"I think he's still a bit in love with you, but that's okay. He's such an interesting set of contradictions, so fierce in the ring and yet so shy out of it, although he tries to pretend he isn't. We're having fun, and wow, can he dance! You should come out with us sometime and show me some of your moves."

"Maybe," Joe replied with a less than enthusiastic tone. "We'd better get back to work." Rhodri stood and put a now drowsy Ellie back in her playpen. "Sorry, angel, the big, bad boss man is cracking his whip."

"She'll go to sleep. Now, let's see what you do with pastry. Dessert is chocolate tart with coffee sauce. We need to make three to be sure."

* * * *

Aron collapsed on his sofa, put his fingers to his temples and rubbed. His headache showed no sign of going away. Margaret had packed him off home.

The others weren't aware of what had happened, but he'd seen the occasional conversation between Margaret and Dai, no doubt speculating about his bad mood. Thankfully, Robbie remained unaware of his and Joe's relationship, which made work easier. He'd told Evan and Beth and been around there for dinner a couple of times. Neither of them had tried to force the baby on him, nor asked difficult questions. He'd also been to a barbecue at Dan and Iestyn's. He'd shaken his head at Iestyn, and nothing more had been said.

Most of the time, he'd simply thrown himself into developing his new gadget, but initial tests had been unsuccessful and he'd began to wonder if he was going to end up being a one-trick pony. Yes, it was a good trick, and it would probably make his firm quite a lot of money, but he had employees to consider and he wasn't one for resting on his laurels. Perhaps he did need a holiday. It had been so long since he'd been away anywhere that wasn't anything to do with work. He could go to see his parents he supposed, but he had no enthusiasm for that idea.

The throbbing started again. He laid his head back and closed his eyes, but his brain kept asking questions. Was Ellie all right? Had she recovered from her infection, or had any more convulsions? He guessed Joe would have sat and watched her every move for some time after. Aron had witnessed firsthand the fear a parent could feel when their child was ill. It had scared him to see Joe so terrified and he'd been glad to help. He missed Joe as well, even though in truth they'd spent little time together, but it had been good to talk and laugh, and feel someone's arms around him. And now he was feeling jealous of a child. Shit, he needed to pull himself together and get over it. Then again, Rhodri would know about Ellie if he was still going out with Joe's friend. He settled back down again now that he'd made a decision.

"What!" He jumped a mile at the banging on his door then dragged himself up. "You'd better not be someone selling me something," he mumbled to himself. A large shape filled his doorway through the patterned glass. He groaned. Only one person could fill a space like that. Pulling the door open, he saw his visitor carried takeaway and wore the most ridiculous Hawaiian shirt he'd ever seen. "Come in, Emrys, I'll get us a beer," he said, turning toward the kitchen before Emrys had a chance to speak.

Aron brought plates and cutlery as well as the beer back to the living room and found Emrys already ensconced on his sofa.

"So, to what do I owe this honor?" he asked more sarcastically than he intended. Emrys simply glanced up at him then continued spooning chicken, rice and chips onto his plate.

"Are you even going to speak to me?" Aron asked. "Or have you run out of plates at your house and decided you'd come and use mine?"

The look on Emrys' face made Aron wonder if he'd gone too far.

"I'll say something when you stop being such an arsehole. Evan said you were living in self-pity city, and you do realize sarcasm isn't the highest form of intelligence — at least when you're doing it."

Aron put his hands up. "All right, I'm sorry. You didn't deserve that."

"No, I didn't. Now, eat some food. You're skin and bone. You could afford to put on a few pounds."

Aron spooned a few bits of everything onto his plate and managed a few mouthfuls. As soon as the salt hit his tongue, he began to eat with enthusiasm. "This is good," he said. "Where did you get it?"

"There's a place near my house — too near, really. You should taste their crispy duck. Man, it's to die for." He patted his stomach and licked his lips. Aron sat back and considered him. Emrys was a giant bear of a man, around six foot five and probably over twenty stone, but gentle as a lamb, and the life and soul of any party.

"Got another beer? I think we need lots of alcohol to soak this up." Aron didn't ask him how he planned to get home, but went to get more. "That's the last," he said, putting the bottles on the table, "but I've wine or whiskey."

"Sounds good either way," Emrys declared. "Now, what the fuck is going on with you? Evan says you're trying to work yourself to death and that you need to get out there and mingle again. This bloke didn't work out, then? And don't give me any of that 'I don't want to talk about it' shit."

Aron explained what had happened with Ellie while Emrys knocked back his first glass of wine along with several pieces of sesame toast sprinkled with crispy seaweed.

"So you went out a few times, you had great sex, but he put his daughter first and finished with you."

"That's it in a nutshell," Aron replied, pushing himself back into the chair as the wine began to have an effect.

"What is it about kids you find so difficult to deal with? I don't get it. If I'd been straight, I'd want a dozen of them, instead I have my dog. I can't wait until Scottie is bigger and I can take him to places and play with him. I'm going to be the best and coolest uncle ever."

"Nothing to stop you from having kids if you want them," Aron said. "Even single gay men can adopt now."

"I know, and possibly I will, but I'd like to find someone to share the fun with first. I guess I'm too picky, or maybe I'm too much for people. I get that I come over a bit strong at times, but that's who I am. I guess I'm a glass is half-full sort of man, and you haven't answered my question about kids."

Aron sighed and swallowed another mouthful of wine. "You and Evan, you get on well with your parents, don't you?"

"Yeah, we're all close. They were fine when I came out, even though I left it until I was twenty to tell them. I see them most weekends as Mum insists on feeding me Sunday lunch. They're made up at becoming grandparents. Dad likes to come and help with my work now that he's retired from the fire service and we go to the club for a few beers and a game of snooker on Friday nights."

"When you were young, Evan told me you used to go on these huge family holidays to various camps around the country with your uncles, aunts and cousins."

Emrys smiled at the memory. "Sometimes there were thirty of us with all the kids and adults — good times."

Aron gazed at his slim fingers clasped around his glass. "I never went on one holiday with my parents." Out of the corner of his eye, he noticed the surprise cross Emrys' face.

"But your parents were doctors, weren't they? You lived in a bloody great, big house. They must have been able to afford wonderful holidays to exciting places."

"They did, to places all over the globe, but I didn't go with them. I stayed at home with the *au pair* to take care of me. Mum said I wouldn't enjoy it as there were no children where they were going and I'd be bored, so I stayed at home."

"Shit, that's harsh. I thought they'd have spoiled you like mad."

"Oh, I had things. I had anything I wanted, except them. They were busy people, always at work, saving others. My mum had fallen pregnant accidently at forty — even doctors make mistakes. Dad was even older than she is. They had set lives, lives they enjoyed. They hadn't planned on having any children, then there I was, large as life and twice as inconvenient. Mum got a nanny to look after me when I was born and went back to work almost immediately. She told me sick people needed her more than I did. I think Dad was more bemused than interested in me. I was this little alien creature presented to them every so often like in a Victorian drama. I grew up thinking it was normal until I went to school and talked to other kids and saw their parents waiting at the gates receiving the paintings and models they'd made with enthusiastic smiles. I never showed my parents anything. Dan came into my life when I was nine, and I fell in love."

"You had good taste," Emrys said. Aron managed a smile.

"I'd fallen over in the yard and this new boy came over and pulled me up. He was already big, but I noticed his hands first—they were huge. Something clicked in me and I discovered I liked boys. I spent more time with him and gained the friends he made and the family he had. I spent weekends at their house. I'm not sure my parents even noticed. Then, one day, years later sitting in my bedroom, I heard them talking. Mum was complaining about a doctor in her department having a baby and saying she couldn't imagine why any woman would choose to have children, especially any woman with a brain and a good career. Children tied you down and were millstones around your neck, capable of stopping a woman's prospects dead. I realized then that she'd never wanted me, and that she was right—children do tie you down. I went downstairs right away and told them I was gay, and d'you know what she said?"

Emrys leaned forward and clasped his shaking hand. "Go on, you may as well tell me everything and get it off your chest."

"She said she was glad because she wouldn't have the bother of grandchildren. I'd be able to have a great career and not be tied down by children, or even a relationship. I'm not sure she even realized what she was saying but—and you have to believe me when I say this—I didn't want to feel the same way. All the same, I couldn't help thinking what if I *was* like her and *didn't* have any desire to reproduce? She was right. Being gay, I didn't have to have anything to do with children. I could have fun. I didn't need to worry. I had a man who I loved and who came to love me. I had everything."

"So why did you and Dan split up?"

"He wanted more. He wanted the family he'd never had. It was obvious when the law changed that he wanted to get married, and that he wanted kids, and I knew I wasn't the man for him anymore, so I let him go. It killed me to walk away, but it was best for him and now he's happy with Iestyn, and I know I did the right thing."

"For him, but what about you? Shit, Aron, what about *you*? Don't you deserve some happiness? Someone to hold you at night? Parents like yours should never have been allowed to have kids." He got up, crossed the floor and wrapped his huge arms around Aron, pulling him so tight he could hardly breathe. Aron leaned into him. Emrys placed a light kiss on his forehead. There was nothing sexual in his embrace, and he fought to keep the tears at bay as Emrys rubbed his back like he was a sick child.

"You don't have to be like them," Emrys said when he finally let Aron go. "Not wanting children isn't in the genes. You've never let yourself get used to one. You grew up thinking you were a burden rather than a joy. I can't imagine how that must have hurt. Evan and I are still the center of our parents' lives."

Aron drained his glass then poured another one and drank most of that. He wanted to try to block all those feelings that thinking about his parents always brought to the surface.

"Hey, go easy," Emrys said.

"What's the point? Now you feel as sorry for me as I do myself. Poor little rich boy whose parents didn't love him. I don't need a man in my life. I especially don't need a man with a child in my life, and he doesn't need me. I'm better off on my own." He knew the alcohol was making its mark.

"Hmm, we'll see about that." He thought those were Emrys' words, but the world had become rather bleary. He didn't fight when Emrys lifted him off his feet and carried him upstairs as if he weighed nothing.

"Need to piss," he warned, as he fumbled with his buttons and zipper. He managed to make it to his en suite, hold himself up then staggered back to the bed.

"You can fuck me if you want," he mumbled.

"I don't think so."

"See, even you're not desperate enough to want to get involved with me."

"I'll ignore your stupidity because you're drunk. Let's get you undressed and into bed."

When Aron woke several hours later, hammers were attacking his skull and Emrys had wrapped his arms around him holding him tightly. Despite the snoring and the pain in his head, he knew he was safe, and that someone cared after all.

Chapter Eighteen

"Don't worry, I was the perfect gentleman."

Aron reluctantly stretched out his arms and legs. A throbbing sensation cha-cha-cha-ed at his temple. He opened his eyes and saw the glass of water on the bedside cabinet.

"Resolve in the glass – drink," Emrys instructed. He flexed his arse and emitted a noise similar to that of a duck being strangled.

"Emrys! Oh, my God, that stinks. Get out of my bed. I need to shower and get ready for work."

Emrys grunted and pulled the sheet over his head.

"Come on. I've got to go to work and so have you." Aron shook him.

Emrys lowered the sheet. "Why don't you play hooky? You work too hard... Come out with me for a while. Get some fresh air. I've got to pick up Boulder and take him to the park. He'll be wondering where I am."

"Boulder? Do I want to know?"

"Boulder, my boxer dog, and he'll be needing a walk when I get home. Come with us. You can go to work later."

"I probably shouldn't ask, but why Boulder?"

"Because he's my rock."

Aron nearly teared up at the thought, cheesy as it sounded. There must be someone out there for this man who had so much love to give. He leaned over, pulled the sheet down, mussed Emrys' hair and kissed his shoulder.

"Thanks for last night. You're a good man."

"I am."

"But you do stink. So use the other shower. First one down makes a huge pot of tea."

Twenty minutes later, they both sat in the kitchen, mugs in hand.

Emrys sighed into his mug. "I'm so glad you're civilized and drink tea at breakfast. Let's go and pick up Boulder. I can get changed, and we can get bacon butties and sit on a bench and feed the ducks. I've got proper duck food. You shouldn't feed them bread—not good for them."

Boulder turned out to be an excitable one-year-old rescue dog Emrys had adopted a month ago. "He needs some training," Emrys explained, as the dog jumped up attempting to lick his owner to death. "His previous owners left him shut up in their backyard all the time. Shall we go walkies with Uncle Aron then, Boulder?"

Aron couldn't help but smile as the dog wagged his whole back end. Emrys picked up a bag of duck food, and they drove to the park.

Despite the early hour, the sun was up and its rays had begun to warm the air. Usually he jogged, ignoring his surroundings, so it was pleasant to stroll through the park until they reached the section where dogs were allowed to run off the lead. Emrys sat on a bench and threw a ball for Boulder to chase.

"He hasn't quite mastered the concept of fetch yet, so I give him the football to push around. I think we've been through at least six already as he tends to burst them."

Aron breathed in several lungfuls of air while watching the dog enthusiastically push the ball with his nose. His head remained decidedly woolly, despite the fact that he'd managed to avoid throwing up his breakfast.

"It's lovely here," Emrys said. "It's especially pretty in autumn when the leaves are turning. I like to come in the early morning when only the joggers are about, and I sit quietly before I go to work."

"How is the carpentry business?"

"Up and down — sometimes busy and at other times less so. I noticed your kitchen needs a facelift. I could give you a good quote."

"Funnily enough I've been thinking of changing it. I'll give you a ring. I want new shelving in the office as well. I haven't done much with the house since I bought it. Work occupies most of my time. All I do there is eat and sleep and I don't always do much of those either."

"Brilliant. You won't regret it. Check out the stuff on my website. Most of my work comes from word of mouth, so I have to do a decent job."

They heard a bark. Boulder and another dog bounced around each other a short distance away. "I'd better go and fetch him. Someone has brought him a playmate, and you never know how the other dog will react."

Emrys walked over to where Boulder was attempting to play with an excitable cocker spaniel. The owner reminded him of Joe. He had the same stocky build and hair coloring. Aron smiled. Dog owners — always talked as dog owners did, and they laughed as Emrys tried to get Boulder to sit quietly. Aron didn't notice the woman who sat on the bench behind him.

"Am I all right to sit here?"

He turned.

"Run. Run. Run"

"It's all right, sweetheart, Granddad won't run away."

Aron gazed more closely at the little girl in the buggy. She smiled back at him and held up her arms. "Run. Up." She wriggled in the buggy, trying to push the strap away and get under it.

"D'you want to get out, sweetheart? Hang on."

The woman freed the child from the seat and picked her up to stand on the bench between them. The toddler wriggled and reached toward Aron.

"Run. Run."

"I'm sorry, she's not usually like this."

"Hello, Ellie," he said, pleased to see she looked so well and happy. The woman stared at him and moved farther away.

"Sorry, that must sound strange," he said. "My name's Aron Roberts. I know her father, Joe. You must be Joe's mother." He guessed she knew who he was when she checked him over from head to foot, obviously interested in the man who'd slept with her son. She held out her hand. "I'm Sue and Andy, his father, is over there. We live around the corner and often bring Ellie here. She likes to feed the ducks and play on the swings. I've never seen you here before, though."

"No, I'm keeping my friend, Emrys, company while he walks his dog. He lives nearby too. Strange how coincidences happen."

"Yes, isn't it?"

He guessed she wanted to say something more, but wasn't sure about it. Emrys and Joe's father came toward them with both dogs now back on their leads.

"Andy, this is Aron." He saw the light dawn in the man's face. Clearly, he'd worked out his wife meant *that* Aron. Aron glanced up at Emrys. Something about the expression on his face told Aron that this meeting might not be entirely coincidental — but how?

"Emrys, these are Joe's parents, and this is his daughter, Ellie."

Emrys immediately knelt so he was eye level with the toddler. "You are beautiful, aren't you? If your dad has your dark curls and green eyes no wonder my friend here fancies him."

Aron shook his head. Emrys had no filters. "I'm sorry about my friend. He has a habit of speaking first and thinking later." He put out a hand to Andy Welsh, who took it somewhat reluctantly.

"She seems well after what happened," Aron said.

"Joe said you acted swiftly and knew what to do while he panicked. I'm glad he didn't have to deal with it by himself."

Aron breathed a sigh of relief. He hadn't been sure how Joe's parents had coped with the revelation about their son's sexuality, but this was his mother telling him it was all right.

"I was glad to help."

Ellie reached her hands out again. "Run."

"No, Ellie, I can't pick you up," he said softly.

"We'd better be going, love. We've got to take her around to Joe's. He was catering a big dinner last night with his new assistant." Andy picked Ellie up and strapped her back into the buggy.

"It was good to be able to put a face to the name. I'll tell Joe we met."

"Thanks, it was nice to meet you too." He desperately wanted to tell them how much he liked their son and how much he wanted to see him again. Instead, he held his tongue as they walked toward the park gates obviously deep in conversation.

Aron stared at Emrys. "That was an interesting coincidence, wasn't it?" he said. "Us being here when they were."

"What?" Emrys replied. "Can I help it if dog walkers talk to each other and happen to mention their son, who's a caterer and has a daughter called Ellie should I ever need any catering. I simply took a chance that they might be here. She's certainly one gorgeous little girl."

"Emrys, please, you know I have no choice. Joe made his decision. He broke it off, not me."

"Bullshit! You want to see him again, don't you?" Emrys said, putting his hand on Aron's arm.

Aron turned back to see Joe's parents disappear around the corner.

"Yes, of course I do," Aron replied, unable to keep the longing from his voice. *I can't get him out of my head or my dreams.*

"Then there's no point sitting here whinging. You need to plan what you're going to do to get him back."

Chapter Nineteen

Joe yawned and swallowed more coffee. It had been a late, but successful, night at the dinner party and he had high hopes of getting more jobs out of it.

"You did well last night," he told Rhodri. He was a great believer in giving praise where praise was due. He removed the now cooled loaves and put them in the slicer ready to make the sandwiches for the Friday run. Gwen would be along later to take them to the various businesses on the nearby industrial estate.

"I enjoyed doing it for real," Rhodri said. "We've practiced with each other at college, but these people had paid and that makes a difference. By the way, I'm seeing Jonno tonight and he wondered if you manage a couple of hours out with him. I told him you don't have a job tonight. Don't worry, I'll behave myself. I know we've got a lot to do for the buffet tomorrow. I guess summer is busy because of all the weddings."

"It is, but I do relatively small weddings, and this one is for fifty people, but there's still a lot to be done."

"Well, if you need more help, I have a few college friends who'd be more than willing. I'd ask Jonno, but let's face it, he'd be useless, and perhaps people wouldn't like food served by a binman stroke boxer."

Joe glanced across at him. They made an unlikely pair him and Jonno, but his best friend seemed happy enough and Joe didn't ask questions about the nature of their relationship or how far it might have progressed. Jonno hadn't asked any difficult questions when he'd told him about Aron either. He wished he could banish all thoughts of Aron from his head, but he kept remembering how wonderful it had felt to have someone pressed against him. Even Ellie conspired to remind him and would say "Run" with a question in her voice as if she was wondering where Aron had disappeared to after their day out. The sound of the front door opening interrupted his musings. His father must have returned with Ellie.

"Joe, Ellie wants you to come in here to see her."

"Be there now, Dad." He washed his hands and went through to the front room. His father knelt with Ellie standing in front of him. When Joe was near enough, his father let her go. "Go on, Ellie, walk to Daddy."

Ellie managed four hesitant steps then fell into her father's arms.

"Oh my God," Joe said. "She did it on her own. Now we'll have to watch her all the time. Who's my clever girl?" He picked her up and they walked through to his kitchen.

"Was she all right last night?" he asked. He still found it difficult to leave her after what had happened, even though she hadn't had another fit. He checked her temperature every night and made sure she wasn't too warm.

"She just walked," he told Rhodri. "We're going to have to keep an eye on her around the kitchen, so don't leave anything where she might reach if she manages to stand up. I'll need to put locks on the cupboards."

"I'll sort that out for you, son, and bring them around tonight. I can fit them for you too."

Aron poured a coffee and put the mug in front of his father. "Rhodri asked if I could get out for a couple of hours tonight for a drink with him and Jonno." He didn't want to take his parents for granted.

"I tell you what," his dad replied. "I'll come round at seven and sort the locks. If you've managed to get her to sleep, I'll do those which don't need any drilling and you can have a couple of hours. I'll see if your mother wants to come round as well." He stopped talking.

Joe thought he seemed worried.

"What is it, Dad? Everyone is okay, aren't they?"

"Yes, they're fine. We took Ellie to the park around the corner from ours this morning when we walked Rumple. It's peaceful out there at that time with not many people about, but we did meet someone."

Joe wondered what was coming next. "Oh?" he asked, concerned that now he'd revealed his sexual preferences they'd asked some random guy for his phone number.

"Yes, there's this bloke we talk to—Emrys—huge build, walks his boxer dog. Rumple plays with him. We've chatted a few times while the dogs played. Well, this morning he was there with Aron."

Joe leaned forward and gripped the edge of the counter. He knew he had no right to wonder about the identity of the man and what he was doing there with Aron.

"It was weird. Your mum said Ellie recognized him. She kept saying 'run' and your mum couldn't work out why she kept saying it and reaching out to this man."

Joe allowed the hint of a smile to turn the corners of his mouth. "She wasn't able to say Aron. Strange he should be there. It's nowhere near where he lives. D'you know anything else about this bloke?" He didn't miss the amused glances exchanged between Rhodri and his father.

"Emrys said they were just friends. He told Ellie it was no wonder Aron fancied her dad if he was anything like her. Look, Joe, I'm not one to interfere in your life and you're old enough to make your own decisions, but this guy seemed pleasant, and Ellie certainly likes him. I know you're worried about taking care of her, but you deserve a life as well."

"In case you didn't notice, Dad, being with Aron is more complicated than normal."

"And? We brought you up to accept everyone. Your mother and I don't care that you got involved with a man if he makes you happy, if you like him, and Ellie likes him, what does it matter? What if a few people might make comments about the two of you? Sod them." He gazed down at Ellie spinning herself around on her bottom. "You didn't hear Granddad say that."

"But there's still the problem of him disliking kids. Yes, he's met Ellie, but that's different from having a child around all the time and dealing with everyday life."

"Well, why not simply have a bit of fun? You both might need some of that. Not every relationship is about the long term. Give yourself a break and get laid, for God's sake. It's not as if you have to marry the bloke!"

Joe glanced across when Rhodri yelped. "Sorry, slipped with the knife. Not serious. I'll get a plaster."

"Now look what you've done, Dad. I hear what you're saying, but I'm not like that, and I still have Ellie's needs to consider. She has to come first."

"She doesn't have to meet him. Get out and have some fun, and if there's anything more to it, then that's good, isn't it? Angie died, Joe, and you didn't. She didn't want you to be lonely. She told you not to build a shrine in her memory."

"I know, and you're right, but I can't simply ring him up, not after what I said."

"I've got his number," Rhodri said. "I'll get him to come out with us tonight. I don't have to tell him you'll be there. My mum will persuade him. She's good like that and he likes her. I'll get her to tell him she's worried about this bloke I'm seeing, and would he give him the onceover. I can go out back now if you want and give her a ring."

Joe glanced back and forth between them. "I don't want you to lie. I'd be pissed if I was him and someone set me up. Maybe you should tell him I'll be there, but only for a couple of hours to have a quick drink." Oh God, he was going to do this. He was going to see Aron again. They didn't have to act like they were planning a future together, did they? Two adults, who knew the score available for no-strings fun—yeah, he could do that. He sighed. Who did he think he was kidding? But he'd loved the sex and as long as they both understood each other, perhaps they could work something out and see where things went.

"All right, get your mother to ring him and we'll see, but tell him I'll be there—and stop bloody smiling, the pair of you. I can't believe my own father is encouraging me to have no-strings sex with a man!"

"Your mum says you've got to invite him to dinner as well."

"I might have guessed she had an agenda. So much for no strings," Joe said, smiling.

"I may not have them, but you know your mother. She said he seemed lonely. Something about a deep sadness in his eyes when he gazed at Ellie and told her he couldn't pick her up. She thinks he's a man with a few mountains to conquer, and she's always considered herself to be a good judge of people."

"I'll see, Dad. Let's not run before we walk, aye."

"Run. Run."

Ellie crawled toward him and he picked her up.

"Even you're getting in on the act now, huh. All right, Rhodri give your mum a ring and we'll see what he says. After that we've got work to do. Oh, and not a word to Gwen about this, all right, or I'll have her giving me advice as well, and there's only so much I can stand."

* * * *

"Will I do?" he asked his mother later that day.

"You look very handsome, but I'm biased. Is the stubble something he likes? I've always found it abrasive when it rubs against some parts."

"Mum! Definitely too much information!"

"What? Did you think you and the rest of your siblings arrived here by stork?" She ran her hand across his chin. "Well, maybe he likes you a little rough and ready."

His father laughed in the other kitchen. "Stop teasing him, love. He's nervous enough as it is."

"You're sure you don't want us to have her tonight? It's no problem."

"No, Mum. I'm going to have a drink with Jonno, and that's it. It's been a while since I saw him. This will give me chance to talk to Aron as well. We can meet on neutral ground without—"

"Sex being on the agenda?"

Heat rushed to his face. "Yes, Mum. He might tell me to get lost for all I know."

She kissed his cheek. "He'd have to be stupid to turn away someone so handsome."

"I'd better get going." He crouched next to Ellie, who was busy stacking blocks. "You be a good girl for your nanny and granddad. I'm sorry she wouldn't go down tonight." He ran his fingers through Ellie's dark curls and wondered again if he'd made the right choice about facing Aron once more.

* * * *

How the hell had Pauline managed to talk him into doing this? He didn't believe her story about Rhodri's new boyfriend. He'd nearly said no when he heard Joe would be there as well, but apparently Joe knew, so maybe he'd changed his mind which scared the hell out of him as well as stirred his cock. There was so much to consider, especially Ellie. There was no ignoring her existence. True, he could have a good time with her father. The sex had been wonderful, but he wanted more. He'd never had sex without some feeling for the other person. For him it had never been simply a desire to get his end away. Was that so unusual? But there had always been something between them, from the moment he'd met him on the side of the road. He wanted to explore that something, to find out if they had any sort of future, all three of them.

They'd chosen to meet in one of the more upmarket tapas bars in the center of Cardiff, and Aron had dressed appropriately in his dark gray suit and pale blue shirt, which he was assured matched the color of his eyes. He'd deliberately left it late, hoping he would be the last to arrive. He hesitated when he reached the door and let other people go in before him.

Stop being so bloody stupid. You're going in for a drink and that's it. See how the land lies and let him do all the running, if there is any running.

He took a deep breath then pushed through the door. The entrance area opened up to a long, narrow space with a bar along the whole of the left-hand side. On the right were tables in various configurations with panels in between to give people privacy. Neon strip lights in red and yellow illuminated the bar and servers rushed around in black trousers and waistcoats with pristine white shirts.

At the far end of the bar, three people sat on stools, and the nearest waved at him. He rubbed his eyes, adjusting to the lighting. Perhaps Margaret had been right when she'd warned him about needing a larger font. He made a mental note to get his eyes tested after all. He walked the full length of the room until he reached the rest of the group and perched on the stool next to Rhodri.

"You got here, then," Rhodri said, putting a hand on his arm. "We were getting worried. This is Jonno. Jonno, this is Aron."

Jonno stood and shook his hand.

"It's good to meet you at last. Joe hasn't said much." The look in Jonno's eye left him in no doubt this man would punch his lights out if he hurt his friend.

He let go of Jonno's hand and stared at the man behind him. Joe was drop-dead gorgeous with a cherry on the top. His hair had grown and had begun to curl at the ends. Ellie had obviously inherited her curls from her father as well as her eye color. Joe waited, saying nothing while Aron studied him from bottom to top, taking in what he was wearing until he finally stopped at Joe's face. For a moment, they simply stared, neither looking away. Aron noticed the deliberate stubble on Joe's chin and shivered at the thought of feeling it scrape across his skin, cheeks and thighs. He had no idea why, but this man spoke to every part of him.

"It's good to see you again, Joe. You're looking well. I saw Ellic the other morning with your parents. Your mum said she's been fine since that night."

Joe blinked, breaking the connection between them, and Aron caught the glimpse exchanged between Rhodri and Jonno.

"Yeah, Dad told me they met you and your friend."

Was there a hint of jealousy in the way Joe said your friend? Aron decided not to explain about Emrys.

"And Ellie's good, thanks. She's begun to walk on her own now. It's just as well I've got Rhodri working with me as we need eyes in the back of our heads to keep her out of mischief."

Jonno got up. "Why don't you sit here and I'll get us another round?"

Aron sat on the stool next to Joe. Feeling a little overdressed, he removed his jacket and folded it carefully over the pole along the bar. "I'll have the same as you," Aron said, noting the bottles of beer in front of everyone.

"So how's he working out?" Aron asked, nodding at Rhodri.

Joe smiled. "Oh, he's fine. I swear he could charm birds from the trees. He had the women eating out of his hands the other night while serving at this dinner, and he can cook, so if he keeps this up, I may have a permanent job for him when he finishes next year."

Rhodri beamed. He wore enough eyeliner to emphasize the shape of his eyes. His fringe, which dangled across his left eye, had also been dyed purple and his ears contained several silver studs. With his slim figure and boyish good looks, he was every gay man's idea of the perfect twink, and he knew it.

"Can I help it if everyone loves me and wants a piece of my fine arse?"

Jonno returned and placed the beers in front of them. "Is he talking about his arse again?"

Aron couldn't help noticing Rhodri was slightly more flamboyant in Jonno's company and fluttered his eyelashes flirtatiously at the man. He leaned forward and whispered something in Jonno's ear, causing him to blush furiously. When Rhodri kissed his cheek, Jonno glance around nervously. Aron smiled. Rhodri obviously didn't care what anyone thought, and Aron envied his confidence and charm.

"Sometimes he acts like he's got a stick up his arse," Rhodri said. "But I'm working on that. And now you're all staring at me."

Joe broke the moment. "I don't know about you lot, but I'm starving and I've got to be back in a few hours, so can we have some tapas now?"

He spoke to a server who showed them to a booth in the corner. Aron found himself sitting next to Joe on the outside of the booth with Rhodri opposite him and Joe and Jonno on the inside. The heat of Joe's thigh pressed against his own warmed him, despite the air conditioning.

"So you can't stay?" Aron said.

"No, I can't expect Mum and Dad to have Ellie all the time, and I wasn't sure about coming in the first place."

"I'm glad you did," Aron said. It was now or never. "I missed you. I kept thinking—"

Joe stopped him. "I kept thinking about us as well. I know there are problems but…" Joe took a big breath as if he was attempting to steady his nerves and glanced across the table to see Jonno and Rhodri absorbed with their own conversation. He waited.

"I want to see you—spend some time together. My family have been great and Mum wants you to come to dinner. She worries about me being by myself too much."

Aron needed to say something before Joe changed his mind again. "My PA Margaret is much the same. Her son lives abroad, so she likes to mother me instead. Do you have any bookings this weekend? We could get a film in and chill out on the sofa."

"I can't do tomorrow. We're catering a wedding and it'll probably go on into the early evening, but I'm free Sunday. Shall I come round to yours?"

"Oh, right, I thought you'd need to stay in with Ellie, but coming round to mine is good." He wanted to say more, but the food arrived and they spent the next thirty minutes eating. Joe made notes on all of the choices.

"Research," he said. "If this sort of thing becomes popular, I can include it in what I offer, especially for canapés and buffet selections."

The conversation turned to Jonno's new coaching job teaching girls how to box.

"Some of them frighten the hell out of me," Jonno explained. "Rhodri sent a few of his martial arts friends in my direction to learn boxing skills—and bloody hell—they are seriously competitive. It's good, though, and I'm enjoying working with them. It helps keep me fit as well now that I'm not training myself every day. That reminds me, I haven't seen you at the gym lately, Joe. You'll be losing that six pack if you're not careful."

Jonno stared directly at Aron. "You should come and work out with us."

Aron understood a challenge when he heard one. Jonno may have been smaller in stature, but Aron guessed there wasn't any ounce of fat on his entire body. He truly was a pocket dynamo, and such a contrast to Rhodri's whippet-like frame.

"I'm more of a runner," Aron explained. "I try to do at least twenty miles a week. It gives me thinking time as well if I have a difficult problem to work out." Talk turned to exercise regimes and what one should eat, and time flew by.

"Time I wasn't here," Joe said. "I told Mum and Dad I'd be home by nine. I'll order a taxi and go and wait outside."

Aron pulled on his jacket. "I need to be off as well. Busy day tomorrow." He had no desire to play gooseberry with Rhodri and Jonno. The intention had obviously been for him to meet Joe again, not to check that Jonno was all right. "It's been a busy week and I'm completely knackered. Let's share a taxi?"

The car dropped Joe off at his house first then proceeded to Aron's. He hoped he'd done the right thing. Maybe, with time, he could overcome his fears. After all, he'd never spent any time with children before meeting Ellie, and she was cute. In some ways, he couldn't believe Joe had agreed to come to his house. He gazed around. A layer of dust covered many surfaces making the place appear messy and neglected. Tomorrow he'd do some long overdue housework. He hugged himself. Sunday couldn't come soon enough.

Chapter Twenty

"You cooked!" Joe said, his incredulity obvious in his tone.

"Hey, I can cook. It won't be up to your standard, but I thought I'd have a go. I found the recipe for dough and decided on toppings, then created these masterpieces myself. I cooked wedges as well, and there's salad and coleslaw." He was babbling. He'd almost cut his finger off chopping the onions, he was so nervous. And now Joe was sitting in his living room with a slice of pizza in his hand. Aron waited to hear what he said before biting into his own slice. Joe chewed in an exaggerated fashion, making noises as he passed the pizza from side to side in his mouth.

"Well?" Aron questioned. "Is it at least edible?"

"It's good, and I'm impressed you used barbecue sauce, not tomato. It's a nice twist. As is the chorizo. I like the heat and combination of flavors. The base is good, crisp on the outside, but with a soft but not doughy interior. I'd give it a good eight and a half out of ten. I'd certainly patronize this establishment again, and be willing to see what else the chef had to offer."

Aron wasn't sure whether to grin or punch him, but his cock stirred in his trousers at the obvious double entendre. He bit into his own piece and chewed. "It's not bad if I say so myself. So what are we going to watch? I've a few you can choose from."

Joe rose from the sofa, walked over to the large DVD-filled bookcase and examined the choices available. "Captain America?" he asked. "I haven't got round to watching it yet."

Joe took the DVD from the shelf. "I'll put it in and join you on your sofa, if that's all right."

A shiver of anticipation ran through him as Joe put the disk in the side of the large TV screen on the wall then sat next to him. Joe had used aftershave, even though his stubble showed he hadn't shaved that morning. Aron let the aroma fill his senses. For a while, they ate and watched, discussing points in the film, enjoying the lead actor's performance and his portrayal of the superhero. Joe gradually edged closer to him and now had his arm laid casually across the back of the sofa. It would be easy to lean over and kiss him. He was still contemplating it and idly watching the film when Joe moved toward him, put a hand around his face and pulled him forward until their lips met in an open-mouthed kiss. It seemed like forever since he'd tasted him on his lips and tongue. Aron allowed his whole body to press into Joe, suddenly aware that Joe's hand tugged at his belt and zipper before reaching into his jeans. He groaned when Joe massaged his cock over his briefs. Okay, he could go with this. Joe removed his other arm from behind Aron's head and Aron lifted himself away for a moment. Joe's one hand remained in Aron's jeans touching his engorged cock, but Joe had stopped moving. With his other hand, Joe undid his own zipper, reached in and revealed his own now fully erect cock.

Shit, the man came here commando.

Aron gazed into his eyes until Joe glanced down making it obvious what he expected. A little niggle of doubt tried to work its way into Aron's brain, but he shoved it away as Joe put his hands on Aron's head until it was level with his erection. Aron stretched his tongue out and licked around the head, then after taking a moment to appreciate its length, he ran his tongue from balls to tip, tracing the vein underneath. A bead of liquid formed on the tip, and Aron licked it up. He moved his hand to hold the bottom of the shaft, covered the rest with his mouth and sucked in his cheeks. Joe groaned and thrust upward. It wasn't more than Aron could handle, but there was that annoying niggle and he leaned back before taking the head in his mouth again.

Joe clasped his hair and pushed him farther down. "Come on, Aron, you know you want to. You liked me being rough that first time. This is why we're here, isn't it?" He moved to grab Aron once more.

Aron lurched away from him. If Joe had shoved a knife in his chest, he couldn't have sliced his heart in two more skillfully. "Is it?" Aron asked. "Is that why you're here, to come then go?"

Joe tucked himself back into his jeans. "I'm sorry. My father said... Well, that doesn't matter now. I shouldn't have used those words. I don't know what I was thinking. That's not me. I'll go." He began to get up.

Aron pulled him back down on to the sofa. "No. You don't get to walk away this time. What's going on, Joe? I know we didn't have the best of starts, but I thought we'd gotten past the angry phase. You sound angry with me, and I don't think I've done anything to deserve being treated like some sex aid. I thought there was more between us. I know it's awkward with everything else going on, but I want to be more than a quick shag."

Joe put his head in his hands, clearly unable to look Aron in the face. "I don't know, Aron. I thought it would be easier for both of us if we had fun together with no strings on either side. I thought that would suit you too."

Aron tensed then sighed. Unsure what to say next, he stared across the room at the TV. There were advantages to what Joe suggested but…

"Please talk to me, Aron. I can't stand this silence. Tell me. I know I've got this all wrong, I can tell that much, but I've no idea what you want from me. If not this, then what?"

Absentmindedly, Aron watched Pepper Potts save Tony Stark for a change. In a way, Joe was right, sex without strings made sense. Just have fun without the complications of a relationship and all that entailed. He could see how he might have given Joe the impression this was what he wanted, but it wasn't. It would be so much easier if he was able to compartmentalize his life, but he'd never believed in sex for its own sake. He could use his hand or shove something up his arse if he wanted to come. There were plenty of choices. He could go to a club and pick someone up, or even book someone online to come over and fuck him into the mattress, but casual sex had never appealed to him. He knew Joe expected him to say something.

"I suppose you have every reason to think of me like that, and in some ways, I guess you're right, we could shag each other senseless when we meet then walk away and go back to our lives with no complications, but I want more. I don't claim to understand why, but

I like you, Joe. I admire how you look after Ellie and your business, and how you weren't afraid to acknowledge me to your parents. Another person would have thought of an excuse, but you didn't. I know I said I don't like kids. However, there are some aspects of my past I need you to understand. There are reasons for my fears, reasons we need to talk about. I know you and Ellie are a package deal, and it's me who has to change."

"But can you change, Aron? I like you too, you know that, but I have other people to consider. I thought this might be easier and we could walk away whenever we wanted."

"Every extra minute we're together makes it less likely either of us can walk away and, cards on the table, I don't want to. Do you? Despite everything, you came back here after you'd made things quite clear. You could have stayed away." Aron placed his hand on Joe's thigh, needing to re-establish a physical connection between them.

"I know, Aron, but I kept thinking what Angie said about loving someone else and being open to anything and anyone. She told me to open myself up to the possibility of finding love. Until you came into my life, I'd dismissed that possibility. I couldn't stand the thought of not seeing you again, whatever the situation. I suppose I attempted to kid myself about my feelings and have my cake and eat it."

Aron moved closer and put a hand either side of Joe's face. He brought their lips together and simply kissed him then edged back. "I need to explain a few things about my life and my past and for you to listen. I know I have issues, but I want to be more to you than a convenient hole every now and again, although I'll not deny you are rather good at filling it. Let me get us more beer, then I'll explain. No doubt I'll ask for lots of help, but I want to try, Joe. I want to be more than your fuck buddy."

Bit by excruciating bit, Aron told Joe about his childhood and his parents in an effort to give context to his feelings and fears.

"Bloody hell, Aron. No wonder you don't have anything to do with your parents. But where does this leave us?" Joe asked. "I want to say more, and you've no idea how much I want to punch someone. Now I understand why you're so frightened of being around kids. It makes me so angry, but I can't change the past for you no matter how much I wish I could. I want to help, and Ellie likes you. She's asked for you a few times, and that's got to be a good sign. But if we're going to have any sort of future together, you know we come as a package deal. Is it too soon to be thinking about the future? I've got to admit, I've never done the dating thing. When are you supposed to decide?"

Aron allowed himself to relax a little and slumped back on the sofa. "I've no real idea about dating either. When I went to America, I did date a man for a while, but I knew more or less straight away it wasn't going anywhere. He was far more interested in himself. Even in bed, he was more concerned about his appearance and kept checking himself out in the mirror. I expect that's what you get for going out with an underwear model!"

"You dated an underwear model?"

Aron nodded. "It's nowhere near as exciting as it sounds, believe me." He took Joe's hand in his. "I guess I'm going to need some help, but I want to try, so more days out and more time round at yours."

Joe smiled. "That we can do, and you'll have to meet my parents properly. Don't worry, I won't expose you to the whole family at once. I have trouble dealing with them all together myself." He leaned forward and kissed Aron, lightly brushing across his lips. "One more thing."

Aron gulped and sat up straight. Joe matched his posture, held both of his hands and spoke.

"We will still get to have sex, won't we?"

Aron breathed out allowing his whole body to subside then began to shake with laughter.

"You bastard! You had me worried." He pushed Joe back into the sofa, lifted up his T-shirt and kissed up his chest, gratified when Joe moaned loudly and thrust his groin forward.

"I bloody hope we still get to have sex," Aron said. "Starting now." He bit Joe's flesh hard enough to leave a trail of bruises then seized Joe's hand.

"Let's take this somewhere more comfortable, shall we?" He picked up the plate of leftover pizza and pulled Joe off the sofa and toward the stairs. "Sex makes me hungry," he explained.

Joe grinned at him. "Well, in that case, I'm not sure that's going to be enough because I'm going to make sure you feel famished by the time I'm through with you."

Chapter Twenty-One

Rhodri told me you're off to meet the parents tonight."

Aron glanced around, hoping Robbie wasn't within earshot. "Keep your voice down, Dai. I'm not sure if Robbie knows yet, and I don't want to out his brother before he's ready. Let's get this thing fitted to the engine and run the tests again. In theory it should work, but after what happened the last time, I crossing my fingers."

"The last few times," Dai acknowledged. "Did you hear from G4P?"

"Yes, they've begun production and will be fitting our part into their new engines. If the results are consistent, they will refit their older engines too and we get paid every time they do."

"We got to be the parents meeting the boyfriend the other night. Rhodri brought this Jonno around. He seems to have his head screwed on right. I'm not sure how serious Rhodri is though. He's eighteen after all — way too young to settle down. He needs to sow a few wild oats."

"What? Like you did, Dai?" Aron replied, grinning. "There got it."

"All right, it's true Pauline got me young and tamed me, but I'd been around the block with a few willing volunteers before then. There's not a lot else to do in the valleys. I bet you're shitting a brick. I remember the first time I met Pauline's parents. Her dad, enveloped by a fog of Woodbine smoke, barely grunted at me, or peered over his paper. Her mum bustled — that's the only way to describe it. She hardly sat, and I don't think I've ever seen her without an apron and flour all over her hands. She's the one who taught Rhodri how to cook. Pauline's dad's not well now — lung cancer — no surprise there, but so far he's lived longer than they projected. I think her mum is determined to keep him alive. Families, eh?"

Aron nodded and went back to the task in hand. It was going to be a long day, and he needed the distraction.

"Right, throw the switch and stand back."

* * * *

Joe had wanted to come and pick him up so they could arrive together, but Aron insisted he would meet him there. He dressed in his freshly cleaned suit with a white shirt and blue tie. At this rate, he'd need to buy a new one. His shoes shone so much they were probably visible from space. He flattened his hair into some sort of shape — he needed to get it cut — then checked himself in the mirror. He wanted to make a good impression. Before he left, he picked up the large bunch of flowers and the bottle of what Joe assured him was his father's favorite blend of whiskey. Gwennie would be there as well, but he didn't get her anything. Instead, he had a suggestion for her. He took a deep breath and shut the door behind him before walking to his car parked on the drive.

* * * *

Joe's phone beeped to tell him Aron had arrived. "He's here," he said to his parents and sister. "Now, please be nice and don't interrogate him about his intentions. And don't let it slip I told you about his parents."

"But it made me so angry. Parents like his shouldn't be allowed to have children. No wonder he's the way he is," his mother objected.

"I know you want to hug him, Mam. And, Gwennie, don't ask him about Dan Morgan, even though you're desperate to find out if he's any good in bed."

His sister shrugged indifference.

"You're sure he's all right with fish?" his mother asked. She'd been faffing about in the kitchen all evening, but wouldn't let him help.

"It's fine, Mam. I checked. There's no need to push the boat out. He tries to eat healthy, but he's got a sweet tooth if the way he ate my donuts is anything to go by."

Gwennie sniggered.

"Oh, for fuck's sake! That was not a euphemism."

His sister glared at him. "Hadn't you better let him in? He'll be shitting himself out there."

Sue glared at the pair of them. "Your language is appalling, the both of you. Joe, go to the door, for goodness sake, before he changes his mind and runs away. Gwennie, check on Ellie. I thought I heard her murmuring earlier."

When Joe opened the door, he could see Aron parked across the road from his parents' house. He waved and watched Aron get out of the car. No doubt Mrs. Evans would be twitching her curtain across the road, wondering about the identity of their visitor.

"Bloody hell, did you buy Kew Gardens?" he said, seeing the huge bouquet of flowers.

"I wasn't sure what to get, so I got one of everything, and this is for your dad. You said he liked Talisker. I also got him these." He showed Joe the tickets.

"Fuck me! Dad'll want me to marry you if you can get rugby tickets. The All Blacks—he'll be over the moon. How on earth did you get them? They're like gold dust. Men would sell their mothers to get hold of these."

"I still have contacts." Aron winked at him. "Oh, don't look so worried. Iestyn is away on a school trip that weekend, so he asked if I could use them. I thought your Dad might appreciate them."

"He'll be speechless. Come on, let's get you in before Mrs. Evans comes out and flashes her cleavage at you." He followed Aron inside.

They walked down the hall past the front room, so at least he wouldn't have to sit in the parlor as a special visitor with the best china. The second door was slightly open, and he hesitated at the sound of voices coming from inside.

"It'll be fine," Joe assured him then kissed the back of his neck.

"Oh, God, stop that. I don't want to go in there with a huge boner now, do I?"

"You're so easy," Joe said, laughing.

"I am around you. I blame you entirely."

A cry came from the front room.

"I bet she heard your voice," Joe said, smiling. "My daughter obviously can't resist you either. I'll introduce you and fetch her in. It won't hurt if she's up for a while.

I expect she needs changing as she stuffed herself earlier."

Joe went in ahead of him. "Mam, Dad, Gwennie, this is Aron."

"It's good to meet you again and you as well, Gwennie. I got you these, Mrs. Welsh, and this for you, Mr. Welsh."

Another cry came from the front room.

"I'll go and see to her," Joe said "She'll have heard Aron's voice.

Joe's mother got up. "Gwennie went in a few minutes ago. You must have woken her. She'll think she's missing something. D'you want me to go?"

"No, I'll go and bring her through. She probably needs changing."

Aron gazed around the room. It was large, with a conservatory leading off French windows and big enough to contain a couple of sofas, an armchair and a table and chairs for eating. One wall contained floor-to-ceiling bookshelves. The color scheme gave the space a warm feeling and he imagined it being cozy in winter with the now fashionable wood burner throwing out heat. The kitchen at the back, next to the conservatory, had obviously been built as an extension at some point in the house's history.

"These flowers are lovely, and it's Sue and Andy. Mr. and Mrs. Welsh are my parents-in-law. Please, take a seat, Aron. Can I get you something to drink? We've virtually everything."

"Something soft, please. I'm driving. Fizzy water?" He took the seat at the end of the largest sofa adjacent to Andy already ensconced in his armchair.

"Gwennie, would you get a drink for Aron while I put these in water? They are beautiful—you obviously have good taste in all things."

He knew she was talking about her son, not the flowers. In the armchair, Andy sat examining the whiskey. "Joe said that blend was your favorite. I'm a complete ignoramus about whiskey, I'm afraid. I also got you these. Joe said you're a fan, and well, I have contacts."

He handed the envelope over and watched with bated breath as Andy opened them.

"Fucking Nora!"

"Andy! What the hell!"

"Sorry, love, but have you seen what these are?"

"Not from here," she said irritably and placed the flowers on the sideboard among the family photos.

Joe came in carrying Ellie. "You've given them to him, then?"

"You knew he had these?" Andy asked.

"He told me when he arrived," Joe replied, taking the seat next to Aron and putting Ellie on the floor.

She immediately pulled herself to her feet and hung on to Aron's knee. "Run, Run, up."

"Will someone tell me what these *things* are?" Sue asked.

Andy held up the two pieces of paper. "Only a pair of tickets to the Wales versus New Zealand game in a couple of weeks."

Sue sat on the arm of the chair and took them from him.

"Bloody hell. I can't wait to tell them at work."

Joe smiled at Aron, leaned over and whispered in his ear. "I think they might want to adopt you now." He put Ellie between them. "You okay to have her on your lap? A few bounces then she'll want to be off again. You don't have to, but otherwise, she'll not let up."

Aron took a deep breath, worried about managing to hold Ellie with Joe's family in the room. They were on the sofa and safe. At least he couldn't drop her here. "All right, maybe for a few minutes," he said.

Ellie sat on his knee quite happily, pulling his tie which she then shoved in her mouth and chewed. It was silk, but he said nothing. She was a mini Joe, who in turn was a mini Andy. He bounced her on his knee. She let go of his tie, giggled then grabbed his nose.

"Sorry, that's her latest trick," Joe said. "At least your hair is too short for her to tug at. Mum, d'you need any help in the kitchen?"

"No, everything is in hand. In fact, it's time we got up to the table. I'll do the fish now."

Aron sat next to Joe and opposite Gwennie with Andy at the head. A wonderful smell of ginger and onions drifted from the kitchen. For a few minutes, Andy interrogated him about the business and how it was doing, and how Robbie had settled in.

Aron turned to Gwennie. "I wondered if you want to come to the factory and see what we do. I realize engineering isn't exactly your subject, but you might find it interesting as we're working with fuel-saving ideas and you're doing organic chemistry."

"That would be great, but you need to speak to Robbie or he'll wonder what I'm doing there."

"I have to talk to him and Idris anyway. I can't say I'm looking forward to it," Joe said as his mother came through and put plates in front of them.

"Steamed sea bass with ginger, and onions with rice. I hope it's all right. If not blame Jamie Oliver. I hope you don't mind chili."

"No, I love hot things." He noted the warning glare Joe gave Gwennie.

"What? I've said nothing." She lifted Ellie and placed her in the highchair. Sue brought through the rest of the plates and some apple sauce for Ellie.

"This is beautiful," Aron said.

And it was.

"Joe mentioned you keep to a healthy diet."

"Most of the time, but I love a pizza as much as the next man. I try to keep fit by running. I'm not a gym bunny like Joe."

Gwennie fixed her brother with a stare then grinned. There was something entirely wicked in that smile, and Aron feared what was coming next.

"Joe says you're very fond of his donuts."

Aron wasn't going to back away from a challenge. "Okay, I admit, you've got me banged to rights. I love his donuts. They're so round and sweet. My favorites are the ones with the creamy filling." He jerked forward as Joe immediately kicked his ankle and was gratified to see Gwennie almost spit out her food and choke. He wondered if he'd gone too far as her father patted her back.

Andy winked at him. "I think Aron won that round, love. Sue, this is wonderful. Now, lad, Joe's told us little about you except what you do. You're a local boy, aren't you, but your parents live abroad?"

Aron didn't go into any detail. "I see them a couple of times a year," he explained.

"Lovely for a holiday, though, the south of France. Sue and I have never been there, only the north and Paris. I expect you've traveled to lots of places. I've always fancied going to the west coast of Canada for whale watching. When Sue can get time off, we're planning to take the train journey across Canada, then a cruise."

"I've been to a few places. I got to go to Australia and New Zealand, which is similar to Scotland, when Dan was playing there, and I'm hoping to get to China soon. Last year I went to India, but it's mostly been for work recently." He put the cutlery on his now empty plate. "Joe said his nan taught him how to cook, but I think he got some of his skill from you, Sue. That fish was tasty and just the right heat level."

She grinned and glanced at her son. "He's a good line in flattery, I'll give you that. However, I have to admit the dessert isn't my own." She got up and cleared the plates away then brought in the cheesecake. "I've cream or ice cream. Yes, Andy, you can have both."

"So," Aron said mischievously. "What was Joe like as a child? I'm disappointed I haven't seen any naked baby photographs yet, or been told any stories."

Joe frowned. "Oh God, here we go."

Sue swallowed a few sips of wine. "Now, let's think. There was the time he played in his granddad's coal hole. They still had the bunker in their yard and it had never been cleaned. Joe was about five. He came in covered from head to foot in soot, and Nan told him to get cleaned up. He came back downstairs in exactly the same state and held out his hands to say he'd washed them. I think we have the photos somewhere."

"There was also the time when he fell in the compost when he was ten, showing off in front of Jonno," Gwennie added. "God, he stank. They were on Granddad's allotment and didn't realize the middle was liquid below the crust. I wish we'd had video of that one. Jonno laughed so hard, and Joe chased him until he caught him. Mum turned the hose on the pair of them and they ended up running around the garden almost naked."

"At least I didn't show the whole school my knickers playing Mary in the nativity play as you did one year."

Aron guessed this is what having siblings was like. He'd never experienced such family banter.

"Idris was the worst, though," Gwennie continued. "He was always in trouble for doing something or another. It's quite ironic he works in a school now, as he always tried to escape. Students were banned from going out at lunchtime, but Idris decided he wanted to get a burger. He climbed over the fence and fell off, landing on a concrete block. Ended up with a compound fracture and in traction, stupid bugger. He hasn't changed. He still thinks he's fifteen playing video games with his friends."

"I play chess online," Aron said.

"Yeah, but that's chess, not shooting people and running over prostitutes to get points. Those games are so sexist."

By now Ellie had put her head down on her tray.

"I'll put her back in her cot," Gwennie said, picking her up. "Before I go off on one."

"Again," Joe whispered.

"I can't wait until she's fourteen and driving you crazy. I can be her mad auntie, the scientist."

A few hours had flown by. Aron didn't want to outstay his welcome and after coffee, thanked Sue for the food and prepared to leave. "It's been lovely, thanks for inviting me." He wasn't sure whether he should acknowledge the elephant in the room, but it had been a good night, so he plunged in regardless. "I know I'm not exactly who you were expecting Joe to get involved with but..."

Andy put a hand on his arm. "It's okay, son, and you're right, but Joe is a big boy. He's old enough to make his own decisions and we respect them. I'll admit it was a shock, but all we care about is what he thinks. We've always encouraged our children to talk to us. It's been good to meet you. Oh, and thanks for the tickets."

Joe grinned at his father. He escorted Aron to the door. "You survived, then?"

"It's been lovely. Baby steps and all that," Aron replied. Joe kissed him gently, touching his face with his hand as Aron leaned back against the wall.

When Joe had finally finished placing tiny kisses on his face and neck and he'd adjusted his trousers, he said, "I've got to spend a couple of days up north this week, but I'll be back on Thursday morning. Weekends can be busy for you, I know, so I wondered if you were available for dinner and a movie on Thursday, or even if you fancied going out to a club, if you can on a school night. I can't remember the last time I went dancing, and I'm sure Rhodri would give us some idea of where to go that's, um — gay friendly. You said it had been a while since you'd been out on the town."

"I know somewhere good," Gwennie shouted from the other room.

"Bloody big ears," he shouted back. "Honestly. Thinks she's an expert on being gay because she reads m/m romance and slash fanfiction. I expect she thinks we're like a real life example of it."

"Slash what?" Aron asked.

"I'll tell you next time." He kissed him again and opened the door. "Call me while you're away," Joe said, remaining on the doorstep while Aron crossed the road.

Aron waved from his car. Driving off, he could imagine the inquisition Joe was about to face as soon as he walked back in the room. Maybe he was lucky his parents didn't give a damn about him after all.

Chapter Twenty-Two

His mother moved forward first and put her arms around him. "He seems…nice, Joe. He said all the right things, and Ellie's comfortable with him, even if he's not used to children. I'm not sure what I expected. He's sort of ordinary and not at all camp."

"Mum!" Gwennie said. "Really! Not every gay man is camp. He used to go out with Dan Morgan and I know lots of people who'd like to persuade the Welsh rugby captain to change teams. I would myself."

"I realize there are all sorts of gay men, but some are… Well…not that it would be a bad thing if he was camp but… And Graham at the office is great fun, but…well, you know what I mean. All we care is that you like him. You do like him, don't you?"

"Yes, Mam. I know it's not going to be easy, but I don't care what anyone else thinks. You lot are the only people who matter to me, and Ellie of course."

His father gestured for him to sit then nodded to his mother who immediately headed toward the kitchen. Stopping at the door, she said, "I think we could all do with a cocoa. Joe, I've made your bed up and put the cot in there. I assume you're staying tonight."

"Thanks, Mam." He turned to his father and couldn't ignore the worried expression. "What is it, Dad? I can tell there's something. Is it Aron?"

"No, son, it's not Aron. I'm making no judgments about him yet. He's got a good head on his shoulders, and he obviously has feelings for you. I'd have to have been blind not to notice how he smiles at you, as if you were one of those donuts he's so fond of eating."

Gwennie sniggered, and Joe cheeks flushed with warmth. He knew the look his father referred too. It was the one that made him feel like he wanted to throw himself at the man and kiss him all over, the one that held promises of what was to come.

"So what is it?" he asked.

"A lot of people won't understand this, Joe. You were with Angie for years and now you're going out with a man. Some people aren't going to be happy and lots will think they have the right to tell you how to live."

"That's their problem," Gwennie said firmly.

"Don't be naïve, Gwennie," her father said, gripping the arm of his chair. "For one thing the Nashes aren't going to be pleased. Have you thought about that? I doubt having a homosexual in the family will go down well with them. They wanted to take Ellie from you when Angie died because her father said single men shouldn't bring up children. I can imagine what he'll be like when he finds out you're in a relationship with a man. What if you decide to move in together? How long before he starts talking Sodom and Gomorrah and God's wrath raining down, not to mention quoting Bible passages at you about man shall not lie with man?"

"I'll have to be careful around them, won't I? At least Ellie is too young to mention Aron to them. But if they want to see her, they're going to have to live with it. She's my daughter and I'll bring her up how I see fit. I told them I didn't want her to be indoctrinated with their beliefs, and if our relationship becomes more serious, we'll cross that bridge when we come to it."

Sue put the cocoa in front of them and sat next to him. "All your dad is saying is be careful. You can't be casual about relationships, Joe, when you've someone else to consider other than yourself. You were ever so lucky with Angie, and I'm worried you're going out with Aron because there's no other woman who will ever measure up to her. You know, despite the fact they've thrown themselves at you, you haven't even glanced at another woman, then Aron comes along and suddenly things change."

He picked up his mug, feeling the warmth in his hand. Every night his parents drank cocoa before they went to bed. It was a family tradition. "I hear what you're saying, both of you, and maybe you're right. You aren't the first to mention this. I can't explain why him or why now, but come on, Mam, your nan and granddad weren't exactly thrilled when you started to go out with a truck driver you'd met in a pub while you were at university. But you married him anyway. No doubt a few people made comments about Dad taking care of us and you going to work, and how unnatural your arrangement was compared to the norm. I'm damn sure I wouldn't have survived Angie's death and looking after Ellie without your help and example. That's why I knew you'd welcome Aron. You two are special." The sting of tears threatened, and Joe wiped his eyes. He swallowed a few mouthfuls of cocoa. "I'll get Ellie and go to bed now if that's all right. Bill and

Penny are taking her for the day tomorrow morning while I go to the gym with Jonno. After I've collected Ellie, we're all going to eat out at the White Horse. There's a new chef there and I want to check out his food. Jonno and I haven't caught up on our own for ages and we've a lot to discuss. Thanks for tonight."

Upstairs, he settled Ellie in the cot and sat on his old bed. His posters and books now gone, the room had been repainted, but his old single bed remained in place and the furniture was the same as he'd grown up with. He picked up the photo of Angie next to his bed. He remembered the day so well down at Barry Island Beach. She'd worn a bikini with ties and the top had come undone, leaving her waving for help in the sea. He hoped she'd understand his relationship with Aron and approve. He still missed her all the time and there was no one he'd rather have talked to about what was happening in his life. She'd always believed in him and supported him. No doubt if she was there, she'd tell him to stop being so bloody maudlin and get on with living. He switched off the light and turned over.

Chapter Twenty-Three

It was an odd thought. If someone had told him he'd be sitting in a pub with his daughter, watching his best friend get them both a pint before they discussed their relationships with the men in their lives, he'd have wondered if he'd been abducted by aliens, or fallen though some door into a parallel universe. Yet, when Jonno returned and put the drinks on the table, Joe knew their respective—what partners would be the central part of their conversation. Nothing would be said about the latest football results, anything on the news, or last night's episode of *Bake Off,* and definitely wouldn't be any talk of the barmaid's obvious attributes. It was a strange and mysterious world both of them had recently entered into.

Joe picked up his pint and swallowed several mouthfuls. Jonno did the same. Neither of them said anything. Joe pressed his palm to his knee to stop it from shaking.

Since when have I ever been nervous talking to Jonno?

In the end, Jonno broke the silence. "This place seems to be all right." He glanced around at the new décor.

Joe had chosen to sit in a booth at the back of the main room, considering the way their conversation might go. He didn't want anyone listening to what they had to say.

"I wanted to check out the food. There's new management in place and I've heard the chef is good. I like to keep an eye on food trends and it's good to get out of the city and breathe some country air."

"Yeah, the smell of manure always makes me hungry." Jonno pulled a menu from its holder and perused the choices. "Starter or pudding?"

"Starter," Joe said. "Then, if we've room, we can have a pudding. We worked off lots of calories this morning. They have baby food choices as well."

"But she's asleep," Jonno said.

"She'll probably wake on her own when she smells the food."

Jonno grinned. "Like father, like daughter. Right, I'm going to have the breaded Camembert, then the steak and ale pie with veg."

"And I'll have the goat's cheese tart followed by the stuffed chicken with their chips cooked three times. The menu has standard fare—nothing fancy. I hope the food lives up to its reputation as it's not exactly cheap. I'll get her macaroni cheese bake. Pasta is her latest thing." With that Ellie stirred in her seat and opened her eyes.

"See? I told you. Any talk of food and madam is alive and kicking, aren't you, angel? I'll ask the waitress for a highchair." He waved his hand and someone appeared immediately to take their order.

"Aw, she's beautiful." The waitress labeled Jess took their order then turned her attention to Ellie. "She's the spitting image of you, so I guess you're Dad."

"Guilty as charged," Joe replied. "Can we have a highchair for her?"

Jess glanced from Joe to Jonno obviously trying to work out their status. From the serene smile Jonno had on his face, it was clear he was about to say something. Joe kicked him before he could speak then glared at him. Jonno lifted Ellie from her carry seat.

"Come to Uncle Jonno then, sweetheart." He tickled her tummy, and she giggled, kicking her legs out until he let her stand on the seat next to him, holding her hands as she bounced excitedly.

"I'll get you that chair, sir."

Joe turned his attention back to Jonno and Ellie.

"She's getting good at standing," Jonno said.

"Tell me about it. Rhodri and I have trouble keeping up with her. I'm investigating putting her into nursery when Dad can't have her. So—one of us has to say it. How's your love life? Rhodri doesn't tell me anything, but he has an annoying habit of grinning at me a lot then staring off into space, as if he's remembering something. I guess things are going well between you."

A waiter brought the highchair, and Joe settled Ellie into it. He got out a few toys, and she played happily, bashing them on the tray and saying their names.

"I told them at work," Jonno announced. "I figured I may as well, so that's everyone."

"How did they take the news?"

"Much as I expected. Some were fine, some huddled together in corners and weren't happy. There have been a few backs to the wall jokes, and Pete has been a complete divvy as always, but he's avoiding me, so that's wonderful, as I can't stand the bastard. My usual crew have been fine about it."

"And Rhodri?"

"Rhodri is fun. It's impossible to feel down when he's around. I've never met someone so up all the time. He sees the good in everything. I swear he could charm the birds from the trees. I've never met a person with so many friends. When we go out, there's always someone coming up and hugging him. Girls throw themselves at him until he introduces me as his boyfriend. I'm getting used to it. I've been to all sorts of places and we've even been dancing."

Joe sniggered.

"Yeah, I know, me dancing, but he's infectious. He drags me out on the floor and rubs himself against me. He has no fear." Jonno looked both ways then leaned in. "I've had so many hard-ons in public I've had to buy roomier jeans or I'm going to get arrested. I'm only six years older than him, but he makes me feel like an old man. And the sex is bloody amazing."

Their starters arrived, and they both tucked in.

"This tart is good. How's the Camembert?" Joe asked.

"As you'd expect, really. So, what about you and Aron? How was the family visit?"

"Run. Run." Ellie gazed around the room. Joe put some cheese on her spoon and gave her a taste. She put it in her mouth then spat it out. "Acky."

"Maybe too soon for goat's cheese."

"Run."

"Aron's not here, sweetheart. You'll have to make do with me and Uncle Jonno. She can't say Aron so she calls him Run and the dinner was good. Mum and Dad like him."

"And the baby issue?"

"We're working on that. He told me about his childhood and I get it now. I'll tell you this, Jonno, some parents shouldn't be allowed to have kids. His didn't want him, and they made sure he knew it. When your parents tell you you're an inconvenience all the time, it's no wonder he thinks the way he does," he explained further.

Jonno put his knife and fork on the plate. "Goes to show you can have an education and jobs which suggest you should know better, but you can still have no nurturing skills at all."

Ellie banged the table again.

"Pasta soon," Joe told her.

"So you reckon there's a future in it? You and Aron?"

"I don't know, and I have Ellie to consider. I don't want a parade of men or women coming in and out of her life, but yeah, I like him. He's a strange mixture. Sometimes, he's the most confident man in the world. Get him talking about his work, or chess, or flying, and he's like a different person — he lights up. At other times, he's so uncertain and nervous. Ellie adores him and won't leave him alone. He's so scared of doing something wrong with her, yet when she had that fit, I fell to pieces and he stayed calm. I can't tell you how grateful I was he was there. And it's been so long since I've had someone. I know Angie told me not to be alone, but I couldn't bring myself to even go out with anyone else. With him, it's like lightning struck and I can't get enough. The first time we had sex was wild. I was angry at the world and allowed all my frustration to pour out of me."

Jonno smirked.

"I know, don't look at me like that. You'll be rolling your eyes next and that's as much detail as you're going to get. But you know how hard it was after Angie died. Only Dad telling me I'd lose Ellie made me pull myself together, especially when Angie's parents tried to get custody. I wouldn't have coped without Mum and Dad and Gwennie and you." He clasped Jonno's hand. "You do realize that I wouldn't have gotten through the last year without you. You have been the best friend a man could wish for. I'm sorry I had no idea you had feelings for me. I had no idea about anything, really, other than getting this business up and running and keeping Ellie healthy. I'm sorry if I hurt you."

A noise made them pull apart. The waiter hovered with the main courses and the baby food for Ellie, who waved her spoon enthusiastically.

Joe grinned when he spotted the young man talking earnestly to Jess at the bar. He'd obviously reported back on the hand holding.

"Here you go, Ellie—yummy pasta." Ellie swallowed the first mouthful then demanded more. He gave her the spoon and she messily attempted to feed herself while Joe cut into his chicken. For a few minutes, they sat in silence eating their food.

"You did hurt me," Jonno said, breaking the silence. "I'd allowed myself to build this fantasy that you'd suddenly realize and we'd live happy ever after. Pathetic, I know."

"No, not really," Joe replied softly. "So, you and Rhodri? You obviously like each other. Is it serious?"

Jonno shook his head. "I don't think so. He's eighteen and has no plans to settle down. Life's fun and I'm having fun *with* him. Few people meet someone when they're so young and stay with them. I've told myself to live each day and see where it goes. I'm new to this as well, new to being out, new to letting other people see us. He'll take my hand in public and not care a jot. We were sitting in a café last week, and he leaned over and kissed me. I went puce. I stared around, convinced someone would want to hit me or throw us out of the place, but all I got was a little old lady smiling at me. When she left, she stopped at the table and said, 'Hold on to love. You never know when it's going to come into your life or when it'll leave'. It turned out her husband of fifty-five years had died a few weeks before. So I'm hanging on to his coat-tails and enjoying the ride." A huge grin spread across his face and his cheeks flushed red. "Sometimes literally."

Joe snorted and barely avoided choking. "I can understand that." He raised his fork. "This chicken is good. I like the haggis stuffing, and the vegetables are a change from the normal fare. How's yours?"

"Meat's good, lean and not gristly at all, and the puff pastry is melting in my mouth. Here," he said, putting some on his fork. "Taste this."

Joe took the food off the fork and chewed, knowing how the gesture might appear to others. "Mmm, you're right and the gravy's got a really good flavor from the ale." He smiled at the mess surrounding Ellie. "She's enjoying her mac and cheese." He fed her the rest then wiped up the excess.

"She's got some in her hair," Jonno said.

"She usually does. It's getting so curly now."

They both finished.

The waiter came to remove the plates. "Was everything all right for you both?"

"Yes, the food was very nice, thanks. Can we have two cappuccinos and the bill please?"

Finally, as they drank their coffees, they did get around to discussing the football and the new season and whether City would bounce back up. They discussed the biscuit sculptures made on *Bake Off* and whether Joe should make something similar for parties. However, they didn't get around to discussing Jess' attributes, although Jonno did mention the waiter had a tight butt.

In the car park, Jonno pulled Joe in for a hug. "It's been good to see you again. Rhodri says I've got to get you and Aron out dancing, so what about some time the weekend after next? Rhodri said you were busy this Saturday."

"We are, but there's nothing in the diary for next Saturday. It's been a while since I've shaken my stuff on the dance floor."

"Will your parents or Gwennie babysit?"

"Gwennie will want to come, knowing her," Joe said. "I'll ask Mum and Dad. I'm sure they'll be all right. It's Aron I'm not sure about. He did mention going out when he's back from his trip, but I think he'd prefer dinner and a movie. I'll do my best to persuade him."

He secured Ellie in her seat, climbed into the driver's side and wound down the window. "I'll ring you, Jonno."

Rhodri would be waiting for him when he got home. He'd left him making pastry for the various pies they'd added to the Friday sandwich run. In the back, Ellie pushed her toys across the rail in front of her.

"Now, it would help Daddy if you didn't throw up your dinner on the drive home."

She gave him a condescending look, as if such a thing was impossible, and went back to trying to pull the head off a dinosaur. He put the car into gear and drove out through the gate.

Chapter Twenty-Four

Aron gazed around the room. Sweat covered his skin, but he had no intention of removing his shirt as many of the other dancers had done already. He wanted to believe he was too old for all this, but many of the men in the club appeared older. He sipped his mineral water and watched Rhodri and his friends twirling round and around in the center of the dance floor. Hot breath tickled the back of his neck. Before he could turn, Joe hugged him from behind then wrapped his arms around Aron's waist. He leaned back.

"I'm not sure this is right for either of us," Joe said. "Jonno's giving Rhodri a run for his money, though. It's too much of a cattle market out there for me and I daren't go into the toilets again."

Aron turned around in Joe's arms. "Never fancied a quick blow job in the loo?"

"Not my thing."

Aron glanced down then up, scanning the body in front of him and ended by staring into Joe's eyes.

Joe stared back, his expression questioning. "You haven't? Really? What, you and Dan?"

Aron nodded and bit his bottom lip. "In my defense, I was sixteen, and it was at our school prom. We nearly got caught as well. These days, I prefer the comfort of a bed to being on my knees on some damp floor covered with God knows what."

"Angie and I nearly got caught in other places. We did it in her dad's shed once on his allotment. He arrived earlier than we expected. Angie stayed as cool as a cucumber while I shook until he left." He took Aron's hand. "Let's get out of here, shall we? I promised you a surprise at home."

"Oh, yeah, so you did." Aron shifted in his seat as his trousers tented remarkably fast.

"Whoa, don't get overexcited yet." Joe grinned. "Save it for when we get to my place. I've prepared a little something."

He moved forward and kissed Aron, taking his bottom lip and sucking on it, unconcerned who might see them.

Aron relaxed into the kiss for a moment then pulled away. "That's not helping my trouser situation, you know."

Joe laughed. "No one's going to notice your erection around here. This place is full of them." He pointed over to where Rhodri wriggled back against Jonno, who had his hands under Rhodri's shirt. Next to them, Gwennie danced with a few friends from university, her hair flying around her head.

"I'll let them know we're leaving and meet you outside. Call us a taxi."

Aron edged past the crowded bar area to the exit. A pleasant breeze cooled his warm skin. He rang for a car while waiting for Joe to join him. He didn't have to wait long.

"All right?" he asked.

"Yeah, Rhodri told us to have fun, even if we were party poopers. I told him we would."

The car pulled up and they got in. A bubbling sense of excitement swirled in Aron's belly. He had no idea what activity Joe had in mind for when they got back to his house. He'd dropped a few hints at dinner when he'd warned Aron not to have dessert because they'd be having something later. Joe was a chef after all. They didn't talk to each other on the way home, but Joe kept his thigh next to his while the taxi driver prattled on about the prospects for the Welsh rugby team in the upcoming World Cup.

"Got to say they've been so much better since Morgan took charge. D'you like rugby?"

An elbow poked Aron in the ribs. "You going to tell him then?" Aron nudged Joe back forcibly.

"Don't all Welshmen love rugby?" he asked.

The conversation continued about Dan's attributes until Aron got another dig in the ribs. "Oi, current boyfriend sitting here, and you're waxing lyrical about your ex and the size of his muscles."

Aron stopped talking and turned to stare at Joe. "Is that what we are?"

The taxi drew to a halt. Joe paid the fare and they climbed out of the back. After the car drove away, Aron followed Joe into the house. When the door closed, he maneuvered him back against the door. "You didn't answer my question."

"Which question?" Joe teased.

"The boyfriend question."

"I'm not one for labels, but we have been going out with each other, and you've met my parents, so I suppose I'm beginning to think of you as my boyfriend. Do you mind?"

Aron stared at Joe. His green eyes shone even in the relative darkness of the hall, but he seemed worried about how Aron might answer.

"No, I don't mind," he replied honestly.

"It sounded like there was a 'but' at the end of that."

"Not really, it's early days yet, and maybe I'm a little cautious. But that's me."

"We both have a lot to think about here, but you know I like you, Aron, and I'm prepared to take the risk that we might have something here."

Joe grabbed Aron's arse and pulled him forward so they were flush against each other, their lips millimeters apart. Aron closed the gap, putting a hand either side of Joe's face and kissing him until both opened their mouths to each other. Joe's growing erection pressed into his. After a while, Aron moved back slightly. "You said you had a surprise for me," he whispered.

Joe grinned and a shiver of excitement caused the hair on the back of Aron's neck to stand at attention. "I need about ten minutes. Why don't you go into the kitchen and get the bottle of wine I left in the fridge and a couple of glasses. Come up when I call you?"

Aron waited eight long minutes for Joe to shout down. He spent the time thinking about anything other than whether this was the right thing to do. An aroma of warm chocolate reached his nose as he made his way up the stairs and along the landing to the large bedroom at the front of the house. At first, all Aron could see was a bare knee through the slightly open door. When he pushed it, Joe was sitting cross-legged and completely naked with a tray of fruit, biscuits and nuts placed on his knees. Next to the bed, on a small table, stood the source of the smell.

"I hoped I'd find a use for this fondue set one day," Joe said. "Why don't you pour us a couple of drinks?"

Aron worked the cork out of the bottle of sparkling wine and filled the glasses. He handed one to Joe who'd placed the tray next to the fondue dish.

"Cheers," Joe said as they clinked the glasses together.

Joe tugged him closer and began to undo the buttons of his shirt. Aron couldn't wait and dragged it over his head while Joe undid his own trousers and removed them and his briefs in one fluent movement. Aron shrugged off his shoes and socks then stepped out of the rest of his clothes until he too stood completely naked. Joe reached over and grabbed of one of the fondue sticks. He ran the chocolate-covered head down Aron's chest. It felt warm, not hot, on his skin.

"I thought the chocolate was for dipping the food?" Aron said, unable to stop his voice cracking. Every nerve in his body was concentrated on that strip of warm skin as Joe ran his tongue up the line of the chocolate. The effect on Aron's cock was instantaneous as it sprang to attention. Aron placed a hand on Joe's shoulder to steady himself and bolster his trembling knees. Having finished the chocolate, Joe reached over, skewered a strawberry from the tray and dipped it into the sauce.

"Open up," he said.

Aron did as he was told, and Joe put the fruit between his teeth. Aron bit into it and the sweet juice and chocolate coated his tongue as he swallowed. Next came mango then raspberry. Aron swallowed them all, savoring the sweet flavors along with the chocolate.

"Try this," Joe said.

Aron hadn't seen what Joe did with the strawberry, but the sensation of flavor on his tongue was wonderfully different.

"Tastes like pepper," he said.

"It is. I told you they tasted good this way."

"That's weird. It shouldn't work, but it does."

Joe patted the bed. Aron sat cross-legged facing him, and for a while they fed each other a mixture of fruit and biscuits covered in warm chocolate and drank more wine. They were none too careful and chocolate dripped onto knees, thighs and chins. Each drip was removed with fingers held out for the other to suck or lick, tongues slowly covering upper then lower lips, making them shine. In the end, Aron could stand it no more. Taking a stick, he flicked chocolate over Joe's broad chest, pushed him backward and began to lick off every drop, finishing by circling each nipple. Some of the drips had landed on the small patch of dark hair between each nub that trailed downward.

"You're going to be so sticky," Aron said.

"So we'll have to finish the evening off in the shower," Joe said, winking.

Aron moved until he was astride Joe, his erection resting on Joe's stomach. Joe's hardness pressed between the cheeks of his arse as he wiggled. Joe reached under the pillow and pulled out lube and a condom.

"Scoot up nearer," he said. Aron didn't need to be asked twice. Joe covered his fingers in lube and prepared him.

"That's enough," he said, changing position.

"Put it on me."

Joe handed the condom to Aron, who rolled it over Joe's leaking cock, then covered it with more lube before he maneuvered himself into the right place and lowered himself until he had Joe buried deep inside him. For a moment, he sat still luxuriating in the feeling of fullness, then he moved up and down, teasing the man underneath him. With a strawberry between his teeth, he leaned over and brought it near enough for Joe to bite one half. Juice dribbled down Joe's chin, and Aron licked it off. Moving slowly, he picked up a chocolate-covered stick and dripped the still warm liquid onto Joe's tongue then onto his nipples. Aron curled his tongue around each nub.

"You do realize I'm never going to be able to have fruit or chocolate again without thinking of this," he said as he increased his movements and met Joe's now insistent thrusts. He steadied himself, covered his own cock with lube and began to stroke. The room filled with the sound of groans and skin slapping against skin as he and Joe increased the pace. Aron let Joe take control, staying still as he thrust up into him again and again. He guessed Joe was close and working hard to come before he did. Without much warning, Aron's orgasm burst from him. He pumped his cock sending streams of white liquid across Joe's stomach. Seconds later, Joe rose up and Aron felt warmth fill the condom.

"Oh, fuck," Joe cried. "Bloody hell, your arse. I think you squeezed that orgasm out of me."

Aron gazed down at the mess across Joe's chest—chocolate mixed with his own spunk. "You're like a marbled chocolate cheesecake," he said, running his fingers through the liquid. He offered his fingers to Joe who sucked on them with enthusiasm.

"Hmm, tastes yummy, like salted cocoa instead of caramel. Maybe it would make a good donut filling after all."

Aron lifted himself and removed the condom, putting it over the side of the bed into the nearby bin. "Shower," he said. "Then sleep."

"Not going to argue with you," Joe said, moving to sit at the edge of the bed. He unplugged the fondue set then got up, taking Aron's hand and pulling him out of the room to the bathroom. Fifteen minutes later, Aron heard Joe snore as he lay spooned against his back. He smiled to himself and wriggled closer to the man behind him. He was happy. Work was good, and he was beginning to fall hard. He needed this, and he wanted it more than words could say. If he had problems to solve, he'd work through them. Joe would help him overcome his fears. He'd begin tomorrow, wouldn't he?

Chapter Twenty-Five

Joe stood at the sink looking out of the window at his garden. A few weeks had passed since their night of sex and sauce. Luckily, the stains had come out of the sheets. Summer would soon be over and the leaves were already turning brown and beginning to fall in the strong breezes.

"I think Daddy will have to cut the lawn this weekend," he said to Ellie, who sat in the corner, trying to put one block on top of another.

His mobile buzzed next to him and he smiled seeing the name — Aron. He'd now met Aron's friends, Evan and Beth, as well as Emrys. Ellie had fallen in love with the big man at once, especially after he'd presented her with a collection of wooden animals he'd carved himself.

Joe picked up his mobile and pressed the green button. "Hello, you," he said, unable to keep the smile out of his voice.

The answering, "Hi," was hesitant.

"Aron? What's up?" Clearly something was.

"Sorry, I needed to hear your voice. Is Ellie all right?"

"Ellie's fine. She's got a bit of a sniffle, but other than that she's busy trying to build a big tower. Penny and Bill will be over later to have her this evening. She's been such a good girl while I've been making quiches and sausage rolls for a party I'm catering. It's got a Seventies theme, so I'm making sausages on sticks, and a cheese and pineapple hedgehog. I've got Black Forest gateaux to make as well. Come on, spill the beans. What are you not telling me? Something's obviously bothering you."

"My mother called. My parents coming to Cardiff for a medical conference next week."

"Do I get to meet them?" Joe asked.

"I wasn't sure if you'd want to, but I invited them to lunch on Wednesday. I know you're not working and I'd like you to bring Ellie as well."

"Are you sure? I'm sure Dad will look after her."

"No, I want them to meet you and her. You come as a pair. I'm not hiding anything from them."

"Right, then I'm going to make lunch for us all," Joe said.

"But…"

"No buts, Aron. I'm not a guest at this lunch. I'm your boyfriend, and Ellie is my daughter. We'll both be hosts, you and I, and I want them to see that. I want them to see us together as a partnership, to know how much you matter to me. I will make them the most gorgeous gourmet lunch they've ever had — better than any five-star hotel meal." He realized how vehement he sounded.

"Thanks, Joe. It means such a lot to have you there, and if that's what you want, that's how we'll do it. Why don't you bring Ellie to stay the night before?"

"She'll love that. I hope you're ready to read several stories. She prefers you reading to her. It must be your voice. I have to say it does things for me as well, and now you're blushing, aren't you?" He loved how he could get Aron all hot and bothered. He lowered his voice deliberately. "I love it when you talk dirty."

"Bastard. Now I'll have to hide behind this desk if Margaret comes in."

"I aim to please," Joe replied. "Now, I'd better get Ellie sorted before the happy couple arrive. I'll plan what we're going to have then run it by you. Don't worry, it'll be fine and if it isn't, it doesn't matter."

"Thanks for doing this."

Joe heard a female voice.

"That's Margaret come in to sort the arrangements for the demonstration we're doing next week. Your brother came up with an idea for something new, which I have to say is brilliant, if we can develop it. We're going to throw some plans around tomorrow. I'll tell you about it later, but for now, it's top secret."

"Good to know Robbie's useful for something. Okay, I'll get off now. See you soon." He pressed the red button and disconnected. "Right, young lady, let's make you presentable for Nanna and Granddad."

Angie's parents were the only spanner in the works at the moment. True, Aron still found dealing with Ellie difficult at times. He still hadn't changed a nappy, or been on his own with Ellie, but he could hold her now—Ellie had insisted on it. She adored him, and went to sleep much more quickly when Aron read to her. But Joe hadn't told Bill and Penny about himself and Aron and he wasn't sure how he would ever find a way. At some point it would come up. Ellie would mention something as her vocabulary got bigger, and Joe didn't want to lie and say Aron was just a friend.

Half an hour later, the doorbell rang. He picked up the bag and took Ellie's hand to walk her to the door. She was much more confident on her feet now and often demanded to walk rather than be carried. He opened the door to Penny. Bill would be at work at the tax office.

"There she is," Penny said. "My, aren't you a clever girl walking by yourself, and don't you look beautiful?"

"Thanks for the dress," Joe said. "The rest of her clothes are in the bag. D'you want to take her?" He lifted Ellie over the step and followed Penny to the car with the buggy and bag, then packed things into the boot and strapped Ellie into her baby seat.

"You be a good girl for your nanna and granddad, and I'll see you tomorrow. She had a runny nose, Penny, but I think she's all right. Keep an eye on her temperature, will you? I've put a thermometer in the bag. If she's gets hot, don't put too many covers on her. I'm sure she'll be fine, though." He said it as much to assure himself as he did them. Part of him hated to see her go. He had no idea what they said to her when he wasn't there.

"We know what to do, Joe. She's in good hands. We've got a fan and it's been quite cold overnight. I've got some baby medicine if she needs something, and your phone number."

Joe shut the door and waved to Ellie through the window. Time to get back to the Seventies, then to the books to find the perfect lunch to make for Aron's parents.

* * * *

Aron's parents loved seafood, so Joe settled on a menu after some research. For starters, he planned a smoked salmon gateau, which always went down well at parties, layering the salmon with cream cheese and a simple little dressed salad on the side. Not too heavy to start a meal with. For the main course seafood pasta with a twist and with mussels and chorizo and other fishy bits in season. He'd be visiting Cardiff market's famous fish stall to get the freshest available in the morning. Finally, dessert would be a classic crème brûlée.

"Let's hope they like it all," he said to Rhodri the next day as they packed the food to take to the buffet.

"Do I have to wear these?" Rhodri asked, swishing his flared trousers to and fro.

"Yes. If I have to, you have to. Come on, you suit those flares, and these wide-collared shirts are something else. At least I haven't made you wear velvet or, God forbid, a tank top."

"Is Ellie with your parents today?"

"Yes, I feel guilty as I won't get to see her until later today. I'll pick her up when we've finished. At least this is a lunch party and I've nothing on tonight. I'm going to do a practice run tomorrow on the food for lunch with Aron's parents if you want to help."

"I guess it's serious with you and him if you're meeting the parents and he's met yours." Rhodri finished packing the plates and cutlery and transported it to Joe's newly acquired van, complete with the company name on the side. Joe followed him out and put in the last of the food then climbed into the driver's seat, conscious he hadn't answered Rhodri's question.

"So, is it serious, you and Aron?" Rhodri asked again. "You can tell me to mind my own business."

Joe sighed not sure exactly how to reply. "I think so. We're building something good together, but I have to say, I'm shitting bricks about meeting his parents on Wednesday. Aron's told me about his childhood and it doesn't make them sound good, but we see life differently when we're children. He spent most of his time with his au pair and Dan Morgan's family. I suppose his parents were both busy doctors. His mum's back over here to give a talk at a medical conference. She still does consulting work in France as well."

Rhodri shrugged. "Sometimes I'm glad my parents are ordinary. Though both of them worked, they always had time for Mel and me. I guess sometimes you don't appreciate how lucky you are."

* * * *

The meeting had gone well. Aron gathered together the notes and diagrams he'd made as people left the room. Robbie's idea, that they should investigate designing something to identify the safe level of dust in the atmosphere for flying, was an interesting one and something that might have legs. He glanced up to see Robbie standing at the other end of the table.

"This is a sensational idea, Robbie. We need to see if we can find out what's out there already. Research is the key." He couldn't help noticing Joe's brother appeared rather uncomfortable as he wrung his hands.

"Is there anything else?" Aron asked.

"Umm, I spoke to my dad last night, and he told me about you and Joe. I thought you should know and it's all right. I didn't want it to be awkward, us working together. I can understand why you didn't tell me, although Joe should have."

Aron let out the breath he'd been holding. "I'm sorry you weren't told before. It was up to Joe to tell you. Anyway, I'm glad. If it makes you feel better, you were hired because of you, not because I knew Joe. Dai had no idea when he interviewed you, and you got the job on merit. I happen to think Dai is a good judge."

Robbie blushed. "Thanks, boss. I'll get going on that research and see what sort of thing we might be dealing with. With the possibility of that volcano in Iceland going up again, I think there'll be competition to produce something as accurate as possible and soon."

After Robbie's departure, Aron leaned back in his chair. His thoughts turned to the meeting with his parents, now only a couple of days away. It had been several months since he'd seen them, during a flying visit between meetings in Europe. Joe would be more nervous than he was, and Aron had no idea how his mother would react to Joe having a daughter. At least she wouldn't feel obliged to play grandmother to Ellie. Even so, he wanted them to like Joe. For some reason their opinion still mattered.

Chapter Twenty-Six

"Stop worrying. You're like a cat on hot bricks this morning." Joe wrapped his strong arms around him and pressed his soft lips to back of Aron's neck. "At least Ellie slept last night, so hopefully she won't be grizzly today. She's recovered from that sniffle she had and her temperature is normal."

"She's certainly in good voice this morning." Aron glanced over to where Ellie made noises and banged her spoon along to the music from the radio.

Joe picked her up and sat her on his lap to give her breakfast.

"Luckily, she's a happy kid. She may be unfortunate and be the spitting image of her dad, but she's got her mum's positive nature, haven't you, sweetheart?"

Aron gazed out of the French doors to the garden. The small breakfast table gave a good view of the birds eating the seed he'd put out in the early morning sunshine. He liked to sit and watch them as he drank his coffee and ate his cereal.

"You don't mind me talking about Angie, do you?"

Aron caught the look of concern in Joe's expression and reached a hand over to touch his arm. "No, of course not. I still talk about Dan at times. It's inevitable that's going to happen. You have Ellie, and Dan is still newsworthy, especially with the World Cup coming up. Right, what do you want me to do this morning? It's warm out there, so we can play outside. It'll be all right if she runs around on the grass. I told Mum and Dad lunch would be served at one, and they're always on time. Being punctual is one of Dad's obsessions."

"Sounds good. She'll love running about out there. Watch her on the patio, though—she's still unsteady at times. We can change her clothes before they arrive, so you can let her play in the mud until then. I'll make the salmon and the crème brûlée early, and do the pasta just before serving. I need to make my special dressing for the salad as well. It's all in hand as long as I can get the ingredients. I checked yesterday about the mussels and they promised they'd have some fresh in today. Are you sure you're okay keeping an eye on Ellie while I'm out? I shouldn't be more than forty-five minutes as long as I get a parking space, and it's early yet."

"We'll be fine. Go on, you'd better get off. I'm looking forward to that pasta dish." He hoped he sounded more confident than he felt. In truth, he was terrified, but this was a test—like some rite of passage. Ellie liked him, which made life easier. Over the last few weeks, Aron had been on his own in a room with her while Joe was busy, and she hadn't cried. He supposed she was used to a variety of faces.

"Right, young lady. You be a good girl for Aron." Joe passed her over and Aron placed her on his hip. Immediately she grabbed his nose. "Run."

"Ouch! She's got quite a grip." Gently, he pulled her fingers down. "Wave to Daddy. Say bye-bye."

Joe kissed them both and headed out of the door. Aron carried Ellie through to the garden and set her on the grass with her toys. He joined her sitting cross-legged in front while she played.

"So, it's you and me, kid, and forty minutes isn't that long, is it?"

* * * *

Joe returned an hour later with the ingredients he needed to find Aron with Ellie sitting on his lap on the sofa reading to her. As one o'clock got closer, Aron couldn't sit without fidgeting and kept pacing the kitchen, waiting for the doorbell to ring.

"For God's sake, take Ellie into the living room and read to her again or sing her nursery rhymes — anything but pacing behind me. The food is ready, and I'll make the main course when they arrive. Ellie's new clothes are great. You did a good job choosing her outfit and it'll last her a while. She's growing like mad at the moment."

"They do that if you feed them," Aron replied, picking her up. "So do you want to hear more stories, little one? Daddy wants us out of the kitchen."

"Come here," Joe said.

"What?"

Joe kissed his daughter, then Aron. "I won't be able to do that for a while. Now, calm down. Everything will be all right and the food will be fit for a king."

Twenty minutes and several nursery rhymes later, the doorbell sounded. He put Ellie on the floor and held on to her hand. Perhaps he should have warned his parents about her, but he thought his mother might not come. They were aware of Joe. His mother had expressed surprise, but also a desire to meet his new boyfriend.

Taking a deep breath, he opened the door. Never casual in how she dressed, his mother had teamed a blue skirt suit with a white blouse and blue, flat strappy sandals, creating an outfit typical of her style. Now slightly tanned, like him she had brown hair and brown eyes — eyes now wide with surprise. His father, unlike his mother, had begun to look his age, being nearer seventy than sixty. His blond hair had gone gray, but his blue eyes were still clear and his skin also lightly tan. He too seemed surprised for a moment until he held out his hand.

"Hello, son, it's good to see you. You're looking well, and who is this lovely young lady?"

Aron shook his father's hand. "Come through to the living room and I'll introduce you properly." He kissed his mother's cheek. "It's good to see you both. The Mediterranean climate obviously suits you both."

They all took seats. Aron put Ellie onto his knee. "This is Joe's daughter, Ellie. She's nearly fifteen months old. Her mother died when she was born, so Joe is a single dad. He's in the kitchen making lunch. He's a chef and has his own catering company. I'll go and get him. Can you keep an eye on her for a minute?"

"She'll be fine, son."

His mother said nothing, but she'd stared at Ellie from the moment he'd opened the door. There was a sadness in her eyes, which puzzled him. He'd expected her to be angry with him for getting involved with a man who had a child, but there was no anger in her face.

"You stay there, Ellie, while I get Daddy." He gave her a couple of her little soft toys and she began to talk to herself.

In the kitchen, he leaned back against the door after closing it behind him. "They're here," he said.

"I gathered that. Are you all right? How did they take meeting Ellie?"

"They were surprised. Mum hasn't said anything at all, and that's worrying me. Are you okay to come and be introduced?"

"Give me a minute and I'll come through. I'll get the starters plated up and bring them to the conservatory. Did you ask them if they wanted something to drink?"

"I forgot. Both of them will have fizzy water. Neither of them drink. I put a few bottles in the fridge. I'd better get back in there. Don't be long."

He paused in the hallway when he heard his mother's voice.

"Aren't you gorgeous? Such a pretty little girl with your green eyes and dark curly hair. She's so like her, Gordon. I can't believe how like her she is. Same hair color — only her eyes are different. Emily had blue eyes like you, although she had my dark hair. She was so beautiful. Oh, Gordon, our little girl was so beautiful. Just like you are, little one."

Aron stood with his hand on the door handle unable to move. Had he heard correctly? Had his mother said he had a sister? How did he not know? He took a few deep breaths and opened the door. His mouth fell open when he entered the room and saw his mother with Ellie sitting on her lap. Both his parents held up toys and were pulling faces as if it was the most natural thing in the world. Tears streamed down his mother's face. In all his years, he'd never seen his mother cry.

Not one tear had ever fallen from those dark eyes, but now they were dripping uncontrollably from her chin.

"Mum?" Aron had no idea what to say. He had so many questions. Instead, he stood riveted to the spot.

Without warning, his mother gave Ellie to his father and got up. "I'm sorry, I can't do this. It's too much." She wiped her face and rushed out through the conservatory doors into the garden. Aron went to follow her, but was stopped by his father's out-shot arm.

"Leave her, son. Give her for a few minutes. It's been a shock, that's all. Been a shock for both of us."

"Dad, I don't understand. I realize Mum doesn't like children, and I didn't think she'd be pleased to discover I'm dating a single dad, but... Who's Emily?"

His father patted the seat next to him. "Sit and I'll explain. We should have told you years ago, but she's never been able to talk about it."

The door opened, and Joe came in.

"Is that your mother in the garden? She looks upset. What's happened?"

Aron's father stood and held out his hand. "You must be Joe. It's good to meet you. I'm Gordon Roberts. I know this is rather rude, but could you give me and my son some time alone? You'd better take your daughter with you in case she gets fractious. I need to talk to him about something personal."

Joe glanced over to Aron. "It's all right. I'm all right," he lied. "Give me and Dad a little while. Nothing will spoil, will it?"

"No, I'm not worried about the food, just you. You're so pale, like you've seen a ghost."

"Not quite. Joe, please, can you take her?"

"I think she needs changing anyway. I'll go upstairs with her then finish off in the kitchen. Call me when you're ready."

Joe gave Aron's shoulder the briefest of squeezes when he picked Ellie up and left the room. Aron pushed away the urge to beg him to stay because his whole world was unraveling before his eyes.

When they were alone his father began. "You had a sister. We called her Emily. She was born in 1975, fifteen years before you appeared. Your mother wanted to have a baby while she was young, then complete her medical training. I had a good job, so would be able to support a family. We had a beautiful baby girl, all blue eyes and dark curly hair. She was perfect. She slept through the night early on and only cried when she was hungry or needed changing. We loved her so much. Her smile lit up a room and she had this way of giggling. She never crawled, but pulled herself around on her bottom. She was eight months old when she died. Your mother got up in the morning and found her in her cot. She wasn't breathing. We both tried to revive her, but she was cold. We blamed each other. We were doctors and we hadn't been able to save our own child. The post mortem revealed nothing—just another cot death they said, but our precious little one was gone.

"Your mother shut down. She didn't cry after the morning we found Emily. She threw herself into her work, and we both began to drink too much. She's never talked about it. I saw a counsellor, but your mother simply worked. Those she worked with feared her, but she was good and got her consultancy post at a young age. She became an authority on transplant surgery. Nothing else mattered. She hadn't been able to save her own child so she dedicated herself to saving as many people as possible. Our marriage only survived because neither of us was interested in looking elsewhere. Then, out of the blue, she got pregnant again. She'd been having gynecological problems and thought she was going through an early menopause. She didn't expect to be pregnant, but she was four months gone when she realized it was a possibility. After you were born, I realized things weren't right early on. She took care of you, but she was afraid of you—afraid of your need. You cried nonstop. I guess you could feel her tension. She found it harder and harder and withdrew from you. I should have insisted that she get help, but I knew she'd have none of it. She threw herself into her work and we got Trude to look after you."

"I thought she didn't love me, but I had no idea why. I thought it must be my fault." Tears streamed down Aron's face. "She was a stranger to me—this beautiful woman who smelled nice when I saw her, which wasn't often. I remember playing with you sometimes, but it was usually me and Trude. She was the person who hugged me and fed me and played with me. I thought every family was like that until I went to school. I asked Trude why my mother didn't take me to school or collect me like other mothers did. She told me my mother had an important job and people needed her and that's why she arranged for Trude to stay with me. I was surprised you didn't send me away to school—it wasn't as if you were short of money."

"Your mother wouldn't have it. She insisted on your going to the local school. She was proud of you of how bright you were and she read your reports from cover to cover. She didn't know how to be close to you, and she wouldn't let herself love you in case you were taken away, so she kept her distance."

"Her behavior made me think children were an inconvenience. I grew up thinking she didn't care about me. It's a wonder I didn't end up a bit mad myself. School helped, and meeting Dan and his family. Dan's nan told me it wasn't my fault, that some people are like that, and if I ever needed a hug, she would give me one."

"I was always grateful you met Dan and his family."

Aron looked up to see his mother standing in the doorway to the conservatory.

"I've no idea what to say to you. I guess your father has told you about Emily. It's one of the reasons why we're here. Tomorrow is her birthday. We scattered her ashes in the park we used to take her to. Maybe we shouldn't have, but she loved the ducks."

Aron wiped his face. Suddenly, his mother was a different person to the woman he'd always known. She sat on the sofa next to him.

"We should have told you about your sister before now. I wanted to love you, Aron, but I couldn't cope with you. I know I was a bad mother. I was older, work was all-consuming. You never stopped crying, and I thought I made you worse, that you'd be better off with someone else, but I couldn't bear to give you away so I got Trude to care for you. I'm not going to ask you to forgive me because it's too late for that—too much water under the bridge for us to go back. You and this Joe, it's serious, then?"

"Yes, it's serious. I love him. It took me a while to get over my worries about Ellie. I grew up wanting nothing to do with children. You'd taught me they were an inconvenience, and luckily, being gay, I never thought

I'd need to worry about them. Then Joe came along and I nearly blew it. I still find it difficult, the responsibility for her, but Joe is a great dad and his family pitch in to help. He's also a great chef and I need to let him know I'm all right."

"*Are* you all right?" his father asked.

"No, not really, but I need to take all of this in and think about it another time. I can't do that now. Please go and sit in the conservatory. I know you're probably not hungry, but he's gone to a lot of trouble."

"We can go if you want," his mother said.

"No, I want you to meet him. He's a good man."

Joe was sitting at the small table when he went back into the kitchen. Aron claimed the seat opposite him, knowing Joe would wait for him to speak. He needed to get everything out quickly.

"The long and the short of it is that I had a sister who died when she was eight months old, fifteen years before I was born. I think it was SIDS. Mum didn't cope well and when I came along, she couldn't let herself love me. Ellie reminded her of Emily — my sister's name was Emily." His voice cracked and he paused. Tears flowed down his cheeks and dripped onto the table. His whole body shook as heartbreak overtook him. Suddenly, only Joe's strong arms surrounding him, holding him together, stopped him from shattering into hundreds of pieces. He heard a little voice breaking through the noise of his sobs as Ellie pulled herself up to her feet and put her hand on his knee.

"Run, Run, up."

He bent and picked her up, putting her on the table with her legs dangling over the side. He wiped his eyes. Joe cupped his face and placed little kisses all over his face.

"It'll be all right, Aron. I love you so much. We have each other, and Ellie, and it'll be fine. We'll love you. You don't ever need to be on your own again."

Aron wanted Joe to hold him and never let him go. He needed to feel his arms around him and his breath on his cheek. He needed to know this was real, and he wasn't dreaming. Joe loved him. Joe wanted to be with him, in spite of everything.

"I love you too." There, he'd finally said it aloud.

"This is probably a stupid question with what's gone on today, but what do you want to do about lunch? Are they staying?"

"I want you to meet them. There's a lot to talk about, but not Emily, not for now. There'll be a time and a place, but this isn't it. Give me Ellie and I'll take her through and put her in the highchair."

"I'll bring the starters. I want to meet your parents too."

"Don't judge her, Joe. She's still my mother, and I sort of understand how afraid she must have been after Emily died. I was terrified of Ellie and the responsibility. Maybe Ellie will give Mum another chance. I don't know, but we've got to try, haven't we?"

Chapter Twenty-Seven

"Well, at least you have an explanation now," Joe said as they lay in bed. Aron had asked him to stay and after a quick call to Rhodri to make sure he would start cooking in the morning, Joe had agreed. He'd said Aron didn't have to be alone and he meant it. To the outside world, Aron was a successful entrepreneur with his own company about to make serious money, but as he lay with his head on Joe's chest, twirling the small, dark hairs around in his fingers, he appeared anything but invincible.

After watching them together, Joe saw Aron was like his mother in many ways, other than how they looked. She'd talked about her work with the same zeal as Aron talked about what he did. They were both dedicated to making life better for people. He had that same obsessive attitude when in the middle of making something new, trying new combinations of flavors to see if they worked and suffering frustration if they didn't. Of course, lives weren't at stake in his work as they were in Dorothy's.

"I suppose that's why she went into transplant surgery," Aron said, interrupting Joe's thoughts. "When Emily died, she couldn't save her, so she saved others instead. She must have changed so many people's lives for the better. I wish I'd known sooner. I don't even know if there are any photographs of Emily."

"D'you want to take her up on her offer? She sounded genuine about wanting us to come to visit them. It's never too late, especially now that everything is out in the open. When are they leaving tomorrow?"

"Their plane leaves Cardiff at ten-thirty."

"Why don't you go and see them off?"

"Do you think I should?"

Joe couldn't imagine not being close to his parents. It didn't matter how old you were or what had happened, you still wanted your parents to be proud of you, and to accept you no matter what. Perhaps Aron would have that chance now.

"Today has been a big day, but this is only the first day. It was never your fault."

Aron raised his head, his features clear even in the darkness. Joe knew from firsthand experience how people coped, or didn't cope, with death in different ways. "It wasn't anything to do with you. Your parents went through a terrible experience. They'll have thought about Emily every day just like I still think of Angie. Your parents will have wondered about how she'd have grown up and who'd she'd have become. She'd have been around forty now, with her own family and career. I dread how Ellie will feel about Angie's death when she's old enough to understand. I don't want her to feel guilty, but she probably will. It's human nature to feel guilty, even when there was nothing we could do. We all wish we'd done things differently. You can begin to rebuild your relationship with them. It won't be easy, but I'll be here for you." Ellie snuffled in the little bed they'd created next to theirs. "And Ellie will be as well, and you'll be there for her. Everyone wants to be needed, to feel special, to be part of someone else, and now you're part of us."

Wet drops landed on his chest. He hugged Aron closer, wishing he could make all the pain go away.

"Are you deliberately trying to make me cry?" Aron said.

"No, but maybe you need to let yourself weep for what you lost before you try to get some of it back. The past is the past and you can't change it, however much you want to, and however many regrets you have. Jeez, look what you're doing to me. I'm talking in platitudes, but you know what I mean."

"Yeah, I do. I'll go to the airport tomorrow. I want to give them something. Tomorrow we need to take a photo of the three of us."

"That's a lovely idea. Now we need to sleep. It's been a long day."

"I'm going to turn over," Aron said.

Joe tucked himself behind and allowed himself a small smile as he gazed at the ceiling. *I hope you don't mind, angel. You told me not to be alone.*

* * * *

Aron waited near the main entrance from around eight in the morning, wanting to make sure he'd get there on time. It had been hard seeing Joe go in the morning. He would be busy over the next few nights, which was good for his business, but not so good for

Aron. Without Joe, he would feel at a loose end. He decided to play online chess. It had been a while since his last game. From the few times he'd tried to teach Joe to play, it was clear playing him wasn't going to be a challenge. Still, Joe had other skills often demonstrated under the covers before Ellie woke up.

They came through the doors at eight-thirty, checked their baggage then went to the coffee shop. Aron waited until they were sitting, then he joined them.

"Aron, this is a wonderful surprise." His father gestured for him to join them. "I'll get you a coffee."

"Is everything all right?" his mother asked when his father had gone to the counter, her concern clearly etched in her features.

"I wanted to let you know I'm okay after yesterday, and I wanted to check you were too. It must have been hard for you, all of the past coming out like it did. I'm glad, though. It's helped me to understand and put my childhood into perspective. Joe and I did a great deal of talking last night."

"I must admit, I was surprised to find out he was a widower, but it's obvious he cares for you, and you for him. I hope you'll come and visit us, and I'm glad you've come to see us off." She reached into her handbag and pulled out a couple of photographs.

"I had copies made at the hotel. This is Emily when she was six months old. We went to a proper photographer for that one. You can see why I was struck by Ellie."

He could. Both babies had dark curly hair and smiling faces. Emily was sitting up, dressed in a pale blue silk dress covered in embroidered flowers. She was beautiful.

"She smiled all the time. Your father said it was wind, but I knew better. She was such a happy child. The other one is of the three of us at her christening."

They were so young, his parents. His mother carried Emily and his father had his arm around the two of them. They had their whole future in front of them. He wiped his eyes as his father returned and sat next to him.

"My goodness! Those flares were bloody awful, and those lapels could take someone's eye out. The 1970s, the time that style forgot."

Aron grinned. His father did look fairly ridiculous in his awful brown suit. "Thanks for these. My sister was beautiful. I brought you a photograph as well. Joe and I took this one of the three of us this morning. We had fun trying to get the timer right and get Ellie to smile at the same time. We'd like to take you up on your offer as well to visit you."

"That would be wonderful, but come for some time, not just a couple of days." She paused for a moment. "I wish we'd told you sooner, but somehow the right time never happened." She put her hand over his. It was the first time she'd done that for as long as he could remember, and his emotions threatened to overwhelm him again.

"I wish you had too, but as Joe told me, there's no point dwelling on what might have been. He's taken advice on how to help Ellie when she's old enough to understand what happened to her mother."

An announcement called their flight, and they drank their coffees. "We've got to get moving, Dorothy."

Aron stood, not sure what to do next. Perhaps it was too soon to hug, but his father put his arms around him.

"Bye, son. We'll see you soon."

He stood facing his mother, leaned in and kissed her cheek. "We can set up Skype so Joe can see where we're going to visit."

The flight announcement blared out again. He glanced in the direction of the flying club and decided to stroll over to visit Mark to find out if he had any free time. Being up there would give him time to think. He waved to his parents as they went through the boarding gate. For the first time in his adult life, he found himself looking forward to seeing them again.

* * * *

"Sorry, is it too odd for you?"

Joe wasn't sure. "I don't know. You've got to admit it is strange, but I suppose it's good you get on well with your ex and his partner, but lunch?"

"All right, I'll tell Iestyn no, then."

Joe heard the disappointment in Aron's voice, and truth was, he was curious to meet both men. After all, it wasn't every day you met the captain of the Wales rugby team, and his family would never forgive him if he didn't get at least one autograph.

"No, don't do that. Will it be all right to bring Ellie with us?"

"Yes, of course it will. They're both great with kids. Iestyn has a niece and three nephews. I haven't been to their new house yet, and I'd like to go. They have a swimming pool too, so bring your trunks."

"You're expecting me to be around Dan Morgan in swimming trunks?" Joe asked. "Please tell me he doesn't wear Speedos."

"I've no idea, but don't let your tongue hang out too much if he does."

"Okay, okay, you win. It'll be good to have someone else make me lunch. I think I'll keep the occasion to myself for now and not tell my family."

"Wear the outfit you wore at the petting zoo. You're seriously hot in that shirt with your tanned skin and a bit of stubble." He smiled at the slight hitch in Aron's voice and lowered his own.

"Are your trousers getting tighter?"

"Might be," Aron replied, breathing heavier. "What about yours?"

"I might have the same problem. Any chance of ringing me later tonight when I'm in bed, rather than in my kitchen trying to make beef stroganoff?"

"The hotel has good reception. We could Skype?"

Joe took a breath and turned to lean back against the counter. His hand itched to move south, as if it had a will of its own. He loved to watch Aron touch himself and the sounds he made. Oh shit!

"I've got to go," he said. "You are a total tease. You know that, don't you?"

"And you love it."

"I do," Joe admitted. He turned back to the food and stirred it once again. "Call me and I hope the meeting goes well. Robbie was made up to go with you. He bought a new suit. He's a fan of yours."

"What can I say? It's my natural charm." Joe paused at the noise in the background. "That'll be him at the door now. Better get off. Love you, and give Ellie a kiss for me."

"Ring me. Love you too. Bye." He smiled to himself and continued stirring and tasting. Was it too soon to use the L word as often as they did? He didn't care. And now he was going to meet Aron's ex, the golden man of rugby. He flexed his arms, checking his muscles, and decided he'd go to the gym in the morning. He wanted to see Jonno anyway, and if he had to get his kit off in front of Dan Morgan, he wanted to be his best. Maybe he'd get a chest wax as well, and a haircut, and a new dress for Ellie. As the list got longer, he laughed to himself, but didn't stop adding to it.

Chapter Twenty-Eight

"You're sure this outfit is all right?" Joe asked again.

"You both look lovely." Aron pushed up Joe's shirt, letting his fingers skim over the soft skin of his now bear chest. "I can't believe you had your chest waxed."

"Hey, Jonno tried to persuade me to get a spray tan as well, but I drew the line at that. You're sure these cargo pants are okay?" He turned from side to side trying to see his own arse.

Aron grinned and moved to stand behind him. "Works for me," he said. "Now, stop worrying. I like them because I can see your calf muscles and toes. I may have a tiny thing for your feet."

Joe knew his face had flushed red from the heat in his cheeks. "Umm, why didn't I know that? I thought it was my arse you liked. I love foot massages, so maybe sometime we could…"

Aron kissed the back of his neck then picked up Ellie's bag. "We'd better get off. You did remember to pack your swimming trunks, didn't you?"

"I did, though I'm not sure about wearing them. Why d'you think I had the wax done? I've seen those shots of Dan in the magazines. It's hard not to feel intimidated."

"You have no reason to worry, believe me. I love you, you daft idiot."

"It's good you're still friends, though. Not everyone manages that after they break up."

"Dan and I were friends for years, and as I said, Iestyn is a good bloke and a good listener. Now, let's get this beautiful young lady loaded into the car while she's still asleep."

* * * *

Forty minutes later, they arrived at the house on the coast. It was the last on a dead-end road, with an outlook over the Bristol Channel.

As instructed, Aron opened the gates, and Joe parked the car on the expansive drive. "His modeling pays for this, not the rugby," Aron said. "Although these days players' wages are a lot better than they used to be."

Joe wondered if Iestyn worried about being with someone so much wealthier than himself. He guessed he and Aron might be in the same situation at some point. Then again, he had his own business, which was doing well, so he would hardly be a kept man if they moved in together. *Shit! Where did that thought come from?* But now that he'd thought it, he found he quite liked the idea of waking up with Aron beside him every morning.

The front door opened, and a dark-haired man in glasses waved at them. A loud yapping noise alerted him to the spaniel dancing around.

"Charlie, sit."

Joe marveled as the animal responded immediately to the instruction to sit and gazed up at its master.

Ellie stirred when he lifted her seat from the car. "Dog," she said and pointed to the doorstep.

Iestyn held out his hand for Joe to shake. "Hi, Joe, it's been a while. We didn't get much of a chance to talk at the wedding, and this must be Ellie, who is the spitting image of her father." He glanced back up at Joe. "Don't worry, she'll be all right with Charlie. He's very obedient."

"So I see. Ellie loves animals," Joe said. "We had a day out at a zoo recently and she wanted to pet everything."

"He used to sniff out drugs but was too friendly," Aron said as he hugged Iestyn. "Where's himself?"

"Would you believe making lunch?"

"Sorry, run that by me again. Dan Morgan, who didn't know how to operate his own coffee machine, is making lunch?"

"Yep, he's made lasagna from scratch, and even made the dough for the garlic bread. No way was I coming home from work to cook at night, so I taught him to cook. He makes a mean curry as well."

"This I have got to see."

Iestyn touched his arm. "He's terrified because Joe is a chef, so go easy on him."

"Hey, I love it when someone other than me cooks," Joe said. He sniffed the air. "Oh, Ellie, already? I'll need to change her."

"The bathroom's upstairs, or you can use a bedroom if you need a flat surface."

Joe threw the bag over his shoulder and picked up the seat. "I won't be long."

Aron couldn't miss an opportunity and stared at Joe as he climbed the stairs, unable to resist lusting after those calf muscles in action.

Iestyn nudged him and laughed. "Come on, get your eyes of his arse for a minute, although I have to admit he's a handsome devil with those green eyes."

"They were the first thing I noticed," Aron replied, following Iestyn into the kitchen.

He could hardly believe his *own* eyes when he saw the tall, blond, handsome figure of his ex-boyfriend dressed in jeans, T-shirt and a very fetching apron, stirring a large, wonderfully smelling saucepan in the beautiful white Shaker-style kitchen. "Bloody hell, it's true, miracles do happen."

Dan left the spoon in the pan and came toward him. He wrapped those strong arms Aron knew so well around his body and hugged him tightly. Dan had been his best friend for so many years, and sometimes he missed him and the way he faced life head on. He'd always admired him for being out and proud in a profession that hadn't been accepting of homosexuality in the past. He admired Joe in much the same way, for how he coped after his wife had died. He patted Dan's back and pulled away.

"It's good to see you Dan, and I'm loving the apron. Iestyn's got you well trained, then."

"Let's say he has some interesting methods of getting his own way," Dan replied cryptically.

Aron turned to Iestyn. "Do I want to know?" he asked.

Iestyn smirked. "Probably not. Now, what can I get you to drink? Are you driving, or Joe?"

"Me, but Joe doesn't drink a lot either because he has Ellie to look after, so we'll have a couple of beers then stick to the soft stuff."

Iestyn got the beers from the fridge while Dan finished preparing the lasagna then put it in the oven. "Should be ready in thirty minutes. Did Iessie tell you I made the bread as well?"

"He did," Aron confirmed. "Bread is one of Joe's specialties. He makes lots of different flavors — even nettles."

The door opened, and Joe came in with the car seat in one hand and Ellie in the other. Aron's heart skipped a beat when Joe smiled and put Ellie on the floor. She was still somewhat unsteady on her feet, but with the help of the kitchen chairs she made her way to Aron.

"Run, Run, up, up."

Aron bent and lifted Ellie into his arms. Immediately, she pulled his hair and giggled. He didn't miss the glance exchanged between Dan and Iestyn.

"Sorry, I should introduce everyone. Joe said you two were rather preoccupied the last time you met."

"Well, it was our wedding day, and we skipped out early that night," Iestyn said.

"I bet," Aron said. "And Dan, this is Joe and his daughter Ellie. Joe, this is Dan."

Joe moved forward and shook Dan's hand with the wide-eyed gaze of a fan unable to quite believe his luck and slightly losing his cool. He held on for a little too long.

"Sorry," Joe said, letting go. "It's… You're… I mean, I know we met before, sort of, but… I was working then. It's different in reality."

"Here," Iestyn said, unable to keep the grin off his face. "Have a beer."

Aron guessed he was used to such reactions by now.

Iestyn pointed to the French doors. "We're eating outside so come and see the view. Ellie will be able to run around safely and we've a few toys about the place for when Megs and the twins are here. We can use the pool, or go to the beach after lunch. There's a gate at the end that leads straight down there."

Aron clasped Joe's hand and led him through to the garden. They both stopped and stared. The panorama *was* stunning. Next to the house was a patio with seating and a huge umbrella, surrounded by a low wall. This gave way to lawn with shrubs on both sides, and a kidney-shaped swimming pool. A small fence enclosed the rear of the lawn, but it was the view of the Bristol Channel that took his breath away. In the sunshine, it stretched out before them with the Somerset Coast clearly outlined on the horizon. He inhaled, and a hint of seaweed filled his nostrils.

"It's wonderful," he said, as Ellie wriggled to get down. He made sure she was on her feet properly then let her go.

"Don't worry," Iestyn said. "The wall will keep her in this area and the surface of the patio is made of the stuff they use in playgrounds. The boys can get over the wall now, but it contains Megs. We have to keep an eye out with the swimming pool, but the twins, Lewis and Lloyd, doggie paddle pretty well."

Ellie made an immediate beeline for Charlie who lolled, tongue out, under the table.

"Dog" Joe said, following her. He glanced back toward Iestyn.

"Charlie, sit," Iestyn said.

The spaniel responded straight away. Aron joined Joe while he showed Ellie how to stroke the dog. Like most toddlers, she sort of hit more than she stroked, but Charlie took it in his stride.

"He's used to Megs," Iestyn said, taking a seat and putting his beer on the table next to theirs. "She jumps all over him, and he's ever so patient."

"I guess the police training helps. He's so obedient," Joe said, still keeping an eye on his daughter now sitting next to Charlie.

"So," Iestyn said. "It's good to meet you for real, Joe. Aron's told me a little about you. The food you made for our civil partnership was fantastic — everybody said so on the night. The business is doing well, I hear."

"It is, and your ceremony did me a favor. It's how I got the dinner at Aron's where we met up again."

Dan came out carrying a beer. "So isn't the view amazing? We couldn't resist it when we saw it, could we, Iessie? I'll give you a quick tour if you want." Aron wanted a moment with Iestyn. "Why don't you show Joe around?" He noticed Iestyn incline his head slightly toward Dan.

"Okay, Joe, you and me it is."

"Go on, Joe, imagine Gwen's face when you say you've been around his house."

He had to admit Joe seemed surprised, but maybe he guessed Aron had an alternative reason. He picked up Ellie. "I'll take her with us, then. The more she walks, the more tired she'll be. Lead on then, Dan."

Dan leaned over and whispered something in Iestyn's ear then kissed his cheek. "When we've finished, I'll get lunch sorted," he continued, standing straight.

Dan and Joe strolled into the house swinging Ellie between them, giving Aron a chance to talk.

Iestyn swigged a mouthful of his beer. "Well, that was as subtle as a brick through a window."

"What did he say?" Aron asked.

"He asked if we were going to compare notes. You've got to admit they have some aspects in common."

"Joe is nothing like Dan," Aron protested.

Iestyn gave him one of those 'you really expect me to believe that?' looks. "All right, I'll give you Dan is over six inches taller and blond, but let's consider other things."

"What?" Aron replied, folding his arms across his chest.

"Okay from the top—broad chest, muscular arms, narrow waist and hips—and I'm willing to guess there's a hint of a six pack under there. He's waxed his chest too, if I'm not mistaken, and no one could fail to notice those calf muscles."

Heat rushed into Aron's cheeks. "That was a quick study," he said, raising his eyebrows.

"Hey, I'm married, not blind. He's got a great arse as well."

Aron choked on the beer he'd been halfway through swallowing. "Jeez, Iestyn."

"Well, I'm at a slight disadvantage. You're all too familiar with my husband's arse." He grinned.

Aron breathed a sigh of relief. "He was more familiar with mine," he said, returning the grin.

"All I can say," Iestyn added, winking, "is that the view of his arse from above never gets boring."

Realizing the implication of Iestyn's words, it was Aron's turn to splutter. "Really?" Which wasn't the question he wanted to ask.

"Oh, yeah."

Aron ran a hand underneath his collar, even though it wasn't tight. He'd suddenly become hot, and needed to pull himself together and fast. He risked another mouthful of his beer then glanced over at Iestyn.

"Sorry, I couldn't resist teasing you. Joe's a nice bloke, and you seem happy."

"I am. Joe and I, we fit. There've been a few ups and down, but he's met my parents and I've met his. His family are lovely and his older brother works for me. They've been more than welcoming, considering their son is going out with a man after being married to a woman. We've not hidden our relationship from anyone, except his wife's parents. My parents came over recently for a medical conference and we talked, really talked. Now's not the time to explain, but a few ghosts were laid to rest. They liked Joe, and they've invited us out to France."

"Wow, but what about Ellie? You were so worried, but you appear to have no problems holding her."

"I wouldn't say no problems. I still find it hard sometimes, but she is so loveable, and she has her own personality and definite ideas about what she wants. Joe is so good with her, and I love watching them together. I'm in awe of the way he copes, looking after her and running his business. There's no edge to him at all. What you see is what you get."

Iestyn smiled and leaned forward. "Seems we both have men we're in awe of."

Charlie raised his head from Iestyn's feet as Joe came out again carrying Ellie. "Dan's finishing off lunch and putting the garlic bread in the oven. He says it'll be fifteen minutes so could you set the table and get the salad and dressing?"

"I'd better get moving then, as himself calls. Why don't you go and see the beach? We could visit later and play in the rock pools, but you have to watch out for little crabs nipping at your toes."

Aron waited until Iestyn had gone into the house. "So did you enjoy the tour?"

"Dan and I had a chat," Joe replied, putting Ellie on the floor. "You should see their shower. I bet they get some interesting use out of that. Dan said they're planning to get a hot tub. He said something interesting as well."

"Oh, yeah?" Aron put a hand on Joe's arm.

"Yeah, he told me about a conversation he'd had with another player when he first started playing for the Giants and had some doubts about being out and open about his sexuality."

"I remember he talked to someone."

"This bloke encouraged him to do what he thought was best for him and said how some good players might cope playing in different positions and make it outside their comfort zone, but that good people always do. He told Dan that by being open about himself, he could do an immense amount of good in the game."

"I've always admired his bravery."

"He told me you were a good man too, and you are. You're my good man, Aron—mine and Ellie's."

Aron gazed at the floor. Iestyn had obviously told Dan of his worries concerning Ellie. Dan's opinion still mattered to him and hearing that he'd said those words to Joe brought tears to his eyes. Joe hugged him and lay his head on Aron's shoulder.

"You know that, don't you?" Joe pulled away and put his finger under Aron's chin, lifted his face and kissed him. "Come on, let's have a look at the beach."

Joe helped Ellie to her feet and they each grabbed a hand and strolled to the end of the garden with her.

"I could get a hot tub if you'd like one," Aron said. "There's room on the patio at mine, and putting a fence at one side would give us privacy if we wanted to get naked."

"Sounds like fun," Joe whispered into his ear.

The room in Aron's jeans suddenly got more constricted as Joe had lowered his voice and turned the full force of those green sparkling eyes on him. They were chock full of mischief.

"I'm not going to tell you any more, you know."

"Not tell me what?" Aron asked, fully aware of what Joe was alluding to.

"Dan and I did compare a few notes while we were going around. He was surprised to hear you'd newly acquired a sweet tooth."

Aron halted midstep and turned to face Joe. "You told him."

"I might have mentioned how much you like chocolate, but he didn't believe me so I had to explain further, didn't I?"

They arrived at the fence and gazed over the mixture of sandy areas and rocks with small pools that made up the beach. Off to the left lay Sully Island, now separated from the beach. Groups of children explored the rock pools with nets and buckets.

Joe picked Ellie up and pointed out various things for her to repeat.

"I like him, by the way," Joe said. "There's no front to him, even though he's famous. He told me to be good to you."

Aron grinned. "He always did take care of me. I must ask him how Betty, his nan, is these days. She was always good to me when I was young, and quite a character. She must have approved of Iestyn, or he'd have had no chance with Dan." Iestyn waved from the house. "Looks like lunch is ready. Now, be nice, even if it's terrible. Dan never made anything when we were together, and he's probably nervous as hell."

Charlie ran toward them then began to herd them back to the house.

"Doggie," Ellie said as Charlie ran around them.

"Clever girl," Joe said. "Time for some pasta, little one."

"Asta."

"That's right, sweetheart." With one arm holding Ellie securely, he reached across and held Aron's hand when they walked back. Aron recognized it was his way of saying 'you're mine'. A warm glow settled in his chest. He liked being Joe's. He liked it a lot.

They shared a pleasant lunch and Joe announced Dan had done an excellent job of making the lasagna.

"Next time I'll make my curry. It was the first thing Iessie made for me on our second date. Joe tells me you've developed a sweet tooth recently, Az."

Aron wasn't sure whether to frown at the use of his old nickname, or blush yet again. Iestyn broke the moment.

"I'm missing something here, aren't I?" he said, glancing at them all.

Dan leaned over and whispered again. Iestyn's grin went from ear to ear. "Really? We need to buy a fondue set, and you'll be able to have your five a day as well."

"I'll get the strawberries and cream for afters, then," Dan said, desperately trying to keep a straight face.

No one succeeded and they all ended up wiping tears from their eyes.

After a couple of hours spent talking and laughing, Ellie had fallen asleep in her seat and it was time to leave. They hugged one other on the doorstep, then Aron and Joe climbed into the car.

Aron wound the window down. "We'll be back soon. You have such a beautiful place. Maybe I'll hunt for somewhere around here, near the sea. Ellie would love it." He spoke without thinking, then realized what he'd said. Joe said nothing, and Aron worried it was too soon.

On the way home, they talked over their plans for the rest of the week and when they had time see each other again, but Aron knew he'd opened a can of worms, which included the possibility of them living together, and there were still questions that needed to be asked, and answered.

Chapter Twenty-Nine

Having to leave Joe and go home on his own had made Aron more certain of how he wanted to change his life, and more determined to set the wheels in motion. That night, although he knew he was jumping the gun and getting into a wild fantasy area, he idly searched through houses for sale on the coast. He would need to talk to Evan about his financial position and that of the company, but most of all, he needed to know if Joe would move in with him. Joe also had a profitable business to consider and he'd admitted he might need to expand into bigger premises and take on more workers. His house wouldn't be needed, but it was the house he'd lived in with Angie, and it was Ellie's home as well. There was also the problem that Joe might be too proud to let him pay for most of the house. Money had never been that important to him, he simply loved solving problems with technology, but he wasn't naïve. He knew how business worked.

Money had come in from the aviation company and he had meetings in the next week to discuss Robbie's idea. The week after he was off to the States for yet more meetings with motor manufacturers. Thank God for Margaret or he'd be in a complete mess trying to organize everything. He and Joe had already worked out they wouldn't be able to see much of each other. Now Rhodri was back at college and only able to help Joe part-time, he needed more permanent help. Aron sighed. If he could show Joe that he was serious, then at least when they had time to be together, they would be in the same house.

He clicked on a page and there it was — the house of his dreams — a few miles away from Dan and Iestyn, but on the other side of Sully Island toward Penarth. It had a view of the sea, four bedrooms and a huge garden.

I need to make this sound more romantic than practical, though. I want to be with him. He glanced over at the space next to him then put the computer to one side and reached out his hand to run it over the sheet. Right then, more than anything else, he wished he could see Joe's strong back and dark curly hair lying there so he could press himself in tight behind, wrap his arm around him and breathe in his smell. He chortled to himself. Man, I have it bad.

* * * *

"So it went well meeting Dan Morgan," Jonno said at Joe's house a couple of days later.

They watched football on the TV and finished the curry Joe had made for them. Every couple of minutes, his eyelids closed and he blinked them back open again — he was so tired.

"Yeah, he's exactly how you'd expect him to be. There's no front to the man. His partner, Iestyn, is nice as well. They suit each other. He is huge. When he's playing and in the line out, there are a few others as big as him, but in the flesh, he's so tall with these massive shoulders, especially compared to Aron."

"The green-eyed monster didn't make an appearance then, meeting his ex, who is not only gorgeous, but famous?" Jonno asked.

"No, and you can take that wide-eyed, innocent look from your face as well. I may not be as big as Dan Morgan, but I can definitely cook better. I get no complaints about anything else, either, thank you very much. So you and Rhodri, how's that going now he's back at college?"

"Don't think I didn't notice that change of subject and as for Rhodri, we're still having fun, but he's young, so I'm not getting too involved."

"You don't always get a choice," Joe said, staring at the TV for a moment.

"Sounds serious."

Joe put his food on the table and turned to Jonno. "I think I'm in love with him. I hate being away from him for even a few days. I won't see him now until the end of next week because he's off to the States. What if he sees his ex from over there and decides—"

Jonno cut him off. "Don't be an idiot. From what you've told me, he's got it bad for you as well. You said he's great with Ellie, even after all his fears, and that she loves him. Your family like him, and you've met his. Granted it's quick, but it sounds serious to me. Maybe you should take the next step and move in together."

Joe sighed. "I've thought about it, but I've got Ellie and the business to consider. If it was just me, I'd take a chance and see, but it's a big step, and I've no idea if he wants to do the same. I wouldn't want to move into his house either, so we'd have to find a place together. And I'd need somewhere to carry on the business. It's getting too big for here. I've decided to advertise for someone to work with me now Rhodri can only do odd days."

"Finally," Jonno said, punching the air.

Joe looked at the screen and saw Cardiff had scored. "At last, all they've got to do is hang on to it now."

* * * *

The next few days were busy. Joe put the advert for an assistant in various places and the applications had rolled in. He had weddings to cater on Friday and Saturday and had to prepare buffets for both. Gwennie and Rhodri helped him serve, and both nights he collapsed into bed and slept like the dead. The following week, he and Aron at least managed a few late-night calls.

"You do realize it's four-thirty in the afternoon here, don't you?" Aron said as Joe lay in bed on Wednesday night.

"But you told me you've just got out of the shower and you're only wearing a towel around your waist," Joe replied. "Be fair, how am not supposed to imagine you half-naked with droplets of water running down your chest and back, your hair all wet and spiky, and the V of your hipbones pointing down under the towel." His cock immediately stiffened when he spoke the words aloud, and the duvet tented enough for him to see even in lamplight. He reached a hand under the bedding and stroked himself lightly. "The thought of you makes me hard and needy."

"Are you pleasuring yourself?" Aron asked, his voice low and sexy and suddenly much more intense.

"I might be," Joe replied. "I might have my hand under the duvet."

"Tell me you've got your hand on your cock," Aron continued, his breath increasing.

Joe glanced toward Ellie's cot. He hoped she was asleep. She's developed an interesting habit of picking up new words recently, and adding cock to her repertoire would not be a good thing.

"Can't, don't want Ellie to hear me, but I'm stroking myself and imagining your mouth on me."

"Oh God, I should not be doing this now," Aron said. "You make me so hard. I've got my cock in my hand, and I'm leaking all over the place."

Joe increased his speed, spreading his own pre-cum to make it easier. "Not going to take long," he said breathlessly. "I miss you so much. I can't wait for the weekend. Your arse will be to be mine."

"You promise?" Aron asked.

"Oh, yeah, I'm trying to decide where in your house I'm going to take you. Maybe over the table with your pants around your feet, or maybe on the stairs. Ever been had on the stairs?"

"Oh God, Joe, anywhere, I don't care as long as I'm full up with you."

He stopped and Joe guessed he'd come from his breathing. A few more strokes and he exploded, sending semen into his own hand as his body arched upward. They lay for a moment in rooms thousands of miles apart just breathing. After a minute, he turned over to check on Ellie, but she was fast asleep and breathing quietly. He pulled some tissues out of the box and cleaned himself up.

"You still there?" Aron asked.

"Barely — feel so sleepy now."

"I love you," Aron said.

Joe's heart leaped at the words. "I love you too. Better go now. I'm interviewing tomorrow."

"No picking someone hot, male or female," Aron said.

Joe laughed. "There's no one in the world as hot as you, and I can't believe I said that aloud."

"I'm glad you did. I've got to clean up again now before dinner tonight with some company exec. I'm beginning to forget who's who, I've spoken to so many people in the last few days. I'll see you Saturday."

"Can't wait. I haven't got a job that day, and Ellie is going to Angie's parents, so I'm all yours." He yawned. "I'm going now. Good night and have a good meeting."

"Night, sexy. I hope you find someone tomorrow."

Joe pressed the red button on his phone and yawned again before snuggling down once more.

* * * *

Thursday, he interviewed several people, finally deciding on a young woman who, like him, had worked in pubs for a while. She was enthusiastic, had great references and had brought examples of her cooking with her to the interview. Joe had nearly swooned when he'd tasted her pastry. She obviously had a light touch and it melted in his mouth. He thought of the sweet and savory tarts she could create.

"This is probably not the way I should do this, but I'm going out on a limb here. At the moment I work from my kitchen, but I'm planning to expand. I have a daughter who is fifteen months old and..." He hesitated for a moment, but he needed to get it out there, to hear himself say the words as much as anything else. "A boyfriend. As we would be working closely together, sometimes day and night, I thought I should tell you a few things before I offered you the job."

She stared at him obviously taken aback. He had to give her credit for thinking about her answer and not blurting something out.

"So you're offering me the job?"

"Yes, I am, if you want it?"

"Okay, in the same spirit of openness. I also have a daughter, who is slightly older than yours. Her name is Melody and she's nearly two. I have a husband who's a firefighter and works shifts, and I'm allergic to seafood which can make things difficult. I can handle it, but I can't eat it."

"I'm sure we can get round that problem," Joe said, putting out his hand. "Welcome to Croeso I Cymraeg Catering, Kirsty. When can you start?"

"I have to give a week's notice at the pub, then I'd like a few days to get organized, so Monday after next? If that's all right."

"Wonderful, so let's get the details sorted and have a cup of tea to seal the deal." He had the feeling he'd made a great choice.

Chapter Thirty

Aron was at the door before Joe got out of the taxi. He'd thought of nothing else but Joe all the way home, and had needed to make judicious use of his suit jacket to cover the obvious hard-on such thoughts produced. If only the older lady next to him on the plane hadn't been so chatty.

The smile he received when Joe saw him made his stomach flip and his heart skip a beat. *I am such a bloody cliché.* Joe looked good enough to eat in his black jeans and white shirt, opened at the neck to reveal his chest. Would it be all stubbly now — not that he cared? His dark hair had grown, and was curling over his collar at the back. Aron had a sudden vision of running his hands through those curls while Joe knelt in front of him. Instinctively, he covered the front of his groin as his cock swelled to attention again.

Joe grinned having noticed the move. "Are you pleased to see me or is that a canoe in your pocket?" he said.

"Oh, I'm more than pleased to see you." Aron stood to one side, allowing Joe to get past him then closed the door. Seconds later, Joe had Aron pressed against the wall in an openmouthed kiss. Joe pulled on Aron's bottom lip, sucking it hard, then he returned to the kiss and plunged his tongue inside Aron's mouth. Aron didn't fight him. He wrapped one leg around Joe, moving it up and down his thigh, and shifted his hands so he could reach under Joe's shirt and rake his back. Knowing Joe could carry him, he raised his other leg, wrapped it behind Joe's arse, and held on as tightly. Joe lifted him and staggered into the living room. Dropping Aron on the sofa, Joe fell to his knees and clutched at the zipper of Aron's jeans.

He gave Aron one questioning glance. Seeing Joe there kneeling between his thighs with eyes as dark as the night sky and as wide as saucers the only word he said was, "Please."

Joe made short work of Aron's zipper and released a now very interested cock. He reached over, removed a cushion from the sofa and put it on the floor. Aron knew, even as his cock was engulfed in the warm wetness of his gorgeous mouth, that Joe was undoing his own jeans and stroking himself like there was no tomorrow. The room filled with the sounds of heavy breathing and groaning. Aron ran his fingers through Joe's hair then held on. Joe grasped the bottom of Aron's shaft and bobbed up and down. Soon the tingling began, and the familiar sensation of his body getting ready to climax engulfed him. It was quick, but there was no stopping his orgasm. Aron tightened his grip on Joe's hair, feeling the suction power of the man on his knees then emptied himself until he could stand no more. Joe milked the aftershocks from him then leaned back and concentrated on his own needs. With his head back, Joe came into his hand, making a few splatters on the cushion beneath, then he fell forward resting his head on Aron's thigh as they both struggled to get their breathing under control.

"Bloody hell, I needed that," Aron said between breaths.

"Sorry about your cushion. I thought it was better than getting jizz on the carpet."

"Very thoughtful of you."

"Semen is a bugger to get out. Laminate is easier I guess, or vinyl." Joe got himself off his knees and lay on his back with his head in Aron's lap, gazing up at him.

"Maybe we should do this in the kitchen next time."

"I don't care where we do it, but I want my cock buried in your arse sometime tonight. I'll do that over the kitchen table if you want."

Aron needed to take this down a notch or two or he'd be testing Joe's power of recovery immediately. He stroked Joe's hair, then his cheek, noting his lover had shaved recently. Finally, he leaned forward and kissed him gently. "I missed you so much. I guess you missed me too."

Joe's grin and shining eyes told him all he needed to know. "Me? I hardly noticed you weren't here. I've got this hot new assistant starting..."

Aron moved his hands and reached to tickle Joe under his arms and across his chest and stomach until the other man wriggled and writhed uncontrollably. "You bastard," Aron said. "I'll teach you." He continued until Joe was breathless once more.

"Pax, pax, enough."

"Are you sure?" Aron replied.

"Yes, I give in. I missed you, all right. I really, really missed you, and your crossed eyes, and your big nose, and your bony chest. Mmm…" His voice softened. "And your soft lips and your seriously gorgeous cock and arse."

Aron fixed him with a stare and pretended to be worried. He touched his nose. "Is it really so big?"

Joe sat up. "No, it's fine."

Aron continued to feel his nose then winked at Joe.

"You had me going there for a moment." He moved to sit next to Aron and zipped himself back up. "I'm starving. I need pizza. Order some while I get us a couple of beers, will you? Then you can tell me all about the States visit, where you went, and if you managed to get out of hotels and offices, that is."

Aron reached for his phone. For the rest of the evening they talked about Aron's trip, Joe's new assistant and the new words Ellie had learned, all while eating pizza.

"Kirsty could bring her daughter over to play with Ellie sometimes, then," he said. "I wonder if her husband knows Jake."

Joe raised his head. "Who's Jake?"

"My, you are a suspicious one, aren't you? I never realized you were such a jealous guy. It's quite a turn-on." He explained how Iestyn had taken Jake, a firefighter, with him to a friend's wedding to make Dan jealous.

"Did that work?" Joe asked.

"Well, Iestyn and Dan are married now, so I guess…" A strange look crossed Joe's face, and he reached a hand over to cup Aron's chin.

"What?" Aron asked.

Joe stared at him, examining every feature of his face. "Can we go to bed now? I need…" He swallowed hard.

Aron stood and held out his hand. "Come on, I need you too." He tried to lighten the suddenly serious mood. "I've this hole I want you to fill."

Joe grinned and followed him up the stairs, taking them two at a time. Both eager, they removed their clothes in record time. "If you're not in me in five minutes, I'm going to survive," Aron said breathlessly, after they'd rolled around kissing and touching every part they could reach.

Joe leaned over and retrieved the lube from the drawer.

"Quickly," Aron said. "I don't need much prep."

Joe pushed in his fingers until Aron was able to take three.

"That's it. Fuck me already." Aron lay on his back and pulled his knees up and wide.

"Greedy bugger."

"I am for you. What d'you want me to do? Beg?"

Joe lined himself up and pushed in slowly until he was balls deep.

"That feels so good," Aron said. It also felt so right to see Joe gazing down at him, such love in those green eyes. He was about to tell him to move when Joe's phone rang. Ellie was with Bill and Penny, so he knew Joe would answer.

"I can't leave it. What if something's wrong?"

"I know. It's okay." Aron hated the emptiness when Joe withdrew and searched for his phone in his jeans. He waited while Joe pressed the button and listened.

"All right, all right. You did the right thing taking her."

Aron sat up. He could see Joe shaking. He picked up his clothes and began to dress, all thoughts of sex now gone.

"I'll be there as soon as possible and you can fill me in then, but you're sure she's out of danger now?"

Joe put the phone to one side and began to dress hurriedly. "Ellie started to have convulsions again, but she also lost consciousness. They've taken her to A & E. I've got to go. She should have been with me." Tears pricked at his eyes.

"It's not your fault. The doctor said it might happen again, and she was fine after she had some antibiotics the last time. Come on, we'll go in my car. I'm coming with you."

"But Bill and Penny will be there," Joe protested.

"We'll cross that bridge when we get to it. You didn't bring your van. No point in waiting for a taxi at this time," Aron said.

Aron put his foot down whenever he could. He pulled up at the entrance. "You go on and I'll catch up."

Joe climbed out and raced away while Aron found a space and got a parking ticket. The situation was difficult, and he was ready for Joe to deny him. Ellie's health was the only thing that mattered now.

Joe rushed through the doors to reception. "My name is Joe Welsh, my daughter, Ellie, Eleanor, was brought in by her grandparents, Bill and Penny Nash. Where is she, please?"

"I'll check now for you, sir." The receptionist picked up a phone while Joe danced from one foot to another. A nurse touched his back, and he jumped.

"Mr. Welsh? I'll take you through to Ellie."

"Is she all right?"

"She's fine now. We've checked her out, and she has an ear infection, so we've begun treatment to lower her temperature and she'll need antibiotics. I see it's not the first time this has happened."

"Thanks goodness." He breathed out. "Yes, she's had this problem once before, but she didn't lose consciousness."

The nurse pulled the curtain aside. Ellie seemed so small. She was awake, and Bill and Penny were sat by her bed. A young doctor had a thermometer pressed to her ear.

"Dadda."

"It's all right, angel. Daddy's here. Can I pick her up?" he asked as Ellie raised her hands.

"Give it a little time so we can keep an eye on her and keep checking her temperature," the doctor replied. "I'll be back in a while, but don't worry. She'll bounce back quickly. I'd suggest more tests, though, to see if there's an underlying condition, such as glue ear. It usually clears up by itself, but she may need grommets if it doesn't."

He sat on the other side of the bed when the doctor left.

"We're sorry," Penny said. "I swear she was fine when we put her to bed. She'd been grizzly but…"

"Did you check her temperature?" Joe asked.

Bill glared at him across the bed. "We told you she was fine. She ate her dinner and played for a bit."

"You need to check her temperature. These fits come on so suddenly." He put his hand to her face. She was still warm. "It's all right, baby."

The nurse came in again. "There's someone here to see you. Says his name is Aron Roberts. We need to check on visitors, and someone will have to go into the waiting area as we don't like cubicles to be too crowded."

"Please let him through," Joe said. He still wasn't sure how to explain Aron to Bill and Penny.

"Who are you?" Bill asked when Aron appeared at the curtain. Joe saw him hesitate before answering.

"Aron brought me in his car."

When she saw Aron, Ellie immediately called his name and reached out her arms. "Run, Run."

"She kept saying that. We didn't know what she meant."

Joe swore he could almost see the cogs turning in their brains.

"I can't now, Ellie," Aron said, still standing at the end of the bed. "Is she okay?"

"Yes. She has an ear infection like last time. She'll need to take antibiotics again. I'm going to take her to an ENT specialist to get her checked out. I can afford to do it privately and get her seen more quickly. Bill, Penny, could you wait outside, please? I need to talk to Aron."

"But who is he?" Bill demanded. "We're her grandparents. We have a right to be here. He's a stranger, to us anyway."

Joe gripped the rail around the bed. "He has a right to be here." He took a deep breath. It was now or never. "Aron is my boyfriend."

"Your what?" Bill said, standing.

"You heard me correctly, but this isn't the place for this discussion."

"You're right, it isn't," his father-in-law said.

Penny glanced from him to Aron. "I don't understand," she said quietly.

"Bill, Penny, I will talk to you, but not now. Ellie wants Aron here and so do I, so please could you wait outside?"

The nurse appeared again. "I heard raised voices."

Joe stared at his in-laws. "Everything is fine. Mr. and Mrs. Nash are going to wait outside, aren't you?"

"This discussion isn't over with. The Bible says…"

"Please, Bill, not the Bible, not now. Just go, will you? The noise is upsetting Ellie."

Once they'd left, he breathed a heavy sigh and leaned into Aron's open arms.

"You didn't need to," Aron said.

"It had to be said sooner or later, and now they know. It won't end here, though." Aron moved a seat to sit next to him.

"I'm glad you're here," Joe said, leaning his head on Aron's shoulder. The curtain opened again. Joe sat up, but kept hold of Aron's hand. The nurse smiled before putting the digital thermometer inside Ellie's ear again.

"It's coming down now. Here are the antibiotics. You need to give them to her three times a day and use the full course. The doctor will be back soon and let you know whether you can take her home."

"Thank you," Joe said. "You've been wonderful."

"I guess we wait, then," Aron said.

Ellie slept while they waited, leaning into each other, almost falling asleep themselves. After thirty minutes, the doctor appeared and confirmed Ellie could go home. Joe put her in the buggy with her blanket loosely around her so she wouldn't get too hot again.

"They'll be waiting," he warned.

"At least they won't make a fuss in public. D'you want me to stay at your place tonight?" Aron asked.

"Please. I don't want to be on my own. In fact, I wish I didn't have to be on my own ever again."

"Then don't be. Let's get a place together. I've been searching online and found the perfect house with a great garden and a view of the sea. I know it's probably too soon and we haven't known each other long, but sometimes you know, don't you?"

Joe thought his heart might be visible pumping through his chest. "It'll need a lot of sorting with the business and everything."

"I've got an idea for that too."

"You have been thinking," Joe said, smiling.

"I'm happy you're not annoyed with me. Come on, let's get out of here."

"Brace yourself," he said and pushed the buggy through the curtain into the waiting area. His in-laws stood as soon as he and Aron got there. Bill opened his mouth, but Joe put up his hand.

"This isn't the place for an argument. Come round to the house tomorrow if you must, but know Aron and I are together and nothing you say is going to change that. We'll be in at ten and expect you both then."

He didn't give them a chance to reply, and walked on out the doors into the car park, following Aron to where he'd parked.

Joe didn't sleep much, checking every twenty minutes or so on Ellie. At seven, Aron got up and made them tea and toast, bringing it back to bed. He pulled up the information about the house on his phone to show him while they ate.

"It's big," Joe said. "And not cheap."

"We can afford it together," Aron replied.

"But it is beautiful and the sea view will be all ours."

"I thought we could get a hot tub for the patio. Less dangerous with Ellie and more fun for us," Aron said.

Joe dragged Aron on top of him. They kissed briefly and Aron lay his head in the crook of Joe's neck.

"You're sure about this," he asked. "I don't want to force you into anything."

He stroked Aron's head. "I love you, Aron Roberts, and Ellie loves you too. Despite all your fears in the beginning, I think she's won your heart."

"She has. I never thought I'd say this, but I love her too. Talking to my parents has helped a lot. I thought being around kids was out of my comfort zone, but I'd never discovered how much you could love a child. Anyway, she's part of you and a lot cuter, so I'm bound to love her."

Joe remembered Dan Morgan's words then slapped Aron's arse playfully.

"Ouch, what was that for?" Aron asked, sucking on Joe's collarbone.

"Just because. Now get your arse out of bed and into the shower, and I'll go in after you. They'll be here soon enough."

* * * *

The doorbell rang at exactly ten o'clock. "Here we go," Joe said.

Aron contemplated the arrival of Joe's in-laws with a heavy heart. Luckily, Ellie lay asleep in her buggy after her disturbed night. At least we'll be able to say not to raise voices or she'll wake up.

Bill Nash had a face like thunder when he came through the door, while Penny had dark circles under her eyes. Aron doubted she'd slept much.

"I'll make some tea," he said, leaving the door open so he could hear the discussion.

"I didn't expect him to be here," Bill said.

"Aron is part of mine and Ellie's lives now, and he has a right to be here."

Aron smiled at Joe's words. He set the cups and teapot out on the tray then poured in the boiling water and put milk in the jug. Steadying himself, he carried the tray back into the main room.

"God says such behavior is wrong. I'll never accept this so-called relationship. How can you expose your daughter to such perversion? Angie would be turning in her grave if you'd allowed her to have one."

Aron wondered what had happened there, but this was obviously another bone of contention.

"Angie didn't want to be buried and you know that, and she most certainly wouldn't turn in her grave. Angie told me not to be alone, but to find someone who loved me and Ellie, and that's exactly what I've done."

"But he's a man," Bill spluttered.

"You noticed."

Aron stared at his knees and tried to suppress his smile. He poured the tea and passed around the cups. Bill looked at his as if it had been poisoned and placed it on the table.

"Please understand, Bill, I'm not going to defend my relationship with Aron, and frankly I don't care what your God says, and neither did Angie. My God, as much as I believe in one, isn't like that. My God believes in love and charity, and Aron is good and kind. He loves Ellie and she loves him. Isn't that what the modern Bible says, that the greatest of these is love?"

"The Bible also says that man lying with man is an abomination. I will never agree with what you're doing."

Penny leaned forward and sipped her tea then put the cup back down. "Joe, I don't understand. You were married to my daughter. You're not gay, or whatever word they use that's politically correct these days. How can you be in love with a man?"

"I've always been attracted to both men and women, Penny," Joe replied gently. "Angie knew about it. Some people are bisexual — they like both sexes equally."

"I'm gay," Aron added.

Joe raised his eyebrows.

Aron ducked his head. Oops, better keep quiet.

"So you could still find a nice woman to be with?"

Aron went to open his mouth, but closed it again when Joe glanced at him.

"I know it's hard to understand, Penny, but I don't work that way. For whatever reason — and I could give you a list — I fell in love with Aron. I didn't look for it, or expect it even, but it happened."

Bill harrumphed his doubt. "There is nothing you can say that will make this right."

Aron saw Joe take a deep breath and wondered what was coming next.

"Then you won't be able to see Ellie alone again. I won't have her mind confused with your poison."

Anger flared in Bill's face as Aron glanced at everyone in the room. He thought Bill might explode, but he struggled to keep control of himself. A tear ran down Penny's cheek, but she stayed silent.

"You can't do that," Bill protested.

"I can and I will," Joe replied adamantly.

"I won't stop you from seeing her, either of you, but you'll have to come to see her here and there'll be no more overnight stays at your house. Aron and I are getting a house together as soon as we can get everything organized. You will be welcome to visit, but that's it. I don't want my daughter's head filled with hatred and bile, and Angie wouldn't have wanted that either."

"We'll consult a lawyer if necessary," Bill continued.

"One of my best friends is a lawyer," Aron said. "I'm sure he'll agree with Joe in this."

"I'm sorry, Penny. You know you are welcome any time without Bill."

"My wife will follow me."

Looking at her face, Aron had his doubts.

She put down her cup and glanced over at Ellie. "No, Bill, this is my granddaughter we're discussing and you're forgetting what Angie was like. I can't say I'm happy about this. I don't know Aron well enough yet to make any judgment, but I am not losing contact with Ellie. She's all I have left of my daughter. I don't care what you say. My God is also a loving God."

Bill stared at her in obvious confusion.

She rose to her feet. "We'll be in contact soon, Joe. Is she all right after last night?"

"She's fine now. I'm going to take her to a specialist as soon as I can get an appointment."

"Right. Good. Thank you. We'll be going now, Bill." She marched to the door, leaving her husband in her wake until he followed her out. Joe got up and stared out of the window to make sure they'd gone.

"That went better than I expected," he said. "Ring the estate agent. We have a house to check out."

Epilogue

Three months later

"And breathe," Aron said, his hands on Joe's shoulders. "You've no need to worry. Margaret has everything under control. You made the right decision borrowing her to manage your move. Best choice I ever made, employing her when I set up Aztechnologies."

Joe glanced over to the entrance where Margaret Pearce stood giving instructions to the extra helpers. "I know you're right, but I can't help worrying."

Aron kissed the back of his neck. "Kirsty's taken the food out and Rhodri is setting up the buffet. Your family is here, and my lot are champing at the bit to get their mouths around your food. The place is packed with people, and you look devastatingly sexy in that suit and tie. It's all good."

Joe tried to calm his breathing and tether the butterflies fluttering in his stomach. Everything was ready, and the place was immaculate. It had taken several months, but the stainless-steel units gleamed in the midwinter sunshine coming through the huge windows at the front of the unit. He and Aron stood by the counter, which would serve those who came in to collect the meals for themselves. As they were on an industrial estate, there would be lots of workers around, all desperate for good food. Joe guessed Kirsty's pies would be more popular than his sandwiches. He sipped champagne and watched Margaret hand out menus to the people coming in through the door. His parents stood talking to Margaret's husband, Harry, and Pauline and Dai Morris. Aron's friends, Evan and Beth, stood with Jonno and the smattering of rugby players Dan had brought with him. Emrys held Scottie and was currently deep in conversation with the surprise visitor of the day. Joe had been so pleased when Penny had arrived without Bill. Holding Ellie in her arms, she was like a tiny sparrow next to Emrys. He wished Aron's parents had been able to come, but he and Aron would be visiting France next year.

"Are we ready, then?" Joe turned to see Dan Morgan behind him. Getting the captain of the Welsh rugby team to open your new business meant press attention, and more publicity was good.

"I appreciate you doing this," Joe said. "And for bringing the other players with you."

"Wild horses wouldn't have stopped Mac. I swear he has hollow legs. The place turned out well."

Joe gazed around the space he'd helped to design and smiled. "Yes, it did. It's been hard work getting the business sorted at the same time as moving into our new house. We wanted it ready before Christmas, and here we are. So, let's get this show on the road."

Joe reached into the drawer, grabbed a large pair of scissors and handed them to Dan. He clinked a knife against his glass and gradually the talking hushed.

"Thanks for coming, everyone. You'll be glad to hear this won't be a long speech, but I have lots of people to thank. Firstly, I'd like to welcome my customers old and new, who I'm sure are only here to meet the hunky rugby players and get a free lunch. I'd like to thank my family and friends for putting up with me while this was being put together so expertly by my newly acquired PA, Margaret, and my new assistant, Kirsty, who I should point out makes the best pastry in the world. Do try the pies and tarts—they are awesome. Lastly, I'd like to thank the two most important people in my world, Aron, who came into my life six months ago, and my gorgeous daughter, Ellie." He leaned in and kissed Aron, something he could never have dreamed he'd be doing twelve months ago. "And now I'd like to ask the captain of the Welsh rugby team, Dan Morgan, to cut the ribbon, then we can get something to eat."

Dan opened the scissors. There were flashes around the room while Dan sliced through the ribbon and spoke. "I'd like to declare the new premises of Croeso I Cymraeg Catering open for business."

Cheers rang around the space, as well as the sound of clinking glasses. Then there was a rush to the back as people piled the free samples onto their plates. Joe felt Aron slide his arm around his waist.

"I'm so proud of you. This is going to be such a success. My workers will be here every day being just opposite, and I'll need to do much more running because of Kirsty's pies."

"I suppose I need to mingle," Joe said, reluctant to remove himself from Aron's arms. He moved around the room finally reaching his parents who hugged him tightly.

"You've done well here, son." Joe's heart swelled at his father's words, and he wiped back a tear.

"I couldn't have done any of this without you both. You are such special people. I'm damn lucky, and I know it."

He left them eating, collected Ellie from Penny and thanked her for coming.

"I'm working on him, but my husband is a stubborn man. I'd better get back. You look happy, Joe, and I'm so glad your business is doing well. Angie would be proud of you."

"I hope so," he said, putting Ellie on his hip. After Penny had left, Joe continued on his way around the room, unable to wipe the grin from his face.

* * * *

Later, after several hours on his feet of meeting and greeting, he was sitting on the sofa in their new home, feeling pleased with the way the day had gone. He'd gained a few more regular orders, and the press coverage would probably bring more if the reporter's face on eating the food was anything to go by. Joe lay his head back and sipped more champagne, aware he was already a little tipsy. The house was quiet except for the crackling of the wood in the burner. He closed his eyes and let himself drift away until he felt the soft caress of Aron's fingers raking through his hair.

"Is she all right?" he asked.

"I read her a story, and she went out like a light after today." Aron sat beside him. "I took her temperature then had a quick shower."

Joe smiled at him, hardly believing this was the same man he'd met for the second time six months ago.

"What?" Aron said.

"You, reading stories to Ellie, tucking her in and checking her temperature. You've got to admit it's something of a turn around."

Aron leaned against him. "I know, but a lot has changed in those months, and sometimes the heart takes you to places you didn't expect to go. I'd only seen the bad before. Don't get me wrong, I'm still in awe of anyone who takes on this responsibility, but Ellie could be anything when she grows up. She has such a distinct personality. She might even be president of Wales."

"There is no president of Wales," Joe said, laughing.

"Of course not, she's not old enough yet. But she is a small bundle of unknown potential. It's exciting imagining who she'll be and what she'll do."

"Talk about born again. You have got it bad, haven't you?"

"I blame her father."

Joe stared at the section of Aron's skin not covered by his dark blue bathrobe then up to his still wet hair. "You look good enough to eat," he said, leaning in for a brief kiss.

"I was hoping you might think so," Aron replied, smiling.

"That is a wicked grin you have on your face, Aron Roberts." Instantly his cock stirred in his trousers as the space lessened. The things this man did to him.

"Perhaps I have something wicked planned," Aron teased. He grabbed Joe's hand and pulled his robe apart. "Feel for yourself."

Joe ran his fingers over his boyfriend's erection, which hardened under his touch. He repositioned himself between Aron's knees and licked around the tip of his shaft. He glanced up. "Is this what you meant?"

"For starters," Aron replied, wriggling under his touch. Joe relaxed his throat and enclosed the whole of Aron's erection. He sucked in his cheeks, happy when Aron arched beneath him, and gave his full attention to licking and sucking for a few minutes before coming up for air and wetting his lips.

"You taste nearly as good as my food." He grinned before moving back up to sit next to Aron on the sofa.

Aron shifted himself until he was kneeling astride Joe, his robe now open, allowing the lights of both Christmas tree and fire to flicker across his skin. Joe put his hands up and ran them down Aron's chest.

"You are beautiful, and I'm a lucky man."

Aron unbuckled Joe's belt and lowered his zipper then reached in and pulled out Joe's cock, now hard enough to punch through concrete. He moaned as Aron dug in his pocket for the lube before finally spreading some on his cock and running his hand up and down the shaft. Aron lifted, then lowered himself slowly until he'd completely encased Joe's cock in that warm, tight space.

Aron winked at him. "I'd like to say I was once a Boy Scout and was always prepared, but that would be a lie. I did, however, use my shower time wisely." He put his hands on Joe's shoulders and moved up and down, creating a delicious friction around Joe's cock as his erection bounced up and down on Joe's abdomen. Aron undid his shirt, exposing his chest with the hair now completely regrown after his experiment with waxing. Joe took hold of Aron's cock and stroked, slowly at first then faster until Aron threw his head back and shot his load over Joe's chest. The tightening around his own cock sent Joe over the edge soon after as he thrust upward, needing to bury himself to the hilt. Aron fell forward and kissed him, laying his head on Joe's shoulder until his breathing was under control before he pulled himself up and off, then turned and lay with his head on Joe's lap once more. He waggled his tongue and Joe bent over and kissed him.

"Hmm, you taste good."

Joe ran a finger over the semen on his chest and sucked on it. "You're not so bad yourself, and that was the perfect end to a perfect day."

He sat there stroking Aron's head while gazing around the newly decorated room with the huge Christmas tree twinkling in the corner. Tomorrow would be Christmas Eve, and they planned to put the presents out around the tree. The next day, his family would be there for their first Christmas Day, to eat and drink too much, then play games, and watch his father fall asleep in an armchair, as he did every year.

"Penny for them," Aron said, gazing up at him with such love, Joe thought his heart might explode.

"I was thinking how wonderful this Christmas will be. Our first Christmas together with my family, and next year we're going to France to visit your parents. Our businesses are going well, and we've a wonderful daughter. You know I love you so much, don't you?"

"And I love you too," Aron replied. He sat up and grabbed the champagne bottle then emptied it equally into the two glasses. "Happy Christmas to us, with many more of them to come, and here's to a great new year — together."

About the Author

Originally from South Wales, Alexa has lived for over thirty years in the North West of England. Now retired, after a long career in teaching, she devotes her time to her obsessions.

Alexa began writing when her favourite character was killed in her favorite show. After producing a lot of fanfiction she ventured into original writing.

She is currently owned by a mad cat and spends her time writing about the men in her head, watching her favourite television programmes and usually crying over her favourite football team.

Alexa loves to hear from readers. You can find her contact information, website details and author profile page at http://www.pride-publishing.com.

PUBLISHING